VENGEFUL VOWS

BOOK 3 IN THE MARITAL PRIVILEGES SERIES

SHANDI BOYES

COPYRIGHT

ALSO BY SHANDI BOYES

Denotes Standalone Books

Perception Series

Saving Noah *

Fighting Jacob *

Taming Nick *

Redeeming Slater *

Saving Emily

Wrapped Up with Rise Up

Protecting Nicole *

Enigma

Enigma

Unraveling an Enigma

Enigma The Mystery Unmasked

Enigma: The Final Chapter

Beneath The Secrets

Beneath The Sheets

Spy Thy Neighbor *

The Opposite Effect *

I Married a Mob Boss *

Second Shot *

The Way We Are

The Way We Were

Sugar and Spice *

Lady In Waiting

Man in Queue

Couple on Hold

Enigma: The Wedding

Silent Vigilante

Hushed Guardian

Quiet Protector

Enigma: An Isaac Retelling

Enigma Bonus Scenes (Two free chapters)

Twisted Lies *

Bound Series

Chains

Links

Bound

Restrain

The Misfits *

Nanny Dispute *

Russian Mob Chronicles

Nikolai: Representing the Bratva

Nikolai: Resurrecting the Bratva

Nikolai: Ruling the Bratva

Asher: My Russian Revenge *

Trey *

Nero: Shattered Wings *

Nikolai: Bonus Scenes (10+ chapters from alternative POVs).

The Italian Cartel

Dimitri

Roxanne

Reign

Mafia Ties (Novella)

Maddox

Demi

Ox

Rocco *

Clover *

Smith *

RomCom Standalones

Just Playin' *

Ain't Happenin' *

The Drop Zone *

Very Unlikely *

False Start *

Short Stories - Newsletter Downloads

Christmas Trio *

Falling For A Stranger *

Enigma Bonus Scenes (Two free chapters)

Nikolai: Bonus Scenes (10+ chapters from alternative POVs).

One Night Only Series

Hotshot Boss *

Hotshot Neighbor *

The Bobrov Bratva Series

Wicked Intentions *

Sinful Intentions *

Devious Intentions *

Deadly Intentions *

Martial Privilege Series

Doctored Vows *

Deceitful Vows *

Vengeful Vows *

Broken Vows *

Omnibus Books (Collections)

Enigma: The Complete Collection (Isaac & Isabelle)

The Beneath Duet (Hugo & Ava)

The Bad Boy Trilogy (Hunter, Rico, and Brax)

Pinkie Promise (Ryan & Savannah)

The Infinite Time Trilogy (Regan & Alex)

Silent Guardian (Brandon & Melody)

Nikolai: The Complete Collection (Nikolai & Justine)

Mafioso (Dimitri & Roxanne)

Bound: The Complete Collection (Cleo & Marcus)

WANT TO STAY IN TOUCH?

Facebook: facebook.com/authorshandi

Instagram: instagram.com/authorshandi

Email: authorshandi@gmail.com

Reader's Group: bit.ly/ShandiBookBabes

Website: authorshandi.com

Newsletter: https://www.subscribepage.com/AuthorShandi

TRIGGERS

Please note this book has the following triggers:
  Child abuse (not on page)
  Sexual abuse (not on page)
  Attempted sexual abuse (on page)
  Rape (not on page)
  Murder (not on page)
  Political sabotage
  Blackmail
  Scarred Hero
  Speech impediment
  Burns (not on page)

1

MARA

*M*y fingers clutch stiff bedding when a door creaking open reaches my ears. I glance up as multiple footsteps clatter over expensive oak floorboards, catch a glimpse of a gold cufflink, and then shift my focus back to the task at hand.

My job isn't to pry into the lives of the wealthy residents who call the Chrysler building home. I am here to wash the sheets, clean the toilets, and only be seen when summoned.

Rarely does the summoning come from the people wearing designer labels and tailored suits. They'd never associate with the "help." They bark their orders at my supervisor, who then passes them on to me for far less than the exorbitant fee charged by the company responsible for maintaining and cleaning the apartments in the most sought-after building in Myasnikov.

A turndown service is the reason for two hours of overtime this evening. It doesn't take two hours to turn down sheets and fluff pillows. The "help" hadn't serviced this apartment in over three years, so the floors needed vacuuming, and the opulent, larger-than-my-apartment bathrooms required restocking.

I could have sworn I overheard Mrs. Whitten telling my supervisor that the building's latest short-stay tenant wasn't arriving until late this evening. It's not even seven. Surely they're not early. I've yet to meet a rich person who isn't chasing their tail.

Curious, I take a second glance at the trio entering the suite from the far entrance. The apartments in the Chrysler building are large enough to require multiple entry points. Only owners and guests may use the main entrance. The rest use the servants' entrances and corridors wedged between priceless paintings and opulence most can only dream of achieving.

Mrs. Whitten, the building supervisor, leads the procession with such animated gestures that she resembles a headless chicken moments from being dunked into a pot. She is slim and a few decades older than me and has a sharp wit and intelligence. I like her, though I doubt she knows who I am.

I am an expert at remaining hidden. No one pays attention to me, not even the stout man with a thick mustache who tosses his bag onto the bedding I recently straightened before he unbuttons his trousers like he is without an audience.

Mrs. Whitten dips her chin in appreciation when I silently move toward the servants' entrance. She often says she wants her guests to feel at home while under her roof. The unnamed man looks ready to do just that.

Once I reach the safety of the alcove, I fumble for the EarPods in my pocket. They were a gift from Mr. Whitten. They were dusty enough to show they weren't new, but they've made my commute home far less boring over the past month, and for that, I am forever grateful.

With my head down, I breeze into the employee locker room, grab my gym bag from its hiding spot, and make a beeline for the shower block. I don't usually change out of my maid's outfit at the end of my shift, but today is different because it's Tillie's tenth birthday.

I promised to meet her and Mrs. Lichard at the bowling alley at 7:30 p.m. sharp. The bus trip home will eat into time I don't have. My schedule is always tight, but it's even tighter this week.

The unisex bathroom is quiet. Only the chefs and lead housemaids remain on the premises at this hour. They're allowed access to the upper levels after hours and take full advantage once their coworkers leave.

While the latest hit from Måneskin blasts my ears, I dump my bag onto an ancient bench inside a wall-less shower cubicle and strip.

Everything in this building is antique, including the radiators. It takes forever for the water to heat up. Since I'm in a hurry, I opt for a deodorant bath instead of drenching my hair as my pounding temples are begging.

In seconds, I smell like one of the women who stand on the corners in my half of Myasnikov late at night, hoping for their *Pretty Woman* moment. My hoop earrings are cheap, as is the comb I hurriedly rip through my hair, but they add a touch of sophistication to my outfit. They make it look more like a date ensemble than a mom hoping the blowout-budget present she bought will keep her off her daughter's shitlist for being late to her first and likely last birthday party.

I'm not dressing up with the hope of securing a date. That ship sailed not long after I gave birth. Barely sixteen with a baby in tow doesn't attract many suitors, and the rare few who assumed my child meant our date would end with more than a kiss never made it past the first course.

I am merely hoping a little glam and a flirty smile will lower the bill of a birthday party for ten of Tillie's closest friends. I didn't consider how inflated non-luxury items had become in the past few years. I wouldn't have suggested a bowling party if I knew it would cost fifty dollars per guest to knock down some pins.

Alas, I promised Tillie she'd enter her double-digits era in style.

I am a woman who keeps her word.

The fact I'm working as a maid announces this tenfold.

My parents aren't wealthy, but they could purchase an apartment in the Chrysler building if they were willing to sit across from a bank manager.

I can barely afford a bus fare to this side of town. I shouldn't complain. Wealth comes with a heap of conditions most consenting adults wouldn't agree to.

I walked away from my family to ensure my daughter would never have to consider their terms, much less follow them to the wire as I was forced to when I was a child.

Although it isn't close to glamorous, we have a good, stable life.

After shaking off haunted memories that will cause more than my vocal cords to shake, I replace my nonslip shoes with heels, stuff my uniform into my oversized purse, and then spin to face the exit.

Partway around, the truth hits me. I forgot to replenish the aftershave in the primary bedroom of the west wing apartment. The grandeur that takes up almost every floor on the west side of the building was serviced first thing this morning.

Although most apartments are stocked with high-end department store cologne, Mrs. Whitten was adamant that this tenant required a special order. She promised to deliver her selected purchase to my service trolley within the hour so I could unbox it and display it before her VIP tenant arrived late this evening.

That was over eight hours ago.

"Shit," I murmur to myself, glancing at the time.

If I don't leave now, I risk missing the 7:15 bus. The next one won't arrive until *after* the time I agreed to meet Tillie and Mrs. Lichard.

I consider ignoring Mrs. Whitten's determination to make this owner's stay as comfortable as possible. The thought doesn't linger for long. I need this job. I can't risk it for anything. I just need to move fast so I can purchase my daughter's birthday cake and eat it too.

"Mara." My supervisor leaps to her feet, shocked when I barge into her office at the speed of a bullet leaving a gun. "Don't you have somewhere to be?"

"I do," I reply, nodding.

Val isn't as stiff and rule-abiding as Mrs. Whitten. Her head is the first on the chopping block when her staff step out of line, so although she hates it, she must pull us into line when necessary.

"But I forgot this."

While flashing Val an apologetic grin, I snatch up a bottle of cologne from her desk and exit her office as fast as I entered it.

Technically, this isn't either of our faults. Mrs. Whitten said she would have the cologne delivered to me. I would have collected it before wrangling an ancient vacuum cleaner into submission if I'd known she wasn't a woman of her word.

As I dart through the door of an office too small to be considered anything more than a broom closet, Val shouts something. I miss what she says, but assuming it is an offer to drive me to the bowling alley to make sure I'm not late for Tillie's party, I shout back, "I won't miss it, but thanks!"

I wave goodbye and sprint down the servants' corridor. My pace isn't graceful, and I'm sweating more than when I wrestle fitted sheets onto mattresses too large for one person to handle, but it's effective. I make it to the west wing in record time.

A second cuss for the evening escapes my lips when I realize I forgot to check the owner's register, leaving me unable to announce my request for access to their apartment.

When you knock on one door in the service corridor, almost all the tenants on the same floor answer. We're supposed to greet the tenants by surname to avoid confusion.

"Hello... h-housekeeping."

I press my ear to the door and wait.

I'm reasonably sure no one is home, but I'd rather be safe than sorry. It took months for me to enter an apartment in this building and not quiver like a bag of nerves. I don't want anything to push my progress back. Even with the profession of over half the residents here scaring the living daylights out of me, I need this job.

Dentists aren't on my list of childhood fears.

Doctors, though, are at the top.

When I don't receive a verbal response, I shake off memories that will make more than my vocals shudder, before testing the latch.

The door is unlocked, saving me from a long walk back to Val's office for the master key that opens every apartment in the building, including the glitzy penthouse.

"S-sir... Housekeeping."

My stutter frustrates me, but it's expected. I can't recall a time I haven't stuttered when speaking with a member of the opposite sex. It's a neurosis I've had since childhood, and it worsened when I was robbed at gunpoint six months ago.

Knowledge that cruelty can come from all walks of life makes me reluctant to speak. If everyone could sign, I'd use that as my sole form of communication.

After a quick scan of the opulent living room, noting it hasn't changed since I removed the sheets protecting the designer furniture from dust and vacuumed the expensive woolen rugs, I make a beeline for the bathroom in the primary suite.

The bathroom door barely creaks under the pressure of my push. It is ten times quieter than the raging of my heart as I tiptoe across pricy marble floors, but it gives away my presence in an instant.

"I don't know what Mr. Kershaw told you, but I'm *not* interested in any pre-interview requisite you seem to *think* I want."

I freeze, shocked by the sheer anger in the man's low, gravelly tone. It's full of anguish and convinces me that I am gripping something more ominous than a pricy bottle of cologne.

My silence agitates him more. "Did you hear what I said? Leave. *Now!*"

While nodding as if he can see me, I stammer out an apology before dumping the boxed cologne onto the vanity and twisting to face the exit.

Since the bottom of my shoes are worn to within an inch of their life, I lose traction on the glossy marble tiles. I skid like a newborn foal, and the brutal collision of my knees on the rigid floor is enough to burst tears into my eyes.

I won't cry. I didn't when I was beaten for a handful of measly possessions, so I won't now, but I'd be a liar if I said my fall wasn't painful.

My knees are cut and oozing blood, but the man I interrupted shreds my ego to pieces worse than any fall could hack up my skin. "What have you done, you silly little girl? Foolish tricks like that don't work on me. You'll need more than a clumsy damsel-in-distress act to gain my attention."

"I'm not s-silly," I snap before I can stop myself. "I'm also not a ch-child."

When the vicious voice returns, a cold wind floats over my skin, producing goose bumps. "Then why do you speak like one?"

"Because I-I... Because..." Realizing I don't owe him an explanation —and that I will never speak without fear when alone with a man in *any* room, so how can I defend it?—I return to my feet, grimacing. "Go-good evening."

I'm almost in the clear when the unnamed man barks out another order.

This one is more sincere than his earlier ones.

"Wait."

My heart pounds in my ears when a shadow falls over the only exit. He was either hiding behind the bathroom door or not in the bathroom when I entered it.

Either way, his positioning terrifies me.

While swallowing hard, I hear him snap, "You're bleeding."

I briefly glance at my thighs before lowering my eyes to my knees. There's enough blood to announce a fall but not enough to fuss over, so I brush off his concern with a gesture my grandmother would have been proud of.

"It-it's nothing."

I don't even get in half a step this time before he thwarts my exit again. "I said wait. You can't leave my presence like this. What will the other residents think if they see you leaving with bloody knees?"

Another bout of silence.

Another step.

Another near heart attack.

This heart stutter isn't solely from fear. It's from parts of the man's face being unshadowed by the bathroom light flickering on behind me.

He's younger than his voice suggests, though still at least a decade older than me. His dark hair is long enough for fingers to get lost in, and a few days of stubble covers a rigid jaw on a deliriously handsome face. His lips and nose are perfectly straight, as level as his brows.

The latter seems more in disgust, as his voice conveys his concern better than the deep groove between his prominent brows does.

This man cannot hide his dislike. His expression reveals his every thought without his lips needing to move. They clearly announce that he isn't a fan of mine.

I can't say I'm surprised.

When have rich, powerful men ever respected the help?

I was fired from my last position because I snuck a mint out of a serving dish in the entryway. It was out of date and ghastly sweet, but I thought it would be better to have minty, fresh breath while my boss was in residence than vomit-laced breath.

I was suffering through a severe case of food poisoning, but when I called my boss to announce I was sick, he told me I either arrive at work on time or don't return to my position at all.

I dragged myself from my deathbed and worked through body aches and chills that made me so delusional I thought asking my mother for help was the right way to go.

I made it to the airport before my smarts kicked back in. Although scared at the idea of adjusting to a new workplace, I'd repeatedly choose that over placing Tillie in unnecessary danger. I'd done it numerous times in the past decade, so what was one more obstacle?

I'm pulled from my thoughts when a creak sounds through my ears. I learn the stranger's concealment isn't as sinister as I first thought when he moves closer.

He's wearing a towel.

That's it.

A.

Towel.

My brows stitch together as I take in the situation. His coverage isn't from the towels I left on the mattress earlier today. It's from the shower mat I placed outside the freestanding multi-head shower cubicle.

The scratch in my throat worsens. Not only did I enter the bathroom of an owner without permission, but I also entered while he was showering.

There's no way I will keep my position now.

Val will have no choice but to let me go.

I try to keep the devastation out of my voice that I will need to rebuild trust with another employer as I say, "I'm s-so sorry. I knocked." I lower my eyes to my hands knotted in my skirt, hoping a painful twist will stop the rest of my confession. "When you didn't a-answer, I assumed you ha-hadn't arrived yet."

The nerves pushing me to the brink of being sick ease slightly when he replies, "Not that I need to explain myself, but I have poor hearing in my left ear."

My eyes dart to his left ear before slowly moving to his narrowed gaze. Even hooded, there's no hiding his frustration.

"Oh."

His explanation is plausible. You have to face away from the faucets to keep your right ear unclogged, which is nearly impossible with six showerheads.

The stranger moves our conversation forward remarkably fast, like he can't wait to get rid of me. "Do you have any Band-Aids?"

"F-for?" I ask, lost.

The mat isn't long enough to wrap around his waist, so it slips between his mannish thighs when he bends down to inspect the cuts on my knees more attentively. I love the crazy tile design they installed when they renovated this bathroom two months ago, but they're a nightmare to clean since they shred any material you glide over them—knees included.

"I think I have s-some Band-Aids in m-my purse."

When he raises his eyes to my face, my breath catches at the full intensity of his narrowed gaze. His eyes are green but could be mistaken for blue since the limbal rings are the color of the deepest ocean.

They're utterly hypnotic, as mesmerizing as his handsome face.

Although he seems unappreciative of my stare, it doesn't come through in his tone when he asks, "And that is where?"

"Huh?" Excuse my daftness. I can't recall the last time a man was this close to me and I wasn't a shaky mess, so my bewilderment is understandable.

I don't understand my body's reactions. Fear should be my first emotion, but for some reason, it isn't. It can't be the stranger's soul-stealing looks. I've been surrounded by captivating men most of my life, though none have ignited such a fierce response from my body that panic has to fight to make itself known with my gut.

The stranger bounces his eyes between mine for a few seconds before he clarifies, "Your purse."

"Um." My nose wrinkles as I wedge my hand between us.

I'm so entranced that I forgot I am carrying my purse.

The stranger's lips tug as if he appreciates my daftness, before he removes my purse from my grasp. He rummages through my limited belongings like he conducts bag searches regularly before he pulls out a three-strip of Band-Aids.

"Two should cover it, but it is better to be safe than sorry."

He zips up my purse, tosses it next to the bottle of cologne, and then nudges his head to the vanity.

I dart my eyes between him, the vanity, and the Band-Aids three times before the truth hits me.

He wants me to sit on the vanity so he can tend to my wounds.

His efforts to "fix" me might appear chivalrous to others.

I am on the other end of the spectrum.

"I sh-should go. S-sorry about the interruption."

Even taking a wide berth doesn't stop me from bumping into him as I race for the exit. The bathroom is massive, but most doorways are similarly wide. It's impossible to bypass someone without touching them. This is why most predators stalk their prey from the doorways.

Mercifully, the stranger's balk when our arms brush is as jarring as mine. It jolts him away from the only exit, giving me unobstructed clearance to safety.

"Mara..." Val shouts when she spots me sprinting down the servants' corridor. "Why are you running? Are you okay?"

I sprint past her fast enough to keep my tears at bay and, hopefully, to ensure I make it to the bus stop with thirty seconds to spare.

2

ARKADIY

*T*he department service head for this building watches the brunette sprint down a hidden internal corridor with as much bewilderment as me. She appears confused, like she too can't understand my ability to look a gift horse in the mouth and turn it down.

For the first time in a long time, my cock roared to life, inspired by the visual in front of it. It was turned on enough to plump out the bathmat I used to shelter myself when I detected a presence in the bathroom with me mere minutes after I had entered it.

It should have been disgusted that I'd allowed someone to sneak up on me unawares. I don't care about the ripeness of her bosom or the tenderness of the usually untouched flesh between her legs. Catching me during a moment of vulnerability usually ends one way—with fierce hostility.

My first thought wasn't sabotage when I spotted the brunette on her knees. Something far more perverse than a wish for vengeance coursed through my veins, which is comical considering the stipulations such thoughts could attract.

Men my age aren't gifted young, fresh women without numerous provisos. My visit to Myasnikov proclaims this without prejudice.

I am here for the wife that I've failed to secure myself.

According to my campaign manager, thirty-nine is too old to be touted as the bachelor of Moscow, so he put steps in place to ensure a "wife-to-be" is by my side during my fortieth birthday celebration, which is a little over three weeks away.

I thought the idea was preposterous until a recent fabricated article in a gossip magazine surged my approval rating by two percent. It wouldn't have been heard of only months ago, but the shine is slowly fading on the Dokovics realm since the patriarch died almost six months ago.

A new cabinet is forming, and I plan to helm it.

I shift my eyes from the now empty corridor when a voice, still timid even without a stutter, trickles into my ears. "Mr. Orlov..." Val waits for our eyes to connect before she asks, "Is there anything I can get you?" Her eyes fall to the bathmat maintaining my modesty, slower than the brunette's did. She takes her time drinking in assets that are the result of early-morning workouts and a vigorous business schedule. "A towel, perhaps?"

She sounds hopeful for a denial, and it agitates my last nerve. I don't liaise with staff, and although I am confident my time in Myasnikov will be short, once on my employment ledger, you're never removed from it.

"Good evening, Ms...."

"Val," she stumbles out, her hand thrusting forward. "Val Maskerta."

I glance at her hand before returning my eyes to her face. Germs aren't a phobia of mine, more touch as a whole, but since mysophobia attracts less fanfare than haphephobia, I farewell Val with a nod before closing the door with her on the other side.

I'm frozen for several seconds, trying to center myself. The brunette's perfume tickles my nose, yet I flare my nostrils instead of opening the door and demanding Val to have my room meticulously cleaned for the umpteenth time this week.

My body trembles as I recall how the brunette's eyes floated up my body and the stutter of her words when she responded to my degrading remarks, how she feared me as much as she revered me. I think about how my first thought was to patch up her wounds instead of doubling them and how Rafael couldn't have chosen more wisely.

Then I consider how I scared her away instead of accepting that not every woman I cross paths with must sign an NDA before associating with me.

My secrets are mine to hide. It just seems impossible when a pair of guarded eyes strips you of all your psychoses in under a nanosecond.

I'm saved from further deliberation on my peculiar behavior this evening when a knock sounds through my apartment.

When I enter the main living area, Rafael's brutish tone rumbles through the entrance door. "Ark, are you decent?"

He snickers like he expects otherwise before he lowers the door handle. He can't enter. Unlike the servant entrance door, I locked the main entrance door to ensure no incidents like the one that just occurred could happen.

I now have another doorway to triple-check before bathing.

Rafael won't be granted permission to enter until I pull on a pair of slacks and dry my hair with a towel I forgot to take to the bathroom. I take my time getting dressed, handing back some of the annoyance he shunted my way only minutes ago.

Raf is a late-thirties political bigwig who has seen too much of the underside of humanity to kiss my ass like the other employees helming my campaign for the presidency do. He's been with me since day one, and despite being a thorn in my backside, he will remain at my side until I take my final breath.

You can't save a man's life and expect anything less.

As Rafael enters the four-bedroom apartment I purchased years ago but haven't stepped foot in before tonight, his eyes widen. He whistles when he takes in the decor that cost more than his first apartment, doubling the heat on the cheeks of the women crushing his designer suit.

Their burn doubles when he offers an introduction, like being offered a low-end appetizer after consuming a five-star entrée is the norm. "Ark, I have the pleasure of introducing you to Ainissa." He purrs out the name of the blonde cozied at his side in a long, wanton moan as his eyes rake her body.

Ainissa is dressed similarly to the brunette. Her skirt is short, her shirt is fitted, and her heels scream the desperation of a woman wanting to be fucked. She just fails to ignite a single throb from my cock.

Rafael is unaware of that since I'm no longer naked. "Ainissa, дорогой, this is my good friend Ark. The man I was telling you about."

I block their entrance when he attempts to guide Ainissa toward one of the spare suites.

Rafael raises a brow, silently questioning my denial. I don't understand his confusion. I turned the brunette down, so why would I be interested in Ainissa? The brunette was far more attractive, and she had a shy demeanor rarely found in the prostitution conglomerate.

When I hint at an early night, Rafael's face can't decide which emotion to display first. "It is barely seven, and our flight was long. You need to de-stress."

"I am. I have."

He huffs like he knows every word I speak is a lie. "You look more worked up now than when Fyodor announced the reason for our visit to Myasnikov." I glower when he laughs, and he backs down. "All right. If you're sure."

I nod before turning on my heel.

It is almost comical when a side of my head I haven't used in a long time surfaces before I can stop it. "Keep the brunette away from the rest of the men."

I don't get jealous. Never have. There's just something about the brunette that has me altering my usually unbreakable stance on no permanent attachments. I want to say that this is the purpose of my trip to Myasnikov, but it feels beyond that.

There's a silence before Rafael says, "The brunette?"

I turn to face him, my jaw working side to side when the faintest flash of her unblemished face curtained by dark, molten hair spikes my pulse. "The woman you sent earlier. Five two. One hundred and twenty pounds. Long, glossy locks." *And far too young for me to even look at, although most likely three to four years older than Ainissa, who is still hopeful of an invitation to my bed.*

The lust in her eyes announces this, much less the greed.

Old money has a scent not many women can ignore. It makes them as rampant as a rat with rabies and has them pulling out every trick in the book to be beneath you.

With Rafael still confused, I thrust my hand to the bathroom. "She brought me my cologne."

This will make me sound fucked in the head, but so be it. I am. Certain smells trigger me. They're usually feminine, so to save any incidents from being reported to the media, I cake my skin with pricy cologne before inviting members of the opposite sex into my domain.

"This cologne?"

This reply doesn't come from Rafael.

It comes from Ainissa, who is thrusting a boxed bottle of cologne my way.

I take in the familiar label before lifting my eyes to Rafael.

Fury burns through my veins.

It is closely followed by intense interest.

3

MARA

*A*fter my third call to Mrs. Lichard goes to voicemail, I leave a message. "I'm sorry. I accepted extra hours hoping it would ease this month's budget." It pains me to think of Tillie's disappointment when she learns I missed the bus to her birthday party.

"My last errand took longer than expected." I glance at the building I fled like my backside was on fire, sparking fresh nerves to bombard my stomach. They're not solely from recalling my exchange with the dark-haired stranger, but also from spotting my supervisor's exit.

"But I have a solution. I should still make it on time." I race for Val, my worn heels clomping the pavement. "If I don't arrive before Tillie's guests, please tell their parents I'm not far away." After a quick thanks, I disconnect our call and wave my hand through the air. "Val!"

Like me, she exits the Chrysler building via the side entrance. Her pace is so brisk that I have to increase my speed if I want any chance of catching her. She isn't purposely avoiding me. Rather, she can't hear me due to the boisterous conversation between two individuals exiting the building from the main entrance.

They don't consider bystanders as they pass through the turnstile door at the front. They proceed without acknowledging the potential impact of their knock to others, including a mother striving to reach her child on her tenth birthday.

"You should really watch where you're going." The woman who collided with me speaks in a nasally, jarring tone. "How will you cope knowing your Wilfred Iwona knockoff is beyond repair?"

"Probably how she lives every other day," comments the blonde standing beside her while noticing the tear my tumble caused my homemade skirt. "Desperate."

They laugh like children in a schoolyard. I don't pay them any attention. My focus is so rapt on Val that I don't realize that I am being assisted off the ground by a man until he responds to their remarks.

"That's enough."

The gravelly tone from earlier has returned, but this time, the stranger's annoyance is directed at the blonde who berated me after knocking me over.

After righting my footing, he glares at her with extreme disapproval. His wordless scorn causes her to step back, forcing her friend to take center stage.

"We're just playing, Ark. We didn't mean any harm."

I can't decide what frustrates me more: her raking her nails over Ark's chest as she replies like they know each other intimately, or watching Val's sedan merge into the heavy flow of traffic.

I focus on the latter when Ark removes her hand from his chest. He does it with as much aggression as he used in the bathroom when I snuck up on him unawares, but this time, there isn't an ounce of remorse in his narrowed gaze when she acts upset.

With her poor acting skills ended by a rueful glare, Ark returns his attention to me. He doesn't speak. Instead, he raises a brow, its arch corresponding with the increase of my pulse when I realize he is still clutching my arm.

Unsure what he wants me to say, I begin stammering out the same excuse I gave Mrs. Lichard when the last time I missed the bus saw me returning home with a black eye and a split lip. "I took on an extra s-shift, s-so..."

My back molars crunch together when the blonde bombshells

snicker under their breaths about my speech impediment. They tease me like they've yet to leave high school, which agitates me.

"Blowing out someone else's candles won't make yours any brighter."

I'm not the only one shocked by my outburst. Ark's cheeks are the color of beets, and a man I hadn't noticed until now howls like a wolf.

I'm glad he is amused. At least someone is benefiting from the erroneous mistake I just made. I need my job. *Desperately.* Snapping at the guests of a man who can afford the outrageous prices of the Chrysler building will make that difficult.

Since my apology is for Ark, I direct it to him. "I'm so-sorry for interrupting your night." I grimace before adding, "*Again.*"

My stutter appears to frustrate him as much as it does me, but he hides it with a tight, stern jaw and a quick chin bob.

I commence my gratitude for his understanding with a brisk smile. "Go-goodnight."

I barely make it two steps away before a snide remark from Bimbo One halts my exit. "Don't forget your broom." Snickering, she hands me the doorman's sweeper. "It'll get you wherever you need to be in no time."

A snarl furls my top lip, but other than that, I keep quiet. The logo stamped on the broom reminds me that she recently left my workplace one step in front of an owner. I have to remain polite despite my anger.

After taking the sweeper from her, I place it back in its holder and then stray my eyes in the direction Val's car went. It's long gone, so I turn back toward the bus stop, confident the number of improvements made to Myasnikov over the past six months means my wait will be done without incident.

When an elegant couple dressed to the nines slips into the back of a cab, I consider flagging down one of the many empty ones surrounding it. I'm only hesitant because every penny in my purse has been counted to the dime. I only have enough for Tillie's party and not a cent more.

The hairs on my neck stand up when a deep, raspy voice floats past my ear. "Was that your ride?"

I turn to face a man who seems more of an observer than an instigator. He's attractive, though not as appealing as Ark.

I doubt anyone could hold a torch to that man.

"No. Uh. I... Ah..." I wait for his eyes to lift from the spot on my arm Ark touched to help me to my feet before saying, "I m-missed the bus."

His expression suggests he is acutely aware of where I was touched, though that seems improbable. The sensation is more a tingle than a painful sting, leaving no visible mark for him to identify.

A grateful smile tugs at my lips when the stranger offers a way out of my predicament. "I have a car. I can take you wherever you need to go."

"Oh. Um. Th-thank you." I briefly consider his offer before declining it. "But I'm okay. There will be another bus s-soon."

Disregarding Ark's muttered comment about taking no for an answer, the stranger steps closer. "Are you sure? You seem like you have somewhere important to be."

"Stop acting desperate, Rafael. It isn't like she's worthy of your time."

Rafael silences Bimbo 2 with a dismissive gesture, his hand shoved in her face, but his eyes never leave mine. It is as if the wolf has found its prey, and he isn't leaving until he's fully devoured it.

The thought should scare me, but it doesn't.

My reaction has nothing to do with Rafael. It stems from Ark's narrowed glare when he notices the predatory gleam firing in his companion's eyes. Rafael's demeanor is pompous, whereas Ark looks like someone whose favorite meal was replaced with a bland soup seconds after being seated at a five-star restaurant.

My eyes shift from Ark to Rafael when Rafael rubs his hands together. "Then perhaps we can have a nightcap once I've gotten you safely to your destination." He licks his lips before cracking them into a broad grin. "We can do that at your place or mine. I'll be satisfied either way."

Rafael's smile widens when Ark moves so quickly that the threads of my skirt, torn from my fall, flap in the briskness of his strides.

"I'll take her." Ark's tone is affirmative, leaving no room for arguing.

Rafael winks at me as if I am a part of his ploy, then turns to face the man who has fallen for his ruse hook, line, and sinker. "Are you sure? I thought you wanted an early night." I can't see Ark's face since he's standing in front of me, but I imagine his snarl when Rafael steps back with his hands raised in surrender. "All right. Keep your panties untwisted. I was just checking."

He spins to face the blondes, who are disappointed to have lost Ark's attention. Their fake lips are lowered into childish pouts, and the scalding looks they're directing at me take care of the cool winds whipping between high-rise buildings.

Rafael acts oblivious to their dismay. "Ladies, shall we continue since Ark is now occupied?"

He doesn't wait for them to reply. After wrapping an arm around each of the women's slim waists, he guides them down the street, leaving me alone with Ark.

Once they're half a block away, Ark turns his focus to me. He stares for what feels like minutes but is barely seconds before he says, "Come. My car is in the underground lot."

His authoritative edge makes it clear he is used to giving orders and having them followed without question. I don't have time to consider the consequences of my actions if I don't comply, because he places his hand on the small of my back and steers me through the main entrance of the Chrysler building before I can utter a word.

The doorman greets us without acknowledging our working relationship. "Sir..." He tilts his top hat to hide his smile when his eyes fling to me. "Ma'am."

His professionalism is so seamless that Ark appears unaware of our association.

"Mateo," Ark replies, his pace unbroken even as he adds more to his greeting. "Ensure he has lost *them* before he returns." He nudges his head to Rafael and the two blondes as he says "them."

His order for the doorman to ensure Rafael gets rid of his "dates" is without a hint of hesitation, and Mateo's response is equally as casual. "Very well, sir."

I'd be relieved he has no plans to entertain guests tonight if I weren't so shocked.

I'm the help—society's belief of the lower class. I shouldn't be prioritized above anyone, let alone two women who can afford the designer clothes I tried to replicate with an old sewing machine and a year of online fashion undergrad studies.

"I can find another mo-mode of transport. You don't need to go out of your way for m-me."

Ark's fingers flex before he says, "It's fine. I don't mind."

"But y-your guests—"

My heart does a weird flip when he interrupts. "Were in the process of being shown out when they rudely knocked you over." His eyes float over my face, categorizing every pore, before he adds, "Let me do this. It is the least I can do after my earlier vulgarity."

I'm about to say I was the only one who was rude, but the elevator attendant's fumble for the call button has me on the back foot. The staff are pulling out all the stops for Ark, and it has me even more panicked about how I will keep my position after having my anger witnessed by coworkers.

The elevator attendant is far from subtle about our working relationship when I'm guided into the elevator he's manning. The corners of his lips tuck at one side as he drinks in the positioning of Ark's hand on my lower back and the shallowness of my breaths.

His smug expression switches to shock when within a second of announcing our floor, Ark demands his exit. "I can take it from here."

"Sir," the attendant gasps in shock.

"Now!" Ark snaps, his voice echoing against the brushed steel walls and mirrored back of the elevator.

After glaring at me as if I yelled at him, the attendant mutters, "Yes, sir. Right away."

As he darts out of the elevator, a shudder I can't suppress rolls down my spine.

Ark seems oblivious.

Or so it seems.

A moment after removing his hand from my back, he walks to the far back corner of the elevator.

It isn't the largest elevator I've been in, but the distance between us is enough for me to feel comfortable riding in a confined space with a man I've only recently met.

We only have one floor to travel, but it feels like a dozen. Seconds stretch into minutes, giving Ark plenty of time to interrogate me.

"Do confined spaces scare you? Or is it not knowing the closest exit?"

I'm taken aback that he's paid enough attention in the short time we've interacted to notice my neuroses, but I try to act nonchalant. "Whatever do you m-mean?"

When his huff rustles my hair, I stare at the panel, silently urging it to hurry to our floor.

My prayers are answered, but even with my mind telling me I am safe, my heart races when the doors open onto an unfamiliar area. I don't own a vehicle, so I've never been in the underground parking lot of this building.

This is as scary as it gets for me.

With fear my highest emotion, I blurt out, "The entrance being blocked is m-my main trigger, but I also like to know w-where they are."

I crank my neck back to face Ark when he says, "They?"

"Th-the exits."

An unrecognizable glint flares through his eyes before he dips his chin. "Noted," he says briskly while gesturing for me to exit the elevator first.

I do, albeit hesitantly.

After catching up with me, he guides me toward a sedan similar to the one Val entered. "There are multiple entry and exit points in the underground garage. I will have someone from my security team mark them on a map for you this evening."

I lose the chance to announce I won't need them after tonight when he opens the back door of a vehicle parked too close to a concrete barrier for us to enter at opposite sides.

"I'll enter first and then scoot to the opposite side. That way, if you need to exit at any stage, you can do so safely without stepping into oncoming traffic."

He misses my surprised gasp that he cares about my safety when he slips into the sedan, startling a middle-aged man behind the steering wheel. The man is reading a newspaper and enjoying a late-afternoon snack. Crumbs are scattered throughout his beard, and a twinkle in his eyes reveals he is enjoying his pre-dinner treat.

"Arkadiy." He swallows his shock and a mouthful of the sugary goodness coating his lips before continuing. "I didn't know you were going out again this evening." Crumbs fall onto his lap as he dusts off his business shirt and tie. "Excuse the mess. I'll clean it up right away."

"It's fine, Darius," Ark says, sliding across the expensive leather back seat. When Darius's steely stare slows his entrance, he adds, "But perhaps you can raise the partition so the crumbs remain in your half of the cab."

"Certainly, sir. Thank you."

Ark dips his chin for a brief moment in response to Darius's silent plea for forgiveness before turning his eyes to me. "The child locks are off. You can leave at any time."

He gestures to the mechanism in the car door, proving the honesty of his words, before he extends his hand to me.

I smile in appreciation before accepting his offer. The car isn't too low to the ground, but maintaining my modesty will be difficult since the split in my skirt is now three times longer than before my fall.

Stitches pop as I step into the car, but with most of the damage already done, further tearing is minimal as I settle into the seat next to Ark.

My eyes lift from the illuminated LED lighting trim on the door when Ark asks, "Address?"

"Um..." I fumble through my purse to find the card the bowling alley owner gave me last month when I booked Tillie's party, then hand it to Ark. "He-here. Please." Realizing how rude I sound, I quickly add, "Or anywhere close to there. You-you don't need to take me the whole way. I'm sure you're busy."

He twists his lips as if considering my suggestion. He isn't. He recites the address in full to the driver via an intercom button next to his seat before sinking back as if settling in for a long commute.

I try to do the same. I rest my balled hands on my lap and let my eyes wander to the scenery whizzing by my window when we exit the Chrysler building at a speed too fast to be classed as safe.

Given how fast his driver maneuvers us through a growing swarm of the press, anyone would think the numerous clicks of paparazzi cameras are for Ark.

Their prying ways remind me of how rudely I trampled over Ark's privacy earlier, and that I've yet to issue him the apology he deserves.

"I'm sorry about ea-earlier. I promise I knocked."

"It's fine," he replies, though I can tell he's lying.

I don't know him well enough to read his expressions, but I feel the groove between his brows is a telltale sign. It smoothed when I mentioned my trigger about blocked exits, but it returned more potent than ever when he told his driver he wasn't worried about the mess.

It isn't as deep as earlier, but it's still very much present.

I choke on my spit when Ark takes our conversation in an unexpected direction. "What is your name?"

I try not to stutter, but it is nearly impossible when corresponding with a member of the opposite sex. "Ma-Mara."

"Mara?" It sounds far more feminine when he says it, and it has me hopeful I can one day share it without stuttering.

When Ark arches a brow, waiting for confirmation of his question, I nod.

He twists his lips into a ghostlike grin. "I like it. It is short and easy to spell."

A breathy sigh whistles between my teeth. "That's exactly w-why I picked it."

I snap my mouth shut, realizing I said too much too loudly.

I've never been so reckless.

My concern about making irreversible mistakes is brief. Ark's laugh is as captivating as his handsome face. It carries through my body before clustering in an area I didn't realize could hold its own pulse.

"Hence me going by Ark." He wets his lips again and adjusts his position to face me more directly. "If I had a nickel for every time someone asked me to spell my name, I'd have..."

When he pauses, I suggest, "Enough to have a driver on s-standby?"

He doesn't take my comment as snarky. I'm glad, as that was not my intention. If you earn your money legitimately, I am more than happy to give you the praise you deserve.

Tall poppy syndrome isn't in my vocabulary.

Ark's eyes gleam with roguishness as he replies, "That, and perhaps a little more."

My confidence feeds off his playfulness. "Do you have a preference for what I sh-should call you? Do you prefer Ark or Arkadiy?" When I recall how the driver and the doorman greeted him, I add, "Or perhaps s-sir?"

He contemplates my question longer than expected before saying, "Ark or Arkadiy is fine. Just don't call me Mr. Orlov. That is my stepfather's surname, not mine."

The groove between his brows is back deeper than ever, so I do my best to dispel it. "No-noted."

Ark doesn't follow my lead in keeping things casual. He forces a similar groove between my brows by asking, "Do you always stutter or only when nervous?"

"Um." I fiddle with my skirt, trying to distract my head from the techniques my speech therapist taught me. "I... ah..."

My breath catches when Ark leans across to still my fidgeting hands. It's the simplest of touches, but instead of adding to the shudders that forever affect my vocal cords, it does the opposite. My shakes ease, and a fiery burn bubbles low in my stomach.

Silence reigns supreme as he holds my hand for the next several minutes. It is the kind of quiet that should feel heavy with unspoken agitation, but somehow isn't.

The longer I sit across from him, the faster my heart thumps.

For the first time in a long time, it isn't panic.

When I finally build the courage to glance up, our eyes meet. Something I've never experienced before sends a shiver down my spine. Shockingly, I savor it instead of fearing it.

While returning Ark's stare, I see the same fiery tension burning me alive mirrored in his hooded gaze. Goose bumps break across my skin, but neither of us speak, words not needed to relay a thousand.

I swallow hard, my throat suddenly dry when Ark's tongue darts out to replenish his lips. Once wet, they shift slightly upward, the corners twitching as if fighting not to break into a smile.

My lips curve in response to his battle, an unvoiced acknowledgment of the electricity surging between us. The chemistry is undeniable, a magnetic pull that neither of us seems to be able to ignore, but I'm still shocked. A man as gorgeous and successful as Ark could have any woman he wants, so why would he pick me?

When Ark's hand suddenly moves for my face, the urge to break our stare down is strong, but I don't want to shatter the moment. Instead, I let the tension that has reached a boiling point hold back my wish to flinch.

It isn't a fight I win easily, but a victory, nonetheless.

Ark shifts his eyes between mine as if he can sense my struggle not to pull back as he says, "You have a... There's..." He cusses before he tucks a wayward wisp of hair behind my ear.

I anticipate for his hand to immediately return to his side of the car, so you can imagine my surprise when he tracks the back of his index finger down my cheek. His touch is as basic as it comes but electrifying. It steals my thoughts as ruefully as it clears my stomach of nerves.

They don't leave my body.

They flutter low—*extremely* low.

I can't think while returning his stare. Can't move. I can barely breathe, and I'm not the only one noticing.

"Breathe, Mara." Ark smirks when my lungs instantly obey his snapped command. "Good girl."

Tingles race across my face when he lowers his hand to my mouth so he can drag his thumb over my top lip. The tension is potent enough to amplify every small movement, shift, and breath.

I should be pulling away. He is an owner on my cleaning ledger and, at a guess, a decade older than me, but for the life of me, I can't. I'm frozen in place with desire and praying like hell I'm about to experience my first true kiss.

The heat turns so excruciating that I am seconds from making a fool of myself.

I'm about to initiate an embrace instead of running from one.

Ark saves me from the shame of rejection. "Who did this to you? Who hurt you so badly that you can't speak without stuttering?"

"Wh-what?"

His fingers remain unfurled, even with the danger flaring through his eyes announcing he is far from composed.

"Who hurt you?" After locking his eyes with mine, he bounces them back and forth, his anger picking up. "He is the reason you stutter, isn't he?"

"N-no," I lie.

Another denial sits on the tip of my tongue when he expresses his dislike of my lie with a growl, but I can't set it free. Nothing comes out but needy breaths. My shock is too high that a stranger cares about me more than my father did when I told him what was happening during my numerous speech therapy sessions.

"Tell me," Ark urges, his composure modeling nurturing if you can look past the murderous undertone in his voice.

His name sits in the back of my throat, but before I can spit it out, the driver announces we've reached our destination, which snaps me out of the bubble Ark's protectiveness placed me in.

If only his sorrowed watch could move my legs just as fast.

As Darius's steely eyes bounce between Ark and me, his confusion growing, he asks, "Shall I circle the block?"

"No," I shout a little too loudly, my mouth finally cooperating with the prompts of my brain. "Here is f-fine." I unlatch my belt and sling it off, my hands as shaky as my vocal cords. "Thank you for the ride. I won't take any m-more of your time."

I stumble out of the car less gracefully than I entered it. It doesn't go unnoticed. We're not surrounded by the glitz and glamor of the Chrysler building, but the people milling on the sidewalk know Ark's ride and the man inside are far too flashy for both this side of Myasnikov and me.

4

ARKADIY

*R*afael peers at me when I throw down the umpteenth manila folder this morning so I can drag my hand through my hair. The internal clock I'm striving to ignore ticks louder with each passing second, reminding me of what is meant to be the true purpose of my visit to Myasnikov.

I am supposed to be finding a wife, not mulling over the possible shady childhood of a woman I hardly know.

I've barely slept a wink in the past three nights. The last time my sleep was this lacking was the weekend before I took a placement in the upper house. Fyodor wanted me to "scratch the itch" rigorously enough to keep my hookups out of the tabloids for six months.

I wasn't featured in almost four weeks.

That was a record within itself. Fyodor, however, wasn't impressed.

Sex is how I blow off steam, but that crutch won't cut it this time around, so I haven't tried. Interacting with women on paper is tedious, and I am too close to the end of my rope to pretend it isn't.

It isn't solely unearthing the cause of Mara's stutter keeping me awake, but also my inability to defuse the ruse Rafael orchestrated directly in front of me.

I took his bait lock, stock, and barrel, and he's been acting like a smug prick ever since.

Even though I knew it was a ruse, the way Rafael looked at Mara still affects me now, three days later. He played his well-versed lion-stalking-his-prey ploy, which he's perfected over the past two decades, but Friday night was the first time I wanted to play the role of the hunter desperate to even the playing field.

To do that, I'll have to ignore the ghosts of my past as if their exhumation won't terminate my campaign for the top job in an instant.

I don't know if that is something I can do. A part of me, a side I've not seen in an extremely long time, wants to cocoon Mara from additional harm before beating the fuck out of the person responsible for the fear in her eyes, but that urge comes with a heap of limitations—limitations I'm not sure even Mara would want me to ignore.

Her flinch when I tried to return a stray lock to its counterparts... *fuck.*

It haunts my dreams.

But the gleam in her eyes when she wordlessly begged me to kiss her... *fuck.*

I'd never felt more torn.

I'm still undecided now.

While muttering my frustration at how quickly Mara dug up my deeply buried nurturing side, I turn to face a window spanning one side of the living room. My impending decision weighs heavily on my shoulders, but I can't rush it. I'll be stuck with the woman I select for years, possibly decades, so I need to choose wisely.

My fists clench, turning white, when Rafael's amused gaze locks with mine in the window's reflection, and he has the hide to chuckle at my riled expression.

When my growl reaches his ears, he plasters a ruthless businessman persona on his face before flicking through the applications I've scarcely perused, too bored with Fyodor's top picks to pay them any proper attention.

A wolf whistle ripples through Rafael's lips when he reaches the glossy Polaroids attached to the first dossier. "Your options could be worse, Ark. This woman is…" His teeth gnawing at his palm completes his reply.

My huff beads the window with condensation when I move closer. The sun is high, casting a warm glow over the foot traffic below. I scan the faces, searching for something, or rather, someone to fixate my attention on before I end my campaign for the presidency before it has truly begun.

It was a close call Friday night, one I'm not sure I would have won if Mara hadn't fled the way she did.

As I stand, torn between the political side of my head and the personal, my eyes are drawn to the side entrance of the building like a magnet. Mara is exiting the building from the service entrance. Her dark locks are cascading down her back in loose waves, and her eyes are fixated on something in her hands.

After stuffing her phone into the hidden pocket in her skirt, she weaves through the clog of pedestrians hogging the sidewalk. Even hurried, her strides are graceful and fluid. They have me mesmerized in under a minute.

Something about Mara entrances me—something I can't quite put into words. It could be that a survivor knows a survivor. However, it feels like more than that.

An unexpected frown plays at my lips when I realize how at ease she seems surrounded by strangers varying in weight and height. Does that mean I was the cause of the shakes that hampered her tiny frame so ruefully she stuttered? I yelled at her at the commencement of our first meeting, but my fury wasn't directed at her. I was angry at myself that I had allowed someone to sneak up on me unawares and while naked.

The last time I made that mistake, it cost me dearly.

I promised myself that it would never happen again.

It hasn't in almost thirty years.

While working my jaw side to side, I watch Mara until she is the size of an ant.

My eyes only unglue from the street below when a familiar voice unknowingly announces he has perfect eyesight. "I can see it." Rafael butts his shoulder with mine, shifting my expression of admiration to frustration. "A modern-day fairy tale. Cinderella and her Prince Charming." He waits for our eyes to align in the window's reflection. "The voters will eat it up. This is brilliant, Ark. A surefire winner. I can't believe I didn't think of this sooner."

When he finally takes a breath, I fold my arms over my chest and shake my head, too off-put by an unexpected pocket of emotions to speak.

Rafael frowns, clearly disappointed. "This is the opportunity you've been seeking." He thrusts his hand at the window Mara commanded like a prima ballerina does a stage. "If she can win you over in less than a minute, she will have the public eating out of her palm in under a week."

I look at him as if he's lost his mind. "I don't know what you think you saw, but you are mistaken."

He scoffs, his tone gentle yet firm. "I saw you touch her... multiple times. *Voluntarily.* That has to mean something."

I'm about to accuse him of lying until I remember how thoroughly monitored my transport vehicles are. It wouldn't have mattered if it were a high-end escort slipping into the back of my town car Friday night or a member of the wealthiest family in Russia. If they're in my domain for thirty seconds, my security team would have started a search on them twenty-nine seconds earlier.

Darius's skills are extensive. He served in the military and the secret service and established a highly successful private security firm in under three years. His role within my empire is just as comprehensive as his previous roles. He's been an asset for as long as Rafael and is just as nosy.

"And that *almost* kiss." Air whistles between Rafael's teeth as he fans the collar of his business shirt. "It made me hard." Laughing, he dodges the fist I throw at his midsection. "I'm joking, Ark." He twists to face me, walking backward. "Not about how quickly she disarmed you, though. I was starting to think anyone not paid to bring the heat wouldn't be able to defrost your icy heart. She thawed it in half a second."

I nod, my expression softening when I recall how quickly Mara lowered my defenses. I'd never felt such an immediate urge to both protect someone and wholly consume them, and the desire had nothing to do with Rafael pretending to be interested in her.

Don't misconstrue what I'm saying. Mara is gorgeous with her thick, glossy hair, a body that could make any man weak at the knees, and a face far too innocent to corrupt. But Rafael's interests have always leaned toward blondes.

My eyes snap to Rafael when he gives reason as to why the niggle in my gut hasn't been soothed in days. "Though I'd be lying if I said I couldn't understand your apprehension."

He moves to my desk before tilting over it to whack his fingers on the keyboard of my laptop. He brings up a file similar to the ones I've been mulling over for several hours. It is incredibly scarce, and although it includes its own set of glossy photographs, they're not glamor shots like the other files. They are of Mara's stumble out of my car Friday night and her arrival at work this morning.

"How is there no employment record for her?"

Rafael smiles, happy I'm paying more attention to Mara's dossier than my prospective wives-to-be to point out an inconsistency. "She is paid under the table. It means she earns less than her coworkers, but without a paper trail every taxpayer would give anything to sidestep."

"So she is hiding something."

I realize I said my comment out loud when Rafael replies to it. "Or just plain hiding." His reply frustrates me, but not as much as what he says next. "Her stutter is a defense mechanism." Unease blasts through eyes that have absorbed many horrid things. "Stammering arises to keep the subconscious off undesirable thoughts." The cause of the painful glint in his eyes is exposed when he adds, "She only seems to do it around men, though."

His theory should firm my stance that Mara isn't the right woman to fulfill the role of my temporary wife, not persuade me to seek further confirmation that I scare the living shit out of her. But words shoot out of my mouth before I can stop them. "All men... or just me?"

The tightness of his jaw could excuse his delay in replying. The stiffness in mine made my question barely legible, so he could be facing the same difficulties.

After a beat, Rafael says, "She hasn't been under surveillance long enough to give an adequate answer."

I appreciate his honesty, but it does little to slacken my anger.

I didn't request that Mara be placed under scrutiny, so why is she?

When I ask Rafael about this, he stammers like he didn't lose his stutter with extensive speech therapy thirty years ago. "She... uh... we..."

The firmness of my jaw strengthens my reply. "Remove the hounds from her scent."

"Ark—"

"Now, Rafael!" I can't believe we're having this conversation. My security team, the people I trust to respect and protect my boundaries, crossed the line. "We came onto *her* turf, not the other way around. She doesn't deserve this level of scrutiny. Her privacy should have *never* been violated."

Some of my anger stems from how hard I pushed Mara Friday night to disclose the name of the person who hurt her, but if my team can't understand the importance of respecting a virtual stranger's privacy, how will they respond if my secrets are ever exposed? Would they protect them? Or undo all the hard work I've done the past three decades to keep them concealed?

With my frustration too high to discount, I snatch up the first four files and dump them onto Rafael's lap. "Have them brought in for face-to-face meetings. Tell them to pack enough clothes for a week or two. I'll need more than a few hours to assess their applications."

I more tug on my hair than slide my fingers through it when I rake my hand over my head while heading for the exit. I don't know where I'm going. My feet move, and I follow them.

After barging through a swarm of media, I walk briskly down the street that leads to Myasnikov Private Hospital. My breaths as I vie to lose the tail of a handful of media members are visible in the cool air. The city is gaining attention as rapidly as my bid for office is alive with activity. Health professionals hog most of the sidewalk, and the voices of students varying in age project out of a high-rise building that doubles as a school.

My thoughts are a whirlwind of anger and confusion, but the bustle simmers when the woman who has held my thoughts captive for the past three days re-enters the frame.

Mara is galloping down the front stairs of a school, holding the hand of a little girl who couldn't look more like her mother if she tried, though her cheeks are far whiter.

I learn why when their hop off the final step sees the child rushing to the bushes hedging the footpath. She loses her morning tea in three stomach-churning heaves before she peers up at Mara with glistening, tear-filled eyes. "I don't feel good."

"I know, sweetheart. It's okay. Mommy will make you feel better soon. We just need to get you home first."

I've barely gotten over my surprise that Mara is old enough to be a mother of a child who looks around nine or ten when I'm struck down with shock for the second time.

She didn't stutter.

Not once.

The knowledge both intrigues and concerns me.

Mara hooks her daughter's backpack onto her shoulder, stuffs the bag she arrived at work with this morning under her arm, and then carefully pulls her daughter into her chest until the collar of her maid's outfit catches her tears. "Let's get you home and into bed."

They make it halfway to the bus stop at the front of the school when Mara's daughter is sick again. This time, the deluge is released into Mara's oversized purse.

I would have been irreversibly scarred for such a senseless act, but Mara takes it in stride like she was born to be a mother. "It's okay, darling. It is nothing a bit of elbow grease won't fix."

She hides her grimace well until the bus they're endeavoring to reach chugs past the bus stop without stopping. With the shelter empty and the school still hours from the final bell of the day, the driver stayed in the flow of traffic instead of conducting a cautious merger.

"Shit," Mara murmurs, glaring at the back of the dirty bus.

Humid air fills my lungs when I tip my head back to take in the clouds that announce a storm is brewing. The dark, ominous sky adds to the concern etched on Mara's beautiful face, but she keeps her daughter unaware of her panic. She gathers her close to her side and continues toward the bus shelter without the slightest fault to her strides.

I can't issue the same verdict when she spots me standing at the side, stalking her. Her pupils widen to the size of saucers as her clutch on her daughter's shoulders tightens. I can't tell if her response is frightened or excited.

If the whiteness of her daughter's cheeks is anything to go by, I don't have time to deliberate. She is moments from being sick again.

With the urgency of the situation in the forefront of my mind, I do something I've never done before.

I go against the cautions of my gut and hail a cab.

When one stops in front of me two seconds later, Mara appears relieved.

Her relief doesn't linger for long.

After lowering her eyes to the bag concealing her daughter's illness from the cab driver, she returns them to my face. "Thank you. Bu-but we're okay. I can't aff—"

A brutal heave cuts her off and has her rushing for the cab like she'd sell a kidney to get her daughter home and tucked safely in her bed.

The gust of her brisk strides brings up the scent still embedded in the interior of my town car. It is still indescribable. It's somewhat floral but not overpowering like most women's perfumes. It doesn't make me sick to my stomach.

It is an intoxicating smell that has me following her into the back of the cab without time for Mara or my head to protest.

5

MARA

*A*lthough I shouldn't, when the cab stops at the front of my apartment building, I sigh in relief when Ark digs his hand into the back pocket of his trousers to remove his wallet. I don't have the funds for additional fares outside of school and work commutes on my MetroCard, so I could never pull together enough funds for a sixty-dollar fare.

"Keep the change," Ark says, tossing the driver almost double the fee.

His generosity is surprising but not unexpected. Tillie was sick again during the drive to the other side of town, and although the cab's floor remains spotless, the smell blooming from my handbag and hair is atrocious.

My hair caught what my bag missed, and when I throw open the cab door to exit, the quickest whiff announces the cabbie will need more than a tree-shaped air freshener to convince his next rider to switch on the meter.

"I'll take her," Ark offers when I almost slip while struggling to maintain my grip on Tillie's school backpack, my vomit-filled handbag, and a child who looks deathly lethargic.

I'm not given the chance to deny his offer. In a swift pluck-and-sweep maneuver, Ark pulls Tillie into his arms and exits the cab from the opposite side.

My panic is so high that I trip over my feet while racing for the sidewalk Ark is commanding like a business mogul would a boardroom. Women slow their steps to admire him, and even a handful of men turn their heads and gawk.

Although I understand their wish to drink in the beautiful specimen in front of them, it does little to settle my panic. "I sh-should take her. She's not well. I don't want you to get s-sick."

"I'll be fine," Ark replies as if accustomed to dealing with vomit.

Fear tears me in two when he walks toward my building like he's been here before. The positioning of his hands as he carries Tillie into our building is nowhere close to inappropriate, and Tillie doesn't seem the slightest bit fazed she is being carried like a child half her age, but I learned the hard way what happens when you accept help from men you assume are meant to protect you.

"Come, Mara." Ark's bark snaps me out of a fear that has rendered me motionless. "You'll catch pneumonia if you remain standing in the rain."

I stare at him in bewilderment. That's how heated my blood is. I had no clue it was raining, even with fat droplets rolling down my cheeks. I assumed they were tears.

I fall into step behind Ark and Tillie just as another brutal heave leaves Tillie's tiny frame. She was born on her due date, but teen pregnancies have multiple disadvantages—the primary: underweight infants. Tillie has always been a head shorter than her peers and several pounds lighter.

When Ark reaches the stoop of the stairs and peers up, I almost tell him that I can take it from here, but the gawk of the building supervisor stops me. Eduard gives me the creeps, and although I've known him a lot longer than I have Ark, there's no doubt who I trust more.

"We're on the fi-fifth floor." When Ark's eyes sling to me, shame overtakes some of the anxiety hammering my voice. "And the elevator is out of order."

His smile lessens my shakes further. "I guess it's lucky I skipped cardio this morning."

An unexpected giggle leaves Tillie's mouth when Ark gallops up the first flight of stairs like she doesn't weigh a thing. I did the same when she was a toddler, but as the years passed and her height crept closer to mine, my back started acting as if it were as old as our building.

Once we reach the fifth floor, Ark steps to the side so I can lead our walk. The minimal floor space means I usually close the gap in eight solid strides, but it takes double that amount this time.

It's hard moving forward when your eyes are constantly darting backward.

My keys clang when I stuff one into the deadbolt I installed against Eduard's wishes, and I crank open the lock.

When Tillie nuzzles into Ark's chest before telling him that her bedroom is the third door on the left, a knot forms in my stomach

We've never invited a member of the opposite sex into our apartment. Not even Tillie's close male friends she's known since kindergarten have crossed the threshold of our front door.

Some of the tension swallowing me whole becomes manageable when Ark seeks my permission to enter my home before doing so. Not a lot, just enough that I stray my eyes to the kitchen at the front of my apartment for only the quickest second before shadowing his walk.

The knife block is full, but the knives aren't overly sharp. They'd barely cause a scratch.

As Ark walks down the long hallway, he takes in my apartment as if it's not a dime a dozen around these parts, his expression neither disgusted nor impressed.

Years of practice allow me to slip my keys out of the lock and wedge the longest between my middle and index fingers without making a sound.

I don't feel the need to protect myself, more that I don't want my daughter to walk down the same scary corridor I was forced to walk in my youth.

Tillie looks so calm when Ark places her on her bed. She doesn't even flinch when he tugs up the covers on her bed like she isn't wearing shoes.

I'm not surprised he's missed them. Her gym shoes are so soleless that she may as well not be wearing any.

"Do you have a bucket? Or are you happy for her to continue using your purse?"

When Ark spins around to witness my response to his witty comment, his eyes lower to the key I'm clutching as a makeshift shiv before they lift to my face. His lips arch at one side as if he's happy I've prepared for a battle, before he glances past me.

"The bathroom is close, but you'd rather be safe than sorry. It isn't hard to remove vomit from carpet, but the smell takes ages to go away." He sounds as if he is speaking from experience, and it eases my hesitation by a smidge.

"I have a bucket." I nudge my head to the bathroom he referenced. "It is above the w-washing machine." The *broken* washing machine.

Ark moves forward too quickly for my stunned head.

I flinch, and I hate myself for it.

The devastation in his eyes cuts like a knife, as does the sheer actuality beaming from them when he says, "I won't hurt you, Mara."

I know sits on the tip of my tongue, but it remains entombed in my throat no matter how often I try to fire it off. It could be because my fear doesn't center around myself. Stopping Tillie from facing the demons of my past is the only thing of importance to me right now.

As if he heard my silent pledge that this isn't about him or me, Ark dips his chin in understanding before he slips past me.

The hairs on my nape prickle when he murmurs, "I will leave the bucket by the door before waiting for you in the kitchen. That way, none of the exits are blocked."

I should tell him to leave, to let us be, but instead, my lungs inhale a shaky breath before I nod. I don't want him to leave any more than I wish I were brave enough not to run from him Friday night.

Even with Tillie sitting between us, sick and clammy, the crackling of energy was undeniable during our cab ride across Myasnikov. Even Tillie's dour mood perked up a smidge after feeding off it.

I can't see Ark's face since my eyes are locked on the emergency escape exit hidden behind tattered curtains. I don't need to. The warmth of his grin makes heating unnecessary. It dots my nape with sweat and has me concerned Tillie's stomach issues are more sinister than her enjoying too many sugary treats.

Her cheeks are the color of beets.

I learn why when a second after Ark exits her room, partly closing the door behind him, she jackknifes into a half-seated position and adopts a look of shock. She did the same thing when John Pearce replaced the previous Purple Wiggle.

The Wiggles are an Australian children's program that Tillie fell in love with several years ago. When I announced the reason behind her Australian name, she became Aussie-obsessed. At the start, she watched shows like *The Wiggles* and *Bluey*. Now, she devours daytime soaps with Mrs. Lichard every afternoon after school.

Although she outgrew her Wiggles hysteria three years ago, her fascination with John has yet to release its hold.

She is too young to have a boyfriend, so I've never discouraged her crush.

I may regret that decision now.

John lives in Australia.

Ark, on the other hand, is only a handful of miles away.

This crush will be more difficult to deter, and I'm not entirely sure I am the right woman for the job. I hardly know the man rummaging through my limited bathroom supplies, yet panic isn't the only thing slicking my skin with sweat. Excitement is there as well.

After placing my keys on a chest of drawers near Tillie's door—and having a stern talking-to myself to get with the program—I walk to her bedside. She's staring at her bedroom door with flushed cheeks and wide eyes. If we were a cartoon, love hearts would be bouncing from her eyes.

"Tillie Malenkov. If Mrs. Pasnov finds out you were pretending to be sick to get an early mark from school, you'll get detention for a week."

Her mouth falls open before it snaps shut. "I'm not pretending." Her voice relays the honesty of her reply, much less the greening of her gills.

"I've had a sore stomach all day." Her lovey-dovey expression is back, though not as strong as it was in the cab. "But not even the worst tummy ache would have me missing how pretty he is."

"Men are not pretty. They're handsome."

I unknowingly walk straight into her trap. "So you *did* notice how handsome he is."

Embarrassed that I'm such an awkward gawker that my ten-year-old noticed, I ruffle her hair before endeavoring to keep my focus on the cause of her stomachache. "Your tummy is sore because you ate birthday cake for breakfast." I push back her curls and check her for a temperature to be sure a gluttonous diet is the cause of her sickness. Her forehead feels warm but not scorching hot. "I told you too much sugar is bad for you."

She folds her arms in front of her chest and huffs. "Mrs. Lichard said the same thing when I packed leftover cake for lunch."

"Tillie..."

"It was fresher than the bread, and I didn't want it to go to waste." Portions of the child I raised hide behind the glint of indulgence in her eyes when she adds, "I know how much you spent on it. I saw the price list at the bakery last week when Mrs. Lichard paid the final payment for you." Her chin balances on her chest, her loved-up gleam nowhere to be seen. "You shouldn't have spent so much on me."

Her quivering bottom lip breaks my heart. "But you loved that cake."

"I did..." She grips her stomach as the color her cheeks have held for only half a minute drains. "But it doesn't taste as good coming up as it did going down."

When she rapidly swallows, I race for the door, snatch up the bucket Ark left there, and then bolt back to her bed with only half a second to spare.

"Mo-Mommy," Tillie cries through a hiccup when the brutal heaves surging through her body spring tears into her eyes. She hates being sick almost as much as she hates when I am right. "I shouldn't have eaten so much cake."

"You're okay, sweetheart. Mommy is right here." I gesture for her to scoot over before joining her on her bed, completely forgetting that I have an unexpected visitor waiting for me in my kitchen.

Desperate to take Tillie's focus off the mess in the bucket, I ask, "What will John think when he finds out you went and got yourself a new crush?"

"I think he'll be okay," she replies through a yawn. "Because I don't want Ark to be my boyfriend..." Her eyes express the words she's too afraid to speak.

I want him to be yours.

6

MARA

By the time I have Tillie settled, the bucket is half-full, and my neck is kinked. I sling my legs off a bed too small for two, stretch out, and then release a big breath. Signs of the fatigue headache that threatened to surface half the day are nowhere near as bad now. They've almost entirely vanished, which is surprising considering the unusual smell in the air.

My body is weird. It can handle inhaling chemically laced cleaning products all day, but something as simple as too much basil on a croissant instigates a migraine.

When I take a whiff of the peculiar scent, my brows stitch. It's not a smell I've sampled before. It isn't sweet like the slosh in the bottom of the bucket, more pungent like burning hair or... *green beans?*

My heart leaps when the fire alarm sounds half a second later.

Tillie is so heavily asleep that my launch off her bed doesn't wake her. She snuggles deeper into her pillow as I race in the direction from which the rancid scent is coming.

I'm taken aback for the second time in under a minute when my entrance into the kitchen doesn't bring me face-to-face with an unmanageable inferno.

A six-foot-three hunk with his sleeves rolled to his elbows and his brows furled, though—there's one of them.

Ark's eyes shoot to mine when my shadow falls over the saucepan blooming enough smoke to warrant multiple windows and a door being opened. Guilt is hardening his features. It's barely seen through his embarrassment, though.

"I was trying to make Tillie some soup." He grimaces while taking in the product, which is burned to the bottom of the pot. "It's been a while since I've cooked. I only remembered that *after* I started cooking."

I almost laugh at the sheer disgust on his face that he is incapable of heating a can of premade soup, but the tea towel he's using to fan smoke out the open kitchen window catching fire stops me.

The setting of my ancient oven is too high.

Flames are licking the edges of the saucepan instead of heating its base.

Ark tugs the tea towel away from the stovetop when he notices the flames. "Shit. I swear I am trying to help."

"In the sink," I shout when his flap almost causes the curtains to set alight. "Put it in the sink."

He hooks the tea towel into the sink like his business shirt is a pitcher's jersey as I tug up the faucet. I blast the flames with bitterly cold water before shifting my focus to the cause of its incineration.

With the apron part of my uniform, I lift the saucepan from the stovetop and carefully edge it toward the sink. My penny-pinching heart feels sick when I water down the meal he was preparing, but no amount of wishful thinking will alter the facts. The soup isn't salvageable.

When I say that to Ark, he looks at the charred remains of what he had hoped would be supper before returning his eyes to me. His expression is mortified. I'd feel bad if it matched his verbal response.

The laughter barreling out of him can only convey one thing.

Utter joy.

His chuckles are loud and wholeheartedly addictive. Before I can consider the lunacy of our exchange, similarly boisterous giggles bubble up my chest. They're not as noisy as Ark's or as thunderous, but the weight they lift off my shoulders can't be denied.

The unease knotting my stomach loosens with every throaty gargle, and within minutes, it is replaced with lust.

I'm not the only one noticing the shift in temperament. Friction sizzles half a second before Ark shifts on his feet to face me.

Just like Friday night, every minute move he makes is amplified. The way his breath catches when he spots my happy tears, the bob of his Adam's apple when his hooded gaze lowers to my chest, and the stiffness of my nipples when it dawns on them that they've secured his attention.

Every move is excruciatingly apparent, and the press of my thighs when he confesses, "You didn't stutter," worsens it. He isn't seeking confirmation, more vocalizing his disbelief. "Not while speaking with Tillie or me."

"Because..." I stop, genuinely lost for a reply.

I can't recall the last time I've spoken a sentence with the opposite sex and not stuttered.

It's been years, decades, even.

Untapped sexual chemistry prickles the back of my neck when pride stretches across Ark's face. He tilts his head to the side and stares at me, a smile playing at one side of his kissable lips.

I squirm as we stand across from each other, staring but not speaking. I've never felt so many sparks. I thought it was something made up by romance novelists to explain extreme carnal desire. I was wrong. The attraction I feel for this man is visible in the air, and shockingly, the hisses and cracks aren't solely coming from my half of the kitchen.

They're just as searing from Ark's half.

My heart drums my ribs when I decide to encourage an exchange I was once scared of instead of shying away.

I step closer to Ark, trembling all over.

"Mara..."

Just the gravelly deliverance of my name sets my skin on fire, and I can't help but moan through the aftermath of its brilliance.

A low hum rumbles from Ark's chest as he tilts toward me like he isn't seeking excuses for us not to act on the tension hotter than the inferno that almost engulfed my kitchen. "This isn't why I stayed. I needed to make sure—"

Unlike Friday night, I lunge headfirst into the lust haze instead of repelling from it.

I kiss him.

I want to pretend I instigated our kiss because I am brave, but we both know that isn't true. I simply can't fight the tension for a second longer.

God himself wouldn't be strong enough to win this battle.

Barely half a second passes before the threat of rejection ceases to exist.

"Fuck it," Ark breathes against my lips before he snakes his hand up my back and sinks it into my knotted locks.

Our teeth clash when he slides his tongue deep inside my mouth. He duels it with mine, sampling and tasting me before he drags it along the roof of my mouth.

I've never been kissed in such a manner. I honestly don't know what to do.

With Ark's guidance, I match the strokes of his tongue and the movements of his lips until he's panting and as breathless as me.

A kiss so violent shouldn't feel so good. It is consuming and blistering, an embrace so all-encompassing that I don't realize we're moving until my back is splayed against the refrigerator and Ark's body presses flush against mine.

He squashes into me so profoundly that the only part of my body capable of moving is my lips.

The inability to move doesn't weaken the intensity of our kiss. We taste and tease each other for what feels like hours but is barely minutes.

My lips feel bruised when Ark pulls away to drag his nose down the throb in my throat. He draws in a long breath, and then an approving sound rumbles from his chest.

"You smell so good."

He licks my neck, sending a shiver down my spine, while the hand not weaved through my hair slides down my back, both pulling me closer and de-suctioning me from the refrigerator.

A desperate gasp leaves me when he kneads my ass before he tilts my hips upward.

He's hard, as lost to the tension as I am.

How can that be?

How can a man so deliriously handsome and wildly successful be attracted to me?

With a confidence I'll never fully embrace, I curl my fingers around the chunky leather material of his belt and then tug him forward, needing firmer contact.

The hiss that strains through Ark's teeth when the most intimate parts of our bodies clash causes an avalanche of kisses and moans.

While kissing me like he can't breathe without his mouth on mine, he grips my ass and rocks his hips, grinding against me. I whimper shamelessly as he drives me to the brink of ecstasy without removing a single article of clothing.

The head of his cock rubs at my clit, sending shockwaves of pleasure spasming through me, while his mouth makes my lips tingle. I'm so mindless with need that my hands seek something to grip to ride through the waves seconds from pummeling into me.

"No touching," Ark snaps out when my hands find solace with his shoulders, his voice pained even while brimming with lust.

With his rhythm unaffected, he gathers my wrists and pins them above my head before his spare hand slides under my skirt.

"P-please," I beg when his fingertips stop just shy of my damp panties.

I should be ashamed he's made me so desperate that I'm willing to beg, but the instant his hand slips between my thighs and his fingers flutter past the sensitive skin between my legs, all cognitive thoughts are lost.

"*Yesss.*"

My thighs shake with more than fear when he rubs the pad of his index finger against my clit. He rolls it ever so slowly, producing sparks strong enough to buckle my knees.

"Ark," I squeak out breathlessly, scared of the sensation rolling through me. I've never experienced it before. It is overwhelming and scary but also blazingly hot at the same time. "P-please."

With a smirk that will highlight my dreams for years to come, he watches me through hooded lids as I squirm and moan beneath him.

The pure thirst in his eyes alone could get me off.

I'm on the cusp of begging, when my imminent orgasm is ripped away from me by a scratchy, sick-filled voice. "Mommy..."

I freeze for half a second before the maternal instincts I should have never been without kick back in.

Almost cruelly, I free my hands from Ark's grip and push him away.

My body hates losing his contact almost as much as my heart loathes his expression when I shout, "I'll be there in a m-minute, sweetheart. Mommy was just..."—I scan the area, seeking an excuse for my erroneous mistake—"making you s-some soup."

My throat works hard to swallow when Tillie replies, "Okay." The unease of her one-worded reply makes sense when she murmurs, "But don't you think it is a little early for dinner?"

Dinner? We've not yet had lunch, so why would I be prepping dinner?

As the patter of Tillie's tiny feet returning to her room trickles into my ears, I stare at the inbuilt clock in the kitchen range, certain we must have had a power outage last week I failed to notice.

I collected Tillie from school a little before noon. It is now 2:55 p.m.

That can't be right. I can't lose almost two hours in the blink of an eye. I know we arrived home around noon because I heard the jingle of Mrs. Lichard's favorite midday show throwing to a commercial through the front door of her apartment. The episodes only run for half an hour.

Ark's kiss was mind-blowing, but there's no way it lasted longer than ten to fifteen minutes. The wave in my stomach would have crested multiple times by now if it had been an hour-long exchange.

That can only mean one thing.

Sickness bombards me when I realize how careless I've been.

I let a stranger into my home while my daughter was here and then fell asleep.

If that isn't bad enough, I kissed him when he made himself at home instead of kicking him out.

How could I have been so reckless?

Lust, instalove, or whatever the hell you want to call my bizarre kinship with Ark should have never overridden my moral obligation to ensure my daughter's safety.

I'm disgusted with myself, but instead of taking it out on the person deserving of my wrath, I do what I do with every man I cross paths with.

I make out my neuroses are his fault.

"You sh-should go."

Ark balks, shocked by the whiplash of my moods, before he smooths his ruffled expression with a frown. "Of course."

Another wave of stupidity crashes into me when he gathers his suit jacket from a chair tucked under the kitchen table.

He wasn't heating Tillie soup from a can. He was making it from scratch. Freshly diced chicken breast, carrots, celery, and beans are spread across the kitchen counter, and there's enough bread to last us a week.

I'm torn on how to respond to his generosity.

How can I build trust and protect my daughter at the same time?

To Tillie, it is as simple as letting Ark in like she did when she invited him into our home.

During our conversation before she fell asleep, she said she likes Ark because our shared cab ride was the first time she'd seen me interact with a man and not physically shake.

Although I tried to push off her observation as me being too worried about her to remember the gender of the person we were sharing a cab with, she said I'll never stop being frightened of the unknown if I don't take the occasional leap of faith.

My online therapist has expressed similarly. She's accused me multiple times of pushing the insecurities and distrust other men gave me onto undeserving victims, and that I'll never be happy until I learn that not everyone is out to hurt me.

Her advice is easy to set aside. She doesn't know what is best for my daughter and me. But Tillie's advice is harder to ignore. She's an old soul. She has been here before and has knowledge beyond her years, so maybe she's right. Perhaps I should stop lumping the distrust a minority gave me onto every man I encounter.

My dive into the deep end minutes ago favored me in a way I could have never anticipated. I can only hope it serves me as well this time around.

"W-wait."

Ark stops partway out my front door but doesn't turn around. He keeps his eyes to the front and his hands balled at his sides, leaving the ball entirely in my court.

It should make what I'm about to say easier, but my voice still comes out rickety. "You can s-stay. If-if you want?"

His chest rises and falls three times before he mutters, "Don't do that." I stare at him like he can read minds when he adds, "Don't ever feel like you need to compromise her safety to make an adult feel comfortable. She"—he cranks his head back to face me before he nudges it to Tillie's room—"comes first. *Always.*"

Since every word he speaks is gospel, I nod without thought.

His smile sets my pulse racing, but it does nothing to ease the tension since it sees him leaving without another word shared between us.

7

ARKADIY

*a*s I exit Mara's building, my steps more reluctant than the ones I used to climb the rickety stairwell, I squash my phone to my ear.

It rings once before Darius answers. "Sir."

My breaths fill the air with a white cloud when I instruct, "I need you to collect me from—"

"I'm out front," he interrupts, humored I thought I could travel anywhere without his shadow.

As I flare my nostrils, striving to cool my skyrocketing body temperature, I scan the street, seeking a blacked-out SUV. My mind is spinning, trapped in a vortex of lust and despair. I love the way Mara looked at me when I pinned her to the refrigerator and kissed her senseless, but her stare when she pondered her daughter's safety in my presence...

Fuck.

It cut me to pieces.

Ten seconds after ripping my fingers through my hair, I find my ride. The ultra-dark tint gives away that it is one in my fleet of many, not to mention the government plates.

My job description isn't a secret. It is just rare to find me in a housing project without news outlets documenting my every move.

When I slip into the back seat seconds after ending our call, Darius's dark eyes find mine in the rearview mirror. When we're without fellow constituents, I usually ride up front. I chose differently this time because I need a second to wrap my head around why I didn't immediately leave Mara's apartment when she fell asleep with her daughter.

Instead of slipping out quietly, I acted like the creep I'm sure her building supervisor is, her belongings untouched but thoroughly inspected.

I thought I could make up for my stalking ways by stocking the bare cupboards I took in while snooping through her possessions, seeking answers to the secrets her eyes hold.

A trip to the market didn't seem like enough. In twenty minutes, I went from purchasing the products needed to improve her daughter's health to cooking them.

I can't recall the last time I cared enough to want to help, but the chance to deliberate further is lost when Rafael asks, "Was that you?"

A cuss ripples through the cool afternoon air. He didn't scare me. I sensed his presence for half a second before spotting him in the back driver's side seat from the corner of my eye.

His head nudge is the cause of my profanity.

A fire truck is rolling down the narrow street with its sirens blazing and lights flashing.

Lying isn't my forte—anymore—so I'll be honest. "I tried to make chicken soup."

Raf arches a brow but keeps the rest of his expression neutral, never willing to give anything away too freely. "Tried?"

"And failed." My huff fills the car's cab with humidity. "Clearly."

He smiles as if he is loving seeing a side of me I've not displayed in an extremely long time, but since my political career is always at the forefront of his mind, he signals for Darius to go around the firetruck, which has come to a stop at the front of Mara's building.

We make it half a block before Rafael's inquisitiveness gets the better of him. "Is she sick?"

I almost nod until the teasing flare in his eyes announces his question isn't regarding Tillie.

It is referencing Mara.

When I shake my head, his brows furrow. "Then why were you making soup?" As he rubs his hands together, he corrects, "Then why were you *trying* to make soup?"

"Because I was hungry."

He doesn't believe my lie.

He never does. It is one of the reasons I don't bother.

My heart hammers my ribs when I give honesty a whirl for the second time tonight. "Mara isn't sick. Her child is."

We cross an intersection and travel another half a block before Rafael's shock clears enough for him to speak. "She has a kid?"

I tilt my chin to hide my smile before bobbing it. "Yeah."

Tillie has a lot of similarities to her mother—the main one is her ability to instantly disarm me. I want to protect her as much as I want to protect her mother. The easiest way for me to do that is to keep as much distance between us as possible. There's just something about Mara that makes that seem impossible. When it's just us, it is like no one else exists.

The way I pinned her to her refrigerator with my crotch announces this without prejudice.

Needing to see the expression Rafael will fight to conceal, I twist my torso to face him before saying, "From the birthday cards on the fridge, she turned ten last week."

"She?" He undertakes the fight of his life to conceal his worry. His act is as woeful as my heart's assurance that my interests in Mara don't stem from a hero complex.

Fixing the mistakes of others was the entire basis of my childhood. Even if I wasn't responsible for breaking it, I was expected to fix it. My endeavors to mend the unfixable only stopped when my gallantry arrived ten minutes too late.

No amount of glue can fix death.

When I nod, Rafael licks his lips, his scrutiny too hot to ignore. "I didn't see anything about a kid in her dossier."

"The dossier I asked you to get rid of?" My fury can't be hidden in my tone or expression.

"An hour ago." When my hands ball, he speaks faster. "Or three. Who's counting?" He continues talking before I remind him that time management is task one of his job description. "Hiding shit takes time, Ark, and I figured since you asked me to get rid of it, you'd want me to hide it deep." Nothing but honesty rings in his tone. "I also thought you'd want to see this before I bury it."

I hiss when he flips open a manila folder and hands it to me.

The images are grainy, but they turn my blood to stone.

"What happened?"

As I flick through still surveillance images of Mara being assaulted at a bus stop not far from the Chrysler building, Rafael gives me a basic rundown. "She stayed back to help clean up a party her last employer held. She was jumped by a low-ranked thug on her way home. He took her purse, a fake tennis bracelet, and this..." He dumps a photograph of a pendant, which I'm confident doubles as an heirloom. It's a family crest I swear I've seen before.

"Was her assault reported to the authorities?" I ask through a tight, stern jaw.

My thigh muscles spasm when Rafael shakes his head. "But the perp was caught and appropriately sentenced."

I'm confused until he encourages me to flip toward the end of the dossier. The final few images show a blonde-haired woman assisting Mara from the ground and onto a bus.

"That's—"

"Zoya Dokovic."

Rafael whistles as if impressed. I don't know why. I thought Zoya's husband would be my biggest rival while running for office, so I've kept tabs on everyone in his realm. I had no clue Kazimir would step back from the role he was born to do when his grandfather died.

I can only hope his father will follow suit. He's currently beating me in the polls, even with him not having a wife at his side during early campaigning.

The widow title will forever triumph over the playboy title when it comes to the minority vote.

"Kazimir took out the trash within hours of the assault being reported to him." Rafael looks confused. I understand why when he says, "Mara is in favor with both the Dokovics and the Ivanovs, so why the fuck is she living in a dump on the wrong side of town?"

I almost shrug until I recall how headstrong my baby sister is. She could be offered the world, and she'd turn her nose down at it. She doesn't want to be handed the keys to the castle. She wants to build it from the ground up.

I can see Mara being just as determined.

The thought makes me hard and pisses me off.

She shouldn't have to fight. It should be her God-given right to live without fear. But I know better than any man that that isn't always possible. Sometimes you need to fight fire with fire.

The reminder sees me shifting my focus to Darius. "Run a background search on the supervisor of Mara's building."

He doesn't seek clarification as to who Mara is, announcing she's been discussed with him sometime over the past three days. The knowledge firms my jaw enough to be heard in my following sentence but not enough to stop it entirely. "Extend your search past the usual perimeters. Just because you don't have a criminal record doesn't mean you shouldn't have one."

The bottle of shampoo I stole out of Mara's bathroom because I thought it would be the only way I could intermingle our scents announces this without fault.

8

MARA

My temples ache while taking in the number of rooms I am rostered to clean this morning. The Chrysler building only has a handful of permanent tenants. Most are fly-in and fly-out residents, so it was surprising to learn we were almost full occupancy when I arrived for my shift this morning.

The number of apartments I need to service is overwhelming because it took Tillie three full days to recover from the stomach bug an on-call doctor assured me wasn't from eating out-of-date birthday cake.

I would have started fresh next week if I were entitled to sick leave.

Since I'm not, I must suck it up.

I can't afford more time off.

I want to scream, or better yet, walk away from it all, but I can't. The indecent length of the split in my skirt persuaded the bowling alley manager to a ten percent discount last week, but the on-call doctor who did a house visit was female and married.

The bill for her visit means I'll have to salvage more than the remnants at the bottom of a burned pot to make it through the next month not hungry.

After stocking my cart with cleaning products and toilet paper that is too soft not to lint in the backside of anyone fortunate enough to use it, I rub my temples, trying to ease the tension headache forming there.

Not all the throb is compliments of staying up past midnight, hand-washing my uniform and handbag for today. A lot of it belongs on the shoulders of the name at the top of my cleaning schedule, and wondering if he's the reason my hair is pulled back into a tight, headache-producing, and highly unflattering bun.

I'd only recently replaced the product I use sparingly since it cost over thirty dollars a bottle, but when I went to wash Tillie's vomit out of my hair Monday night, my shampoo was nowhere to be seen.

I couldn't call Ark and accuse him of stealing my shampoo. That would be preposterous considering he'd spent four times that for a cab to drive us home, and don't get me started on the food he left behind when I kicked him out. But I'd be a liar if I said I wasn't a bit peeved.

My cocoa butter and rose shampoo is the only luxury item I kept from my childhood. It reminds me of the innocence that was cruelly stripped from me and how keeping some memories of my past unlocked will ensure Tillie never faces the same hurt I did.

I shake off thoughts that will strengthen my headache before checking my cleaning cart is appropriately stocked. The more I try to keep my focus off Ark, the more my temples pound. The guests Ark is anticipating have requested things most men don't use.

Makeup-removing wipes have numerous purposes, but sanitary pads are a little more telling of the gender of the people about to plump out Ark's apartment from two bodies to six.

I can't help but wonder when Ark's invitation went out. Was it before or after we kissed?

My ego wants to say it was before, but considering I've not heard hide nor hair of Ark since we locked lips, I assume it is the latter.

After a quick shoulder roll and a prompt reminder that Ark is out of my league, I ensure I have everything in order before heading to the first apartment on my cleaning roster.

When I reach Ark's apartment, I take a deep breath to clear my voice of nerves before gently knocking on the servants' entrance door. "H-housekeeping."

I wait a moment. Then, when no one answers, I use the master key to enter.

Not wanting to burst Ark's privacy bubble for the third time in under a week, I continue to announce my presence while heading toward the primary suite. "Arkadiy?"

We usually address tenants by their surnames, but the disdain on Arkadiy's face when he gave me his preferences ensures Arkadiy will be as formal as my greetings will go.

"Are you h-home?"

I startle when a voice from the side breaks through the thudding of my pulse in my ears. "He isn't here." Rafael smiles to assure me he is remorseful for my jump before he says, "He had a handful of errands to run before... he... ah..."

I nod, saving us both from the embarrassment of him admitting I'm the cause of Ark's absence.

Gratitude flares through Rafael's kind eyes before he asks, "Is there anything I can help you with?"

"No. Thank you." I hook my thumb to the primary suite, my hand's shake noticeable. "I sh-should get a start. My s-schedule is full today."

Rafael smiles like he isn't disgusted that I clean strangers' messes for a living or that I speak with a stutter. "All right. Let me know if you need anything."

I mimic his gesture before making a beeline for Ark's room, my pace fast. The quicker I get this apartment sparklingly clean, the faster I can move on to wallowing in another million-dollar abode I could have lived in for free if I had accepted Maksim Ivanov's generosity six months ago.

I declined his offer of a rent-free apartment because I firmly believe in karma. If someone helps you, it is your moral obligation to help someone else. If you do something bad, expect something bad in return.

That's how life should work. Does it always transpire as intended? Not always, but for the most part, the odds have swayed in my favor, so I will continue with my beliefs until they are proven inadequate.

The scent of someone recently showering fills the air when I enter

Ark's room. The towels dumped at the foot of the bed announce that the bathroom is void of a soul, but I still check, just in case.

It's empty—of people.

The bottle of shampoo I've been seeking for the past three days is present, though, and it makes me confused about Ark's game plan.

It isn't like he can't afford his own shampoo. The produce he purchased from a local market wasn't from the bagged seconds stock I usually veer for every payday. It is top-shelf produce that comes with a surcharge. Even the sparkling water I stacked in the bar's mini refrigerator last week cost more per gallon than my favorite haircare brand.

My nails nick the label of the shampoo bottle when a voice sounds from behind me. "Before I forget, I was meant to ask you..." Rafael stops talking when my jump can't be missed. "Sorry. I didn't mean to scare you."

"Yo-you didn't."

He did. He snuck up on me so agilely that I didn't hear his steps, and it has made me mindful that Ark had every right to be furious last week. I'm not naked, and I still feel somewhat violated since I am in a bathroom. It is usually a place of sanctum.

When Rafael's sigh announces he heard my lie from a mile out, I twist to face him. I both loath and admire the way he leans against the doorjamb like he doesn't have a care in the world.

If only his worldly eyes announced the same.

They're broken, though not as guarded as Ark's.

"What did you want to a-ask?" I hate myself for stuttering, but it can't be helped. He is in the doorway, blocking the only available exit. That's as triggering as it comes for me.

The tightness spreading across my chest slackens when he steps deeper into the bathroom. "I wanted to ask you about *that*." At the end of his sentence, he lowers his eyes to the shampoo bottle I've almost crushed. "I was hoping you could tell me where I can buy it." Again, I don't recognize his expression. "Ark is almost out, so I thought I should grab him another bottle before he returns for his fifth shower of the day."

When I roll the bottle in my hand, my heart rate quickens. Its lack of weight exposes it is almost empty.

Ark would have had to use it at least three times a day to deplete the almost full bottle he took from my bathroom. His hair is thick, but washing it even once a day is excessive.

"He knows this is sh-shampoo, right? It isn't body wash." When images a chambermaid shouldn't have of one of her clients inflame my cheeks with need, I return my focus to the core of Rafael's question. "I purchase this brand from a local sa-salon. I can jot down the address for you if you'd like?"

Rafael gleams like a hunter who has locked in on their prey. "You use this same brand?" He sounds shocked. He needs to take acting classes. His stirring expression doesn't mimic the bewilderment in his tone.

"Yeah. Um..." With words eluding me, I complete my reply with a nod.

My throat works through a hard swallow when Rafael pads closer. His shoulders aren't as broad as Ark's. I could easily squeeze by him if needed. My limbs just feel suddenly too heavy to attempt an escape.

Or perhaps I am intrigued.

Ark didn't just steal my shampoo.

He's been using it as well.

That's shocking and somewhat enthralling. I took so long to wash Tillie's vomit from my hair because I didn't want to lose the scent of Ark's aftershave on my neck. Could he possibly be trying to maintain the same infused scent?

I'm pulled from my thoughts when Rafael removes the bottle from my hand and inspects the label. It shouldn't give anything away, but he homes in on the evidence as if he is Sherlock Holmes. "Is this your shampoo, Mara?"

"No," I push out. "I don't think s-so."

I am a terrible liar.

I know this, and so does Rafael.

Mercifully, he doesn't call me out as a liar.

Not directly, anyway.

"I was just asking because if it was yours, I could replace your bottle while buying Ark a new bottle." The walls slowly close in on me when he says, "That would be the right thing to do in a situation where someone's shampoo was stolen."

"It would be," I agree, nodding. "But that isn't m-my bottle."

He watches me for several heart-whacking seconds before he says, "All right. If you insist." He twists to face the exit. "I better leave you to it. You said you have a full schedule, and who am I to question your word?"

I let out the breath I'm holding in, confident the screams of my lungs demanding air will stop me from nibbling on the bait he's dangling in front of me.

I'm not strong enough to withstand the flames of hell.

"It's my bottle. I-I think." My last two words are nowhere near as confident as my first three. "It went missing from my apartment the afternoon Ark drove m-me home."

I can't see Rafael's face, but I can feel his smile.

The heat of covetousness is as hot as the inferno I was endeavoring to sidestep by being honest.

Not speaking another word, Rafael exits the bathroom, leaving me dumbfounded.

Again, I'd love a few minutes to deliberate, but that option is even more out of my reach now. I accused an owner of stealing. Things can't get direr on the job front for me.

After rolling up my sleeves and breathing out a handful of butterflies my stomach hasn't been without for the past week, I get to work.

I first strip Ark's bed and gather the high-thread linen into a bundle before placing it into my cart. Time moves fast since I'm bobbing along to the tracks Tillie added to my playlists yesterday afternoon, instead of contemplating my many erroneous mistakes.

Tillie was in that stage of sickness where she was no longer contagious but not quite herself enough to go to school. While we did a jigsaw puzzle, she doubled my assurance that her birthday party was the best party she'd ever attended.

She doesn't have much to go off. My shameful theatrics in my apartment Monday afternoon prove when your trust is low, you palm the neurosis onto more than your children.

I've declined every invite Tillie has received in the past five years.

The pure bliss on her face when she recalled how loudly her friends sang "Happy Birthday" has me hopeful I can loosen the reins enough that she will have both a safe and happy childhood.

A smile plays at my lips when I recall another part of our conversation yesterday. We made it halfway through the puzzle before Tillie queried about the weird smell that hadn't left the kitchen in days.

I tried to make out I had burned the pot making hot cocoa the night she was sick, but Tillie knows me better than that. She immediately saw through my bluff before unashamedly declaring she knew Ark was the perfect match for me.

She only stopped teasing me when I reminded her that I hadn't yet cleaned her vomit out of my work bag, and if she had enough energy to rile me, perhaps she had enough to help clean up the mess she made.

Her focus never veered from her Nintendo Switch for the rest of the day.

As I move through the motions of a thorough yet hurried clean, I think about the owner of this apartment and how he would never have to save for two years to buy a console that's discarded the instant the latest model comes out.

Most residents of the Chrysler building are either wealthy businessmen or part of the healthcare conglomerate. One of Russia's leading private hospitals is only half a mile away, meaning the serviced apartments attract world-renowned surgeons and their patients.

My fingers tighten around the corner of the sheets firmly when my thoughts stray to Ark for the umpteenth time today. He couldn't be sick, surely. Excluding the time my nails dug into his shoulders, clamminess never dulled his natural olive skin coloring. His eyes are bright and without pain, and he is physically fit—*extremely* fit.

Someone on their deathbed wouldn't have an eight-pack.

Or a monster dick.

I cough to clear my chest of the tingles spasming there before I finish making the bed. I can't have these types of thoughts about an owner. It's against the rules. Mrs. Whitten would have my head if she heard even a snippet of my thoughts. I'd hate to consider her response if she learns about our kiss. Just the thought doubles the output of my cleaning skills.

Confident the sheets are tight enough to bounce a nickel off, I vacuum the carpet, scrub the sink and toilet, and then wipe down the mirror and shower walls.

Once the products on the vanity are replenished, I take a step back and survey my work.

Everything is clean and orderly.

I can't say the same for my heart when a shadow falls over the only exit of the bathroom for the second time in under an hour. "All done?"

My head bob is submissive, but it hides my nerves. "Yes. This room is r-ready."

Rafael acts as if I didn't stutter. "This room?"

Again, I nod. "I have four more rooms on m-my roster for this apartment."

My heart pounds in my ears when he straightens his spine. His height is more imposing when it is at its full stature. He is an inch or two taller than Ark but around twenty pounds lighter. "You're servicing the rest of the rooms here?" He points to the floor at the end of his sentence.

I nod, too confused by his unmissable bewilderment to speak.

Cleaning isn't a housemaid's sole skill, but it is very much a part of their job description.

Shock hits me half a second before disappointment when he asks, "Does Ark know?"

"I assume s-so."

Rafael twists his lips as if he isn't convinced. "I highly doubt that."

"Why?"

Don't worry. I am as shocked as you that I didn't stutter. The shortness of my reply helps, but it is still surprising. I guess I shouldn't be shocked. Rafael isn't Ark, but who you surround yourself with is as important as how you present yourself. I trusted Ark enough to fall asleep in his presence *and* kiss him. That means Rafael's name will most likely soon be scribbled at the bottom of a very short list of people I trust.

Interest blooms in my chest when Rafael says, "Because he has a far more important task he needs your help with."

"He d-does?" I sound daft. Rightfully so. I am.

And desperate.

Very desperate.

I breathe a little easier when Rafael nods before he returns to the central part of the primary suite. I follow him, my nerves instantly dispelling since there are two exits and only one person capable of blocking them.

The odds are back in my favor.

Rafael moves for a desk at the corner of the ample space while saying, "Val said she'd give you this at the same time she gave you the map."

I'm lost in his meaning until I recall my interaction with Ark last Friday night. He said he would have his security team draw up the entry and exit points of the underground parking lot for me. I've seen him since then, but when a sick child is demanding your attention, you don't have time for anything else.

"I haven't se-seen Val this morning. She wasn't in her office when I arrived."

"Probably because she's doing this instead." Rafael gives me a hand-drawn map of the foyer. "The meetings have already started, but you still have plenty of time."

"For?" I ask when he fails to elaborate on his reply.

"For... whatever it is that you do."

"C-clean?"

This shames me to admit, but that is the only thing I am skilled at. When I was fired from my last job, I tried to find something different. Nothing came up. I only stumbled onto this position when I returned the check Maksim Ivanov hand-delivered to me for helping his wife.

The amount cited on the check would have had Tillie and me living comfortably for years, but I genuinely don't believe in spending money I haven't earned.

Again, my life isn't close to glamourous, but it is ethical.

Rafael waits a beat before lifting his chin. "Yeah."

"When does the me-meeting end?" I move to the cleaning cart to remove my schedule, hopeful I can squeeze in Ark's request without too much reshuffling. A disruptive routine is as dangerous as no routine. "I could probably clean the me-meeting room—"

"Ark doesn't want you to clean up *after* the meeting. He wants you to..." He strays his eyes around the room, his lips twisting when he takes in the portable coffee station at the side of an inbuilt bar. "He wants you to serve refreshments. These meetings are a snoozefest. Without coffee, he'll never make it out alive."

The dramatics of his reply twitches my lips, but it doesn't alter the facts. "I don't do catering. There is a bakery n-nearby that—"

When Rafael interrupts, I stop searching for a brochure I tucked away with the hope of future use. "Ark *specifically* asked for you. He needs *you* there, Mara." The sheer honesty in his last sentence weakens my hesitation. It sounds gospel.

"Val—"

"Has already given her approval." He pulls his phone out of his pocket. "I can call her again to check if you don't believe me."

He only dials two numbers before I end his campaign. "I-I believe you." *Ludicrously.*

He looks at me as if all his Christmases have come at once before he says, "Great." His eyes drop to my uniform. "We should probably get you something more appropriate to wear. First impressions count." Before I can object, he adds, "The people attending these meetings are *extremely* important to Arkadiy. We don't want to give them the wrong idea."

I'm about to say they're not here to judge me, but something stops me. I want to blame the woman in the living room, rummaging through designer clothes on a wheelable clothes rack. However, it feels like more than that.

Goldilocks has once again entered the bears' house without permission, but it feels like more than a burnt saucepan is on the line this time around.

9

ARKADIY

*A*s I sit across from one of the most recognizable faces in Russia, I wish I were anywhere but here. Veronika is stunning, with blonde hair, piercing green eyes, and a body often featured on magazine covers, but I've never met someone so dimwitted.

She's droned on about her latest skincare line nonstop for the past hour. I'm bored out of my mind, and her voice, the equivalent of nails being dragged down a chalkboard, is so grating that my head is throbbing.

The one between my legs isn't close to having the same pulsating response as the one between my shoulders. There's no interest on my cock's behalf whatsoever, which isn't surprising.

I'm only here because a member of the media I thought I'd lost snapped a picture of me opening the cab door for Mara and Tillie before I slipped in behind them.

He was an hour away from splashing Mara's face across the glossy front pages of gossip magazines as my latest fling when my offer for an exclusive interview landed on his desk.

The promise of an all-inclusive interview with one of Russia's most sought-after women and me is why Mara isn't being defamed by the media right now.

The interview concluded twenty minutes ago, but Veronika has yet to notice the journalist's absence.

As the social media influencer harps on about her latest fashion campaign and the designer clothes she will be rewarded for it, I think about the deals I could be closing instead of being here.

My mind shouldn't immediately deviate to the hearty hum of Mara's refrigerator that came from nowhere near the motor, but it does.

I've never heard a more erotic sound.

Not wanting Veronika to get the wrong idea about the heat creeping up my neck, I drift my eyes to the two-way mirror at the side of the meeting room before tapping my watch.

If Fyodor notices the signal we devised for when I want our meeting interrupted, he doesn't pay any attention to it. None of the multiple doors surrounding the meeting room shoot open as they have numerous times today.

Fyodor remains behind the two-way glass, no doubt devouring the double espresso I requested Rafael bring down almost an hour ago so I'd stay awake while listening to the ramblings of a woman who hasn't worked a hard day in her life.

When Veronika launches into a monologue about her ex-boyfriend and how their breakup affected her influencer status, I slice my hand through the air.

She barely pauses for half a second before focusing on how our collaboration could boost her follower count to celebrity-level status. "We don't even need to be in the same room. Photoshop can do wonders. I know a guy who knows a guy who…"

I tune out again before locking my now-narrowed eyes with the two-way mirror. My expression announces that despite Fyodor's seal of approval, Veronika is *not* the woman I want at my side during my fortieth birthday celebrations.

Just the thought of being subjected to her nasally whine for another thirty seconds has me wanting to damage the hearing in my right ear as poorly as the incident that stole the hearing from my left ear.

A pen to the ear would be less painful than another update on Veronika's follower count.

The tightness in my chest alleviates when a tap sounds from the main meeting room door; I'm optimistic relief is moments away. "Come in."

The clinking of silverware drowns out Veronika's adenoidal tone. It isn't a noise I am anticipating, but I welcome it when I learn who it is coming from.

While smiling hesitantly, Mara approaches the boardroom table, juggling a large silver serving tray. Because the tray is overloaded with coffee, milk, mugs, a sugar bowl, and a handful of pastries, her arms are rigidly robotic.

Their stiffness teasingly tugs up the risqué hem of a fitted pleated pencil dress I'm certain isn't on any chambermaid's uniform list. It is from a designer I know well.

The label, not as meticulously stitched as the one Mara was wearing Friday night, shows off her legs in a way her maid's outfit never will.

It also displays that she is a woman who should be served, not serve others.

Follower count has nothing on natural grace and sophistication.

Mara's eyes move to Veronika for the quickest second before they return to me. I can tell she is uneased about approaching me in general, much less when I'm seated across from a woman known worldwide for her beauty, but she hides it well with a friendly smile and a professional edge.

"Ex-excuse me, sir," she says softly, her words barely above a whisper. "I have your order for you."

"Oh... coffee. Yippee." Veronika claps her hands together twice before signaling for Mara to come closer. "I've been dying for a drink. My throat is on fire."

"Because you speak in run-on sentences, and you've barely paused to breathe in almost an hour."

It dawns on me that I said my last statement out loud when the corners of Mara's chunky lips tug upward. Her smile only lasts for the quickest second, but it hangs around long enough to reduce the shudder clanging the ceramic mugs together.

Unlike Rafael's Friday-night guests, Veronika doesn't ridicule Mara when she asks if she'd like sugar in her coffee. She eagerly nods, blind to Mara's stutter, before she thanks her for her hospitality. "This is the most scrumptious coffee I've ever had."

Her polite response ensures she won't endure the repercussions Ainissa and her friend faced Friday night. I'll keep my mouth shut about the sleazy bowling alley owner. He isn't worth the breaths I'd need to update you on what happens when you try to barter sex for a woeful fifty-dollar discount.

Mara's perfume tickles my nose when she moves to my side of the table to serve the coffee. It isn't the same scent that held me captive in her kitchen four days ago, but it is almost identical to the one that's kept my cock in a constant state of erection for the past week.

The urge to come has been so intense that I've stroked my cock to Mara's scent multiple times over the past four days.

I'm almost out of shampoo.

That's how much the quickest sample of her mouth has invigorated me. Don't get me started on her fuckable body and beautifully stunning face, or we will be here all night.

Even without an ounce of makeup, her face is fresh and radiant, a handful of freckles adding to her youthful appearance. Her thighs tell you she will be a dream to fuck, and the tilt of her mouth, along with the fire in her eyes, promises not a moment of dullness will be endured while in her presence.

She is fascinating, a true sight for sore eyes, and she tastes even more scrumptious than she looks.

After sinking back from the table, her strides wobbly, as if she heard my private thoughts, Mara locks her eyes with mine. "Is there anything e-else you require?"

She's served the coffee she arrived with. There's nothing more she can do. But for the life of me, I can't dismiss her from the room.

It is easier to walk away than to demand that she do precisely that.

I don't solely want her to save me from another torturous minute in Veronika's presence. I also want to know how she'd answer the many questions Veronika dodged at the start of our interview and why her stomach growled even though her shift only started an hour ago.

Did she not eat breakfast this morning?

I'm saved from showing a nurturing side I don't want publicly announced when a knock sounds through the conference room for the second time.

Rafael's broad frame fills the doorway that separates the security office from the boardroom. His grin is hugely telling.

A ruse is about to begin, but I have no intention of dodging it this time.

"V, I have Riley Valentine on the phone. She heard you were in town and wondered if you had time to squeeze in an appointment at the boutique?"

Veronika's squeal is more ear damaging than her voice. "*The* Riley Valentine? As in the understudy of Wilfred Iwona?" When Rafael nods, Veronika leaps up from her chair and sprints out of the room, screaming that she can't believe *the* Riley Valentine reached out to her.

My ego is saved from being scalded when she spins around to farewell me with an air kiss. Don't mistake my reply. I'll happily live never exchanging another word with Veronika. I am responding to the jealousy that has slipped over Mara's face from Veronika's loved-up farewell.

Jealousy has never looked more ravishing.

An amused huff rumbles in my chest when Mara whispers, "She se-seems nice," a second after Veronika exits the conference room, slamming the door behind her.

When my chuckle reaches her ears, her pretty eyes snap to me. She drinks in my riled expression like she knows not a groove between my brows belongs to her before she wrinkles her adorable nose.

"If you needed a ruse to escape her clutches, you could have just t-told me." She hints at an interest in fashion by adding, "Her scarf cost over five thousand dollars. It w-would have only taken a wayward drop of coffee to have her running for the closest washroom." As quickly as jealousy was etched on her beautiful face, it is replaced with remorse. "I'm sorry. That was uncalled for."

"Not necessarily." I slouch low in my chair as if I weren't mere seconds from vacating it before draping my arm across the one next to me like I have all the time in the world. "I was seeking an out." She looks pleased, and it thrills me immensely. "And I'd be a liar if I said I wasn't as equally invested in learning how you developed your date-skirting techniques as I was to skip this date."

"Date? You were on a d-date?"

She looks set to run when I nod, but the fire she's endeavoring to relight in her eyes keeps her feet firmly planted on the ground.

There's that fighter I've been endeavoring to unearth.

"Do you always take your dates for filtered c-coffee in a conference room?" She doesn't call me a cheap ass, but her humorous expression most certainly does.

Before answering, I take a moment to relish the resurrection of some of the wittiness her attack six months ago stole. "Not always. Sometimes I offer them lukewarm tap water instead of coffee."

Fuck, she's beautiful. Her lips are as ruddy as her cheeks, and her eyes glisten with life regardless of the secrets they hide, but neither of those points has anything on her sheer beauty when she smiles.

It knocks down my defenses hard and fast and has me thinking with the personal side of my head instead of the business side. "How's Tillie?"

I have to adjust my position when she can't help but respond to the sincere interest in my tone. Her kissable lips furl, making them more plump, as a handful of her teeth are exposed.

"She's better." A hint of shyness impinges on her cheeks. "Despite al-almost burning down our kitchen, you've gained yourself a new fan."

I don't know the man seated across from her when a warmth tracks across my cheeks. I could never be accused of being shy, but recalling Tillie's commentary seconds after I left her room warrants some sort of response.

It isn't that Tillie is crushing on a man almost four times her age blooming my cheeks with heat. It was Mara's lack of retort when her daughter tricked her into admitting she found me attractive and the fire-sparking kiss we shared in her poky kitchen only hours later.

Desperate to shift my thoughts from how kissable her mouth looks, I ask, "Is she eating?"

When Mara nods, stealing my focus from the second grumble of her stomach, I'm tempted to ask, *Are you?*

I lose the opportunity when she glances at someone over my shoulder. Panic surges in her diamond-shaped eyes when she locks on Mr. and Mrs. Whitten in the building's foyer, but it is only half its strength when she returns them to me.

"I sh-should go. I'm already behind schedule."

My hand shoots out to grab her wrist before my head can warn me against it. I don't grip her painfully. She can remove her arm at any time. I just can't let her leave without ensuring she knows my regret about how I ended things Monday night.

She sees my remorse and lets me off with only a slap to the wrist. "If that's all, sir, I will l-leave you to your guests."

I want to tell her no. I want to force her to stay and share every sordid detail her eyes hide, but with our duo about to be plumped out to a quartet, I act like a coward instead.

I dip my chin, granting her permission to leave, before I stray my eyes to the conference room table so I don't have to witness her brisk retreat.

After diverting Mr. and Mrs. Whitten's focus to another resident, Rafael enters the office from a door across from the one Mara exited half a second earlier. He props his shoulder against the doorjamb before folding his arms over his chest. His expression is filled with sappiness.

"She's the one, Ark. She is the ideal wife for our future president."

I *pfft* his blatant stupidity. "Veronika couldn't—"

"Not Veronika." While twisting the end of the sleazy mustache he's been reluctant to shave since a silver screen starlet once told him it was sexy, he joins me at the table, his eyes unmoving from the door Mara walked through seconds ago. "*Her.*"

There's a bout of silence, and for a brief moment, a flicker of hope.

Then clarity forms as to why I am apprehensive.

Mara is a mother. Her daughter is the same age my sister was when our world was upended. That automatically removes her from the list of possible candidates.

Since I need to lock down my thoughts before they get carried away, I don't object to Fyodor joining our discussion. "I disagree with your findings, Rafael. From what Darius unearthed during their brief interlude Friday night, she has no pedigree, no online status whatsoever, and no knowledge of our world." My hands ball into tight fists that I hide by stuffing them into my pockets. "Mrs. Orlov would *never* approve."

Rafael doesn't give in without a fight. He never does. "Their chemistry is undeniable. The sparks bouncing off them could cause an inferno." He steps closer to Fyodor, willing to fight for what he believes in. "If you want your plan to work, Fyo, she"—he points to the door Mara walked through moments ago—"is the woman Ark needs at his side."

"She speaks with a stutter, and I highly doubt she knows the difference between a salad fork and a regular one."

"All things that can be taught," Rafael yells, his voice echoing.

Fyodor scoffs. "Class cannot be taught, and that lady has none."

I shoot up from my chair, my fists ready, prepared, and willing to maim. "Enough!" I glare at Fyodor. "If you're pissed none of your lap dogs lived up to their hype, take it out on me. Leave Mara out of this. She didn't ask for your critique, and neither the fuck did I."

I snatch up my suit jacket and head for the door before I do something I can't take back.

Knocking my campaign manager the fuck out can't be taken back.

"Ark..." Fyodor's swallow is audible as he stalks my trek to the door. "I thought I was supporting your decision." His confused eyes bounce between mine. "I thought you were disinterested. Isn't that why you requested me to keep you away from her?"

Rafael's laughter booms into my ear, freezing my steps. "You did a shit job of that, Fyo." His eyes are on me, hot and telling. "Where the fuck do you think he's been running off to every afternoon?"

I wordlessly warn him to shut his mouth, but I've never given him any reason to fear me, so my bluff does little good. "He sure as hell ain't visiting the gym." My nails dig into my palm when he steps closer to ensure his words are only for my ears. "Though I'm pretty sure he's getting a *thorough* workout every time he enters the shower with *her* shampoo at the ready."

He waits for an objection. When he fails to get one, because every word he speaks is true, he shifts his focus back to Fyodor. "If you truly want this, if you want him to lead this nation out of the trenches it's been buried in for the past thirty years, you need her at Ark's side."

He doesn't need to stray his eyes in the direction Mara went to announce who he is referencing. The absolute honesty in his tone exposes every detail of his plan and hides how much I am terrified that he is right.

10

MARA

"I'll see you in the morning, okay?" Tillie nods before she loses her fight to hold back a tigerlike yawn. It's been a big day for us both. "I love you, Tillie."

"I love you too, Mom," she replies before she hands the phone back to Mrs. Lichard.

"Don't," she warns when she spots the numerous apologies beaming from my eyes. "I love having her here, and we have almost a week's worth of *Home and Away* and *Neighbours* episodes to catch up on." My worry eases from the excitement in her tone. She loves Australian soap shows as much as Tillie does. "I just wish you weren't taking the late bus home. You know it isn't safe."

"I'll be fine," I assure her, confident in how well Maksim has cleaned up the streets of Myasnikov since he made it his hometown. "Are you sure you don't want me to collect Tillie when I arrive home? I don't mind."

Air whistles between her teeth when she waves off my offer. "And have you interrupt my sleep? No, thank you. Unlike you, some of us need our beauty sleep." Her expression switches from playful to mothering. "We will see you in the morning. Travel safe."

I promise I will before disconnecting our FaceTime chat.

After tossing my phone into my bag, I rub the kink in the back of my neck. I'm exhausted. My roster was already bursting at the seams, but Rafael's lie set it back an hour.

I had to scramble to finish all my assigned apartments, but I did it. All the residents on my ledger are sleeping in freshly made beds, and I'm a fifty-minute bus ride from doing the same.

I just have one last task to tick off first. I need to return the dress Rafael gifted me earlier. I can't accept it since Ark was unaware it had been given to me. He purchased those clothes for his guests. They were not Rafael's to give away.

With the hour late, and since my visit is more personal than business related, I close my locker before heading for the main elevator.

"Ma'am." The elevator attendant finalizes his greeting with a glare before he pushes the call button for me.

I breathe a sigh of relief when he doesn't shadow my entrance into the car. It could be because he doesn't deem me a threat to the residents here, but my intuition pleads with me to look deeper. His decision feels like it centers more around Ark than me.

After selecting the main floor of Ark's apartment, I check my face in the mirrored wall. I look wretched. Dark circles plague my eyes, and my cheeks look gaunt. It is understandable after recalling what I had for lunch.

Air isn't overly filling.

I hesitate to exit the elevator when it arrives at Ark's floor. Someone is ending their week surrounded by friends. Four apartments spurt off this hallway, and its echoing design makes it impossible to work out which apartment is being overrun with guests—guests I will most likely have to clean up after in the morning.

The cleaning staff have a seven-day roster. Weekends are not guaranteed days off.

While grumbling about my dislike of my position, I stomp down the carpeted hallway. Music carries through my ears the further I encroach on Ark's apartment. It leaves no doubt as to who is keeping the other tenants awake.

Ark is entertaining guests—many of them.

Confident they'll all most likely be as attractive as the female giving him gaga eyes this morning, I pivot on my heel and stalk back to the elevator.

I'm halfway there when a familiar voice says, "Hey, Mara. Ditching already?"

I muster up a fake grin before spinning to face the voice. "I'd have to be invited to di-ditch."

Rafael shrugs as if science is an unnecessary part of physics. "Tomato, *tomato*."

He bands his arm around my shoulders before he twists me around to face Ark's apartment. I try to dig my heels into the carpet. It is a woeful waste of time. Rafael is too strong, and I'm not exactly putting up a fight.

I've been dying to see how the other half lives, and with Tillie already in bed, why not live a little?

When I enter the foyer, I anticipate being hit with narrowed glares and snarled lips.

To my surprise, my arrival goes relatively unnoticed. The only person who pays me any attention is the blonde from earlier, the one who had a date with Ark in the conference room of this building.

"Did you two officially meet?" Rafael asks after stealing a glass of champagne from a server's tray and handing it to me. "Or did I hatch my ruse too early for an introduction?"

"Ah..."

I'm saved from looking like a blubbering idiot when he waves the blonde over. Her excitement about his wordless invitation announces she is clueless that Rafael orchestrated her demise, or she doesn't care.

I don't know how the latter could be plausible. I was devastated to have lost Ark's attention, and I'm to blame for the injustice.

I guess she has no reason to fret. She is gorgeous and successful. I could never compete with her.

As Rafael offers an introduction, I wipe my riled expression. "Veronika, this is Mara, the woman I told you about earlier."

Veronika's mouth falls open as she playfully slaps Rafael's chest. "You weren't joking, Raf. She's totally gorg."

Gorg?

I'm left floundering when another faultless specimen joins our trio. This woman is brunette and approximately the same age and height as me. "Who is your designer?" She lowers her familiar eyes to my skirt, their trek slow as she takes in the outfit I handcrafted. "That stitchwork is impeccable, and I've not seen that fabric anywhere. Is it vintage?"

"Ah. It's a c-custom piece." I'm such a liar. The fabric is from one of Mrs. Lichard's old tablecloths. She was throwing it out, assuming the material was useless since it had a tear. I made myself a skirt and Tillie two dresses from the one swatch of material. "I made it."

"You made it?" Veronika bumps the unnamed brunette out of the way when I bob my head. "Very mode. I totally approve." She twists her torso to face Rafael like he oversees my schedule. "She must accompany me to the boutique to help pick out some items." Her whine reminds me of the tantrums Tillie used to undertake when she was five. "*Please*, Raffy. She clearly has an eye for fashion." Her eyes return to me, begging and wet. "Wilfred Iwona's garments are exceptional, but the stitchwork doesn't show this skill level. If you could fix them for me, I'll never be on another worst dressed list."

"Wilfred Iwona?" I choke on my words instead of stuttering them. "You're go-going to Wilfred Iwona's invitation-only boutique?"

"Uh-huh," Veronika answers, clearly impressed I know who she is referencing. "And you could be there right with me if you say yes."

I nod before considering the consequences of my actions. Then I shift it to a headshake.

"I can't. I have to work."

The unnamed brunette's interests are as piqued as Veronika's impeccably manicured brow. "Making more custom pieces?"

"Ah. No. I—"

"Will be there with bells on."

Veronika claps, missing the scald I hit Rafael with from acting as if he is my boss.

"I can't go with her. I can't mi-miss more days of work," I whisper to Rafael when he guides me away from Veronika and her equally attractive friend.

"Then I guess it is lucky doing anything I ask is now a part of your job description."

Huh?

He waves at two blondes eyeballing him from the other side of the den before lowering his eyes to me. They're full of mischievousness but, somehow, still friendly. "Ark hired you to service his apartment permanently until he returns to Moscow later in the year."

Excitement scuttles through my veins.

They're overrun by disappointment only seconds later.

It isn't solely the knowledge Ark has no intention of making Myasnikov his home that has me floundering. I am wondering if his company has a strict nonfraternization policy like the one that the maintenance and cleaning department in the Chrysler building undertakes.

Our kiss was so blistering that my lovesick heart is hopeful of a second chance to seduce him.

Shock that a nonfraternization policy shouldn't be seen as a negative when contemplating a job offer scarcely registers when Rafael ensures there's no possibility I can turn down the opportunity. "The pay is double your current rate, and the four days on, three days off roster is during school hours."

It sounds too good to be true, which can only mean one thing—it is.

"I—" I choke on my reply for the second time when the man offering me an opportunity I never anticipated enters the den from the opposite side.

Ark smiles at me like I'm welcome in his space, and it instantly facilitates my worries that most nursery rhymes are based on heinous acts.

11

ARKADIY

"*I*f you want anyone to believe you hired her because of her cleaning skills, you need to alter your expression." Rafael butts shoulders with me before he joins my stalk. To an outsider, it appears as if he picked the side closest to the bar. I know that isn't true. He always stands to my right to ensure I hear every snarky comment he mutters. "You look hungry."

I am.

I'm fucking starved.

It just isn't for food.

Rafael winks at a brunette prancing past us like her hair coloring won't see her left in the cold before he says, "This isn't what I meant when I said you needed her at your side. I meant—"

"I know what you meant, Raf," I interrupt. "But this is better for all involved. Safer." My next sentence leaves my mouth before I can stop it. "It will give me time to make sure the headrush I face every time she looks at me won't cause unforgivable mistakes."

He shakes his head, his expression a mix of disappointment and confusion. "You're not *him*, Ark. You'd never...." He can't finish his sentence, and I am glad. I'm not sure how I'd respond with eyes identical to the ones from my nightmares on me.

Needing to change topics before my somewhat playful mood nose-dives, I ask, "Why is she here so late? She usually finishes no later than five."

I want to add, *And where's Tillie?* But I know Mara wouldn't have left her in incapable hands. Unlike my mother, she cares about her child. The way she weaponed up against me on Monday proves this without a doubt. The reminder has me pushing aside my worries faster than they can surface.

Rafael shrugs. "She didn't say." He leans in close. "Want me to kick her out? I'd hate to disrupt your routine. You'd usually be half a block from her apartment by n—"

I rib him with my elbow, stopping his rile midsentence. He chuckles, loving seeing a side of me he's not witnessed in an extremely long time.

I'm not opposed to a changeup. Occasionally thinking with your heart can't be a bad thing. I just wish it wasn't occurring during one of the most pivotal times of my career.

If my skeletons are exposed, my campaign for office is over.

I won't be able to come back from that.

Haunted memories see me removing my eyes from Mara for the first time in almost thirty minutes. "Make sure she gets home safely." My snapped tone announces the words I don't need to speak to a man as protective as Rafael, but I articulate them anyway. "And don't let it be on a fucking bus."

His jaw is as firm as mine. "I'll be sure to announce her new employment contract has a no-public-transport stipulation."

I smile, grateful there's no chance Mara will face the injustices of a dangerous world for the second time this year before I turn toward my office. The interview to keep Mara out of the tabloids set me back by half a day, but I'd do it again in an instant if it achieved the same results.

It is not my intention to strip Mara of her cloak of invisibility. I simply want to learn who forced her to wear it, and how much it will take to free her from it.

I don't even make it two steps away before Rafael thwarts my wish to flee. "What if she wants to stay?"

My eyes stray to Mara, who is being introduced to a handful of fashion icons by Riley, my baby sister, before they shift back to Rafael. "Let her stay. But if your eyes leave her once—"

"They won't," he interrupts, walking away.

The possessive edge beaming from him should piss me off. It was as claiming as they come. But since it is Rafael, the man I owe my life to, I tuck away my flare of annoyance before continuing for my third-floor office. I have paperwork to endorse and a headache to massage away.

The latter sees me making a quick detour to my bedroom for supplies.

Pain relief tablets won't touch the surface of this ache.

Buttery, floral goodness, though. It works a treat every single time.

My bedroom is on the far side of my apartment, away from prying eyes. All the sleeping quarters are similarly sized, but I picked this one because no one bothers to wander far from the action and free booze during impromptu mixers like the one Fyodor organized today.

I'm left alone when I venture to this side of the building, so I'm somewhat taken aback when my entrance is flanked by an appalling amount of overspray of a woman's perfume and another scent I can't quite describe.

"I thought you were never going to show up."

My jaw cracks when I flick my eyes toward the feminine voice. Veronika is sprawled across my bed. Her lingerie is see-through, her panties are crotchless, and the perfume killing my sinuses was so recently placed on it is still wet on her neck.

After loosening the firmness of my jaw with a quick grind, I turn to close my door. Not because I am interested in anything Veronika has to offer, but because I don't want my dirty laundry aired for the world to see. That is all Veronika is about—publicity at any cost.

The tightness of my jaw is heard in my question. "What are you doing here, Veronika?"

"Waiting for you, silly." She rakes her teeth over her lower lip while dragging her eyes down my body in a slow, dedicated sweep. "I thought we should get to know each other a little better."

Whatever she thinks her childish voice is doing to my cock couldn't be further from the truth. My dick is shrinking, not knocking at the zipper in my trousers, begging to be freed like it does any time Mara's scent fills my nostrils.

"A conference room meeting is just so... *stuffy*." Her nails make a mess of my bedding when she drags her hand across the sheets. "I work best on my back, being served a healthy dose of d—"

"Did you miss the alterations I made to the proposed contract today?"

They weren't explicitly made for Veronika, more to get Fyodor off my back long enough to wrap my head around how many backflips I've made over the past few days, but I'm glad I pushed them through.

Veronika's pose would put her in breach of contract if I were to accept it.

Veronika jackknifes into a half-seated position, thankfully removing her puffy pussy lips from my peripheral vision. "You made those changes?" When I nod, she scoffs. "Why?" She doesn't give me a chance to speak. "It isn't like you're gay. I've heard stories—many of them. You're not called the playboy minister for no reason. Your dick pic trended for six months straight. Six. Months! That's a record. Not even a porn star with a thirteen-inch wang got that much online love."

When she pauses to take a much-needed breath, I gather up one of the towels Mara left on the tallboy drawers and toss it at her, covering the rest of the unsightly image. "If you can't follow the one term I said wasn't negotiable, Fyodor is wrong. You are *not* a suitable applicant for the *position* advertised." I say "position" in a way she cannot misconstrue. Our proposed arrangement was never about feelings.

I freeze partway to the bathroom when Veronika whispers, "It's her, isn't it? The maid. That's who you put the rule in for?"

She stares at me as if I am insane when I don't cite an objection. Her response is understandable. I must have rocks in my head. That is the only plausible reason a man would turn down a walking wet dream to stroke his cock over his cleaner.

But that's precisely what I'm planning to do. I'll show Veronika out before snagging Mara's shampoo out of my bathroom and hotfooting it toward my office, where I plan to act like it is perfectly acceptable for a grown man to have a childish crush.

12

MARA

A squeak pops from my lips when a voice behind me says, "Ark had the locks changed earlier today." I recognize the voice, and although he's been nothing but kind to me, a snippet of fear still runs down my spine when I realize I'm trapped in a room with no viable exit. "He hates not being able to deadlock every entry point of his home." Rafael moves to the side of the living room, clearing the exit, before folding his arms over his chest. "You weren't sneaking out, though, were you?"

"No, of course not. I just need so-some air." Since my last sentence is honest, it sounds that way.

Rafael has been the perfect party host, and although the conversations he encouraged me to participate in rarely veered past skincare lines and eyewatering endorsement deals I could only dream of, he ensured I was welcomed into Ark's team with open arms.

I still feel like an outcast, though.

The women filling the ballroom-like den of Ark's multi-floor apartment are glamorous, and the men are gorgeous, so I shouldn't be surprised that I didn't stumble onto a single person not wearing a custom piece of jewelry that cost more than I earn a year, but I am.

Very much so.

I'm swimming in waters out of my depth, and the drowning started the instant Ark left the festivities.

That was a shameful forty minutes ago.

Rafael knows I'm lying, but he pretends he's clueless. "That's good, because I would have hated to interrupt Ark's *self-care*"—he air quotes his last word—"routine again for the second time today." After banding his arm around my shoulders, he guides me back to the party. "I haven't had time to replenish his shampoo yet, so he'd be extra grouchy if I were to interrupt him now." He stops walking, his brows furrowing. "Unless..." My heart launches into my throat when he hands me an invitation out of nowhere. "We're about to head out for a bite to eat. You should grab Ark and join us. Last I heard, he was heading to his third-floor office."

"I—"

I lose the chance to get out another word.

As quickly as Rafael snuck up on me, he points out Ark's office like I'm unaware of the floor plan of his apartment before he races into the den to tell his guests it is time to eat.

They're nowhere near as apprehensive as I am. They gather their coats almost immediately and file out of the apartment until only two people are left—Ark and me.

I contemplate leaving as well, but I've yet to do what I set out to achieve fifty minutes ago, and it would be rude to leave Ark in the lurch as to where his guests went.

I'll tell him of Rafael's plan, hand him back the dress I'm praying hasn't been poorly crinkled enough to require dry cleaning, and then leave. It is the polite thing to do, the right thing to do, and the very thing I don't want to do.

Ark's guests are out of my league, but when Ark was eyeballing my arrival, it was nice to pretend I was in the top one percent of the country.

Elite is too tame of a word to describe Ark's friends. They're top tier in all the rankings—looks, personality, social status, and wealth.

The reminder slows my steps toward Ark's office, their lack of briskness not a contributor to the wailing of my heart when I rap my knuckles against his office door.

"Ark?"

I knock again, louder this time. Rafael mentioned shampoo and self-care in one sentence. I'm not the sharpest tool in the shed, but I am reasonably sure that was code for Ark being in the shower. With all the showers in this apartment designed the same way, he won't be able to hear my knocks.

When my request for entrance is denied with silence, I press my ear to the door and listen for any signs of life.

I get that and so much more.

I hear my new boss moan my name—twice.

13

ARKADIY

*A*s flashes of Mara's gorgeous face roll through my head like a movie, I squeeze my eyes shut and tighten my grip on my cock. I couldn't find Mara's shampoo; it wasn't where I left it, but I don't need it to bring myself to climax. Having her here, under the same roof as me, is all the incentive I need.

In a way, my plan is as brilliant as it is dangerous. I get to help Mara by giving her a steady, stable income, and her presence will ensure I keep my hands to myself—*literally*—which will keep both Fyodor and media-hungry harlots like Veronika off my back.

My unexpected brilliance sees me stroking my cock faster. It reacts as if it is Mara's fingers circling my shaft, jacking me off like she is hungry for my cum.

I'm seconds from release and moaning like there aren't a dozen guests in my den, drinking my liquor and partying like I took the lead in the polls instead of a dive.

The fact I'm stroking my cock instead of mulling over votes still a year from being cast is already lurid, but doing it here, in a bathroom, blows my mind.

Only a week ago, if you had asked me about the possibility of me getting myself off, I would have deemed it impossible. My fear of touch isn't solely fixated on strangers. It is, as a whole, for both strangers and me.

Yet here I am, stroking my dick for the second time today, in a shower of all places.

My shock should have my cock sitting limp against my thigh. It shouldn't be rocking in and out of my fist at a pace quick enough for release to be imminent. But since my focus is on her, the woman with eyes that seemingly can see through to my soul, my balls pull in close to my body as my cock pulsates with want.

Mara's scent, pert tits, and fuckable body feature heavily over the next several minutes. I think about how she looked up at me when my hand slid inside her panties and how she moaned my name when my thumb found her clit. I think about her smell and how I used her shampoo as bodywash for days to ensure I didn't lose it.

"Fuck."

I'm right there, on the brink of release, picturing how she'll moan my name when I take her bare for the first time.

It won't be with a stutter.

Her voice will be crystal clear and without fear.

"Oh..."

As I strangle my cock, desperate for a quick release so I can get back to the party before Mara leaves, my spare hand braces against the sparkling clean tiles of my office bathroom. My hips piston as I think of all the ways I could take her without the restraints my hookups are never without.

Her tits will bounce when I take her hard and fast, and her lips will be cracked and swollen from the number of kisses we'll share.

She'll taste so good.

Moan so hard.

She will fuck me as much as I will fuck her.

And I won't punish her for her sneaky touches, scold her, or end our exchange when her desire to touch grows too rampant for her to ignore.

I could encourage them. That's how unhinged she makes me. How unique. She makes me think I can have my cake and eat it too.

The theory wouldn't be in limbo if she weren't a mother.

That is the *only* thing holding me back from going gung-ho on Rafael's suggestion to make Mara my wife.

It may make me seem like an ass, but you can't judge me until you've walked a day in my shoes.

My childhood was... *fuck.*

My cock softens.

"No."

I thrust my hips faster, trying to strangle both my dick and my thoughts back into submission. I need this release more than my lungs need air. I won't have a single lucid thought if I don't release the lusty deluge Mara's presence forever causes.

Nothing works.

My cock is as limp as it was meant to be only moments ago, and I've washed too much of Mara's scent off my skin for it to convince my head into a second hiatus.

Frustrated, I throw my fist into the tile before relishing the snippet of pain it rewards me with. I'm not a sadist by any means, but pain is a salutary reminder of my goals and why I strive so hard to achieve them.

With my shoulders hanging as flaccid as my dick, I switch off the faucet and exit the shower. Blood is pissing out of my hand from where it split while colliding with the tiles. It dots the vanity sink with droplets of crimson and has my thoughts shifting back to my youth.

There was so much blood then, so much gore, yet the silence was the most painful part.

It still haunts me now.

Talking about silence, the noise booming from the den before I entered the bathroom no longer exists when I dress before entering the central part of my office to search for something to clog the graze on my hand. It soaked through a hand towel in less than a minute, so I don't see cotton swabs doing any better.

My apartment resembles a graveyard at midnight.

It is deadly quiet.

Blood drips on my desk when I hit the intercom button and say, "Rafael?"

I don't get a response, so I try again. "Rafael—"

"He left twenty m-minutes ago," replies a voice I would immediately recognize even if she hadn't stuttered.

Mara's throat works hard to swallow when I march to my office door and swing it open, stealing her temporary cloak of invisibility. My third-floor office hovers above the den, a perch to overlook all the debauchery below, so it can't hide the emptiness of my apartment.

It is just Mara and me.

My cock roars back to life as the scent I'm becoming obsessed with filters through my nostrils.

I drift my eyes away from the ghost-town-like den to Mara when she says, "Y-your hand. What happened?"

She doesn't give me a chance to reply. Quicker than a heartbeat, she pulls me into my office, plops me onto my chair, and then empties her purse onto my desk.

It's brimming with an assortment of items—including the Band-Aids I sought when she slipped on wet tiles the night we met.

I huff, amused, when she commences ripping open a strip of Band-Aids. I entered my office seeking a stapler. A sterile strip isn't going to cut it.

"Y-yes, you're right," Mara says, tilting to my right to ensure I have no trouble hearing her whispered words. "You need something more d-durable than Band-Aids."

Her search ends when I nudge my head to the stapler, and then her cheeks whiten.

"We can't s-staple your wound together."

"Why not?" I ask. "I've handled worse than a staple piercing through skin."

I cuss under my breath when sympathy sparks through her eyes. I said too much, but mercifully, Mara is as adapt at making people feel comfortable as she is beautiful. "Be-because every seamstress knows you only pin before s-sewing to ensure you get the perfect seam."

I'm lost on her metaphor until her hand moves for a mini sewing kit hidden under a travel-size bottle of hand sanitizer.

When I nod, approving of her plan, she opens the lid and threads one of the needles. Once she has everything ready, she moves in close and gathers my injured hand.

Her briefest touch jolts electricity through my body. Mara's response seems the opposite. A rush of nausea makes her giddy, and she sways uncontrollably.

"Are you okay?"

She stumbles before nodding as if she didn't. "I just realized I can't st-stitch your wound. My kit isn't sterile. You should probably go to the h-hospital."

"I don't want to sit in the ER for hours for a handful of stitches." The shield she is trying to force between us slips away when I curl my uninjured hand around her stuttering ones, and I say, "And as I said previously, I've endured worse."

I stare at her, and she stares back, the intangible string between us growing stronger with each passing second.

Honesty does that. It has you knocking down barriers you were certain would never topple.

"I don't want to hurt you," she eventually whispers, her dour tone incapable of weakening my excitement that she's more concerned about me than the reason she stutters.

He isn't on her mind right now.

I am.

With the knowledge of that sending all the blood to the lower extremities of my body, my wound seems more superficial than life-threatening. It doesn't drip a droplet of blood when I raise my hand to Mara's face to free her lip from her menacing teeth.

Her moan when I drag my thumb over her lips coagulates my blood, mending both my wound and my heart. Not an ounce of consideration is given to any consequences I may face when my thumb fills the gap between her parted lips.

My cock knocks at my zipper when she sucks on the tip of my thumb before she swivels her tongue around it. When I picture her mouth doing the same to my cock, another first I can't wait to experience with her, it leaks pre-cum from the crest.

Almost desperately, I lunge for her.

My kiss is violent. Needy. It shows how unhinged she makes me and how desperate I am to let go of the reins as Rafael is suggesting.

I've lived my life governed for years, long before I started my political career. Not a single decision I made was for me. It was to keep my family's secrets and bury them deeper than anyone could find them.

It was to hide years of shame.

They aren't featured in my exchanges with Mara. Nothing matters but how many moans I can entice from her and my hope that they'll be delivered without a stutter.

14

MARA

*W*ith his fingers knotted in my hair and our tongues dueling like they've danced together for years, Ark kisses me until his office window fogs up and my needs are too potent to ignore for a second longer.

It is hotter than our exchange in my kitchen, blistering and panty-wetting.

I groan when he pulls back. My disappointment doesn't procrastinate for long. It switches to excitement when he drags his arm over his desk, dumping the contents of my handbag onto the floor, along with a laptop and a stack of paperwork.

Any worry left lingering in the back of my head that I'm placing my livelihood on the line disappears when he lifts me to sit on his desk before he wedges himself between my splayed thighs.

My heart skips a beat when he floats his eyes over my face before they slowly narrow down my body. My positioning is unladylike. I'm reasonably sure my panties are exposed, but for the life of me, I can't close my legs.

I love the way he looks at me. I crave it more than my lungs do air.

His scrumptious voice rolls through me like liquid ecstasy when he says, "Keep your palms flat on the desk. If you can do that, I won't need to restrain you."

The thought of being bound should scare me, but it doesn't.

I'm not myself when I'm with Ark. I am fearless, as if my nightmares never came true.

Desperate for air, I roll my shoulders back and tilt my chin. It makes the situation worse. It thrusts my breasts in Ark's direction and exposes even more of my damp panties.

I'm not the only one noticing.

"You're so wet, Mara. Your pussy is salivating for me."

I moan when he plays at the wetness between my legs, and my thighs shake. Neither point has anything to do with his next set of words.

"You heard me, didn't you? You heard me stroking my cock while pretending I was using your shampoo as lubricant."

I try to shake my head. It is an impossible task. The messy situation between my legs isn't solely because of how skilled he is at kissing. It was from listening to him moan my name. It was so virile and hot that I struggled to harness my excitement.

Ark drags his thumb over the hood of my clit, doubling the shudders wracking through me. Half his thumb is calloused, with raised scars making it smooth and rough. It reminds me of his confession about how staples to the skin seem like a walk in the park for him.

The reminder that abuse comes in many forms should weaken the intensity of our exchange. It should suffocate the fiery embers and scatter them in the ashes I was sure were mere seconds from being dispersed when Ark unearthed my hiding spot.

It seems to do the opposite.

My right to sexual enjoyment was stolen from me at an extremely young age.

Ark's attention is returning it tenfold.

I've never felt more wanted and needy.

After only a handful of rotations, I'm on the verge of climax. *I think.*

I've never orgasmed, so I can't testify that the tingles racing through my core are that or something else.

I think it's that.

It could be the start of a climax.

"You'll know," Ark murmurs, making me panic I said my private thoughts out loud. "There will be no doubt. It will make you feel angry and sad the first time. Maybe even a little dirty." He locks his eyes with mine. They're searingly intense. "But I will be here to guide you through it. You just need to trust me. Can you do that, Mara? Can you trust me to make it feel good?"

I nod without a second thought, and my submissiveness is rewarded tenfold. After hooking my panties to the side, Ark returns his thumb to my clit. His strokes feel ten times better now that there is nothing between us. Direct and purposeful.

My shoulder blades join when he murmurs, "I want to taste you here." I scratch at the varnish on his fancy desk, frantic for something to clutch, when his voice comes out as needy as the pulse hammering my clit. "I bet your pussy tastes as sweet as your mouth."

As his words make me hot, my hips instinctively gyrate upward, toward his mouth.

"No. That won't work." Instead of my sprint to climax slowing in momentum from his rejection, it catapults to an unmanageable level. "I need your words. Tell me how badly you want me to eat you."

The thought of begging would usually disgust me.

Not today.

I never once wanted what was forced on me.

I begged them to stop, not to touch me.

This is entirely different.

"P-please."

Ark's moan rolls over my clit for half a second before his tongue follows it.

When he sucks the nervy bud into his mouth, I lose all sense of control. I shatter like glass on a hard-tiled floor, and Ark's name rips from my throat.

Even with my body surrendering to a madness it's never faced, Ark's pursuit to unravel me doesn't taper. He devours me with greedy licks and hungry sucks until the stars he danced in front of my eyes explode into fireworks.

"Oh..." I moan, stunned by the length of my orgasm.

Are they meant to last this long and be so violent?

It is intense.

Blinding.

And as Ark hinted, scary.

I don't know whether to burst out crying or scream his brilliance into the air, and I lose the chance to do either when a strangled cough announces we're no longer alone.

15

ARKADIY

"*I*'m so s-sorry."

With her cheeks ashen and eyes brimming with remorse, Mara slips off my desk and hightails it to the door. My brain screams at me to go after her, to remember the pledge I made to guide her through what I am certain was her first orgasm. But I'm not a man when the eyes from my nightmares are glaring at me.

I'm only a boy.

After adjusting my cock so it stops pitching a tent in the crotch of my pants, I shift on my feet to face the doorway Mara raced through.

Riley's cheeks are as white as Mara's, but the fury in her eyes has nothing to do with lust.

"What the hell, Ark?" She enters my office with her hands balled, ready and willing to battle for a woman she has only recently met. "Why was she crying? She's not meant to cry when you're... when she's..." She looks me dead set in the eyes. "She's not meant to cry. Period. So what the fuck did you do?"

My words are as hostile as the tension radiating from her. "Nothing. I did nothing."

"Then why was she crying!" she screams, her words bouncing off the walls slowly closing in on me.

Her words echo ones I've heard before, and they instantly sour my mood. "Perhaps she was crying because you walked in on her when she was vulnerable. Did you ever think about that?"

"Don't you dare," Riley snaps out, her voice as seething as the spit sizzling from her mouth. "Don't you dare try to pin this on me. I am not this family's scapegoat."

"Neither the fuck am I!" I lash back, too overwhelmed with emotions I don't know how to handle to act cordial.

I'm not the ruthless tirade most people believe I am right now. I'm a brother and a son, and another one of the endless victims of an unfair world.

"I wasn't hurting her. I wouldn't do that to her. I am not him. I'm not a monster."

"Unlike me?"

My eyes snap to Riley so fast they burn. "That isn't what I meant. I've never said that. I have *never* compared you to him."

Pain and anger flood her impressive eyes—*his* eyes. "Words aren't the only way to express yourself, Arkadiy. You display that better than anyone." After shaking her head, announcing her disgust without words, she reveals the reason for her interruption. "Mother called. She saw this…" She dumps the photograph of Mara, Tillie, and me onto my desk before she heads back for the door. "I told her you were busy, but you know what Mother is like. If she asks you to jump, you ask her how high."

She isn't generalizing her parody. She used "you" on purpose because she knows I can't deny the actuality of her scorn.

My mother rules the roost in our family, and I've yet to cut ties because I'm too scared of the backlash it could cause.

What once seemed unachievable is nowhere near as daunting with the taste of Mara's pussy still stimulating my tastebuds.

Three short words slow Riley's brisk exit. "She's like us."

Her back remains facing me for several long seconds before she eventually turns around. I don't know what she is seeking when her eyes bounce between mine, but she must find something, because her tone is completely different than it was minutes ago when she whispers, "Us?"

I could force her to elaborate on her reply, but I won't. For the first time in her life, I refuse to let her carry the sole burden of our childhood.

It is *our* burden, not hers.

Air whizzes between her quivering lips when I dip my chin.

Then her tears fall freely.

16

MARA

The coolness of the winds that forever batter this part of the country reduces when I stuff my hands under my arms. I hug myself tight while continuing down an isolated street, seeking a bus service that runs at this time of night.

After being jumped at gunpoint, I should be scared to take public transport at this hour, but my embarrassment is too high to let something as insignificant as fear in.

I can't believe I almost cried while climaxing.

Who does that?

Who freaks out during a sexual activity that's meant to make you feel your weight in gold?

I'm horrified Arkadiy was subjected to my near blubbering, so my emotions blew over when I discovered he wasn't the sole witness of the farce.

At least Riley interrupted us and not Rafael or I may never recover. It will take more than a forty-minute walk to let gratitude seep in, though.

On top of my shame, I also feel guilty. I didn't mean to barge past Riley, but with my emotions scrambled and the exit blocked, I went for the bolt-now-answer-questions-later coping mechanism I designed after I found out I was pregnant with Tillie.

Riley balked when I accidentally touched her as much as Ark did the first time I fled from him. It caused a million questions to flood my head and has me so confused it takes longer than I care to admit to notice that I am being followed.

I move to the far shoulder of the road, giving the driver plenty of room to maneuver past me.

He doesn't. He follows me down a side street before flashing his headlights. Their brightness is as blinding as the flashes of the paparazzi cameras when they mistook me during my exit of the main entry door of the Chrysler building as someone of importance.

I crank my neck back, preparing to serve the driver some of the anger bubbling in my veins. My words entomb in my throat when the car's internal light flicks on, and I spot the desolate face of the man seated in the back passenger seat.

Ark looks as tormented as I feel.

Heartsick, I slowly approach the idling car and slip into the back seat.

I've barely latched my belt when Ark snaps out, "Term one of your contract was that you were not to use public transport, so what the fuck are you doing walking to a bus stop at this time of night?"

His anger momentarily shocks me. Then, as I work his words through my head, I realize it isn't anger they're projecting. It's panic.

"I am s-safe on these streets."

He huffs as if I said more, and it instigates a lengthy period of silence between us.

I don't know what to say to make things less awkward. I'm not the best communicator in general, but it is worse in hostile situations.

For every mile we travel, the more withdrawn Ark becomes. The distance between us is so great that I don't bother tilting toward him when Darius turns down the street my building is on. I say my farewell from where I'm seated before curling my hand around the lock mechanism.

"Thank you for the opportunity, but I think it will be best if I s-stay with my current employer."

A click sounds two seconds before I yank on the lock. It doesn't budge an inch. I'm trapped in a car with a man teeming with anger and on the verge of hyperventilating.

"P-please let me out."

Ark acts as if I never spoke. "Running won't solve anything, Mara. Hiding won't solve anything."

"Please let m-me out," I repeat as if his words aren't gospel.

Running hasn't gotten me anywhere fast, but it is better than staying and being abused.

When I say that to Ark, his thighs twitch and his hands ball. There's no doubt of his emotions. He's furious. Not at me. At himself.

"Ark—"

"Your schedule will be forwarded to you tomorrow morning. If there is anything you need to adjust, you can either contact Rafael or myself. Rafael's schedule is erratic, but I will be available all weekend. I don't have *any* planned engagements."

Is that his way of telling me he is prioritizing me above anyone else or that I'm merely an employee to him?

It seems a bit of both, and it makes me more angry than grateful.

"As s-stated previously, I appreciate the offer—"

"I need you, Mara," he interrupts, freezing both my words and my heart. "I won't be able to do this without you." His whispered words burrow into my heart, deep down where no one has touched. "I won't survive it."

"It" seems like so much more than his political career. It appears personal, extremely personal, and it squashes my objections to microdot in an instant.

"Okay," I murmur, choking back a sob before I repeat myself, a more heartfelt response above me. "Okay."

The carnage left of my heart tries to pull itself back together when the clank of the central locking system disarming booms through the cabin of the car. I'm relieved my exit is no longer blocked, but I am also torn about leaving.

I'd stay if Ark asked.

He doesn't, though. He presses his lips to the edge of my mouth before he orders Darius to walk me into my building.

Confused and emotional, I farewell Ark with a tight smile before shadowing Darius's somber exit.

17

ARKADIY

*H*ow is it only Monday? The past weekend was the longest in my life. It dragged, easily the equivalent of a month. I'm tired and moody since my sleep schedule has been just as lagging, and the only thing I was looking forward to this week is late.

Where the fuck are you, Mara?

Forever impatient, I pull my phone out of my pocket and select a frequently called number.

Rafael answers two rings later. "I was beginning to think you had lost my number." His laugh hacks my nerves. "Run out of shampoo already? I only restocked your bathroom Saturday morning."

After working my jaw side to side, I get to the source of my frustration. "Where is she?"

I haven't spoken to Mara since my disastrous attempt at acting like I wasn't choked with fear that it took my team over an hour to find her Friday night, but she gave me her word that she would be here today.

I never considered the possibility she would change her mind. She seems too honest for that, too determined, and I hate that I don't know her well enough to be one hundred percent confident in my assessment of her traits.

I hear Rafael twist his seedy mustache before his tone switches from teasing to understanding. "We adjusted her roster, remember? You wanted to give her more time with Tillie, so you changed her schedule so she could drop Tillie off at school and pick her up." The unease making my skin hot soothes when he murmurs, "She's looking good. A little tired, but *definitely* good."

When a growl finalizes his statement, one rumbles in my chest.

Rafael's laugh is cut short when I say, "When she arrives, send her to my office." I try not to look desperate. "The bookshelves need dusting."

"Bullshit. It is because your office is like your bedroom. Out of bounds for anyone not named Ma—"

I disconnect our call before shifting on my feet to face the floor-to-ceiling window of my office. The hope of witnessing Mara's arrival at work trickles through my veins and doubles the output of my heart.

I have an obsession I'm confident isn't healthy, but I have no clue how to alter it. I have had infatuations before, but not like this. Mara truly fascinates me. I don't think, drink, or eat without her beautiful face sneaking into the picture. She is the first thing on my mind when I wake up and the last thing before I sleep.

Before you ask, hardly any of the things I imagine include her stutter or how she got it.

I'm pulled from my thoughts when I sense I am being watched. The heaviness of his footing announces who it is half a second before I turn around to greet him.

Fyodor is a little overweight in the midsection, and since he must counterbalance his stomach, he walks heavily on his heels. His stomps could wake the dead.

I'm shocked when Fyodor isn't the only soul in my office. The woman who forced me to stroke my cock in my office bathroom the past three nights because her perfume is too distracting to discount is standing at his left, looking smug.

"What the fuck is she still doing here?"

Veronika isn't turned off by either my scold or the fact I spoke as if she isn't present. "Saving you from making a mistake." She steps closer, her overly floral perfume hammering my sinuses. "I get it. The maid—"

"Mara." My bark announces I wouldn't allow my mother to disre-spect her, so there's no chance in hell I'll stand aside and watch her be belittled by a woman who'd sell her soul for half a million Instagram followers.

"Mara"—Veronika's eyelids twitch as her eyes roll—"is beautiful. I understand your fascination, Ark." She should stop there. It may be the only way she will make it out of my office in one piece. "But she is *not* wife material." My fists stiffen as rapidly as my cock when she says, "That's why I'm giving you a free pass. Fuck the mai—" She recovers quickly. "Fuck Mara, get her out of your system, and then we can move on to a mutual collaboration that will shoot our stardom to superstar status."

A mutual collaboration?

That's what she calls a possible eight years of marriage—a mutual collaboration.

I'm so shocked I can't speak.

Fyodor mistakes it as a consideration. "Veronika is right, Arkadiy. Early polling this morning has forecasters predicting a surge in your approval rating." He fumbles through an oversized newspaper and reads from an article printed several pages in. "If predictions remain ingenuous, Arkadiy Orlov could enter the race ahead of his main competitor." He backhands the newspaper, his chubby hand tearing through the page before he lifts his eyes to mine. "The articles printed over the weekend about your flourishing relationship with Veronika are responsible for this. The voters love the idea of you settling down—"

"Yes, settling down. They don't care with who."

Veronika huffs but remains quiet, leaving the floor to Fyodor. "They approve of *this* relationship"—he thrust his hand between Veronika and me during the "this" part of his reply—"because of the excitement of possible future endeavors. The courting, engagement, wedding, and commencement of fatherhood." He lowers his tone to barely a whisper. "A ready-built family is *not* what the voters are looking for." I'm already on the verge of blowing my top, so you can picture how perverse it becomes when, instead of going down with a sinking ship, he throws others overboard so he has something to cling to. "Your mother agrees with me. She saw the struggles your father faced when they wed—"

"That man was *not* my father."

Fyodor swallows, shocked by my outburst. He can be because he doesn't know the hell I went through under *that* man's reign and how badly it still affects my life to this day.

If it weren't for *him*, Mara would already be mine.

"Leave." My narrowed gaze is for Fyodor, but my demand is for Veronika.

She tries to lessen the tension pilfering the air of oxygen. "Just think about it, Ark. That's all we're asking. We could be amazing together and do many wonderful things."

While batting her lashes, she places her hand on my chest and leans in to kiss my cheek goodbye. I pull away, causing her to almost stumble. Just her hand on me makes me furious. I wouldn't be responsible for my actions if her overly glossed lips were to touch me. And don't get me started on her choice of perfume.

It reminds me of *her*.

I wait for Veronika to leave before walking around my desk. I need something bulky between Fyodor and me to ensure I use words instead of my fists while announcing my anger about his blatant disrespect.

"Who do you work for, Fyodor?"

He looks at me in shock, and it pisses me off.

"Who do you work for?" I ask again, louder this time. "Me or my mother?"

"You," he answers, his reply just as loud, his anger as apparent. "Of course you." He tries to soothe tempered waters, his paycheck as vital to him as his life. "I only brought up your mother because she contacted me last night." Stupidly, he steps closer. "She said you told her to back off and that you need space."

"Because I do!"

I've never spoken a bad word about my mother in my life. If she says something, even something I disagree with, I keep my mouth shut. It isn't that I trust her word and know she would never lead me astray. It is because she knows all my deepest, darkest secrets.

Pacifying her pacifies my worry that she will destroy any chance I have of power. Not the power some men wrongly believe they have. The ultimate power. The top tier of the ladder. I want to rule the nation because those on the top perch will never be shit on again.

But I couldn't do that Friday night. My mother doesn't know a thing about Mara, her background, or the fight she displays with nothing but a glance, yet she tore her to shreds by assessing her credibility through a paparazzi image.

I went to war. I fought for a woman who scares me as much as she intrigues me, and I was winning... until my mother noticed Mara wasn't the only female in the photograph.

Tillie's whitened face is barely visible in the image the paparazzo took of us in the back of the cab, but once you notice her in the crook of her mother's arm, you can't miss her. Her face is as precious as her mother's, and her eyes are just as soul-stealing.

Not even my mother could deny those facts. She used them against me multiple times throughout her two-hour tirade. Her belief that I am moments away from becoming the monster from my nightmares was so on-point not even a fifth of whiskey and a recently replenished bathroom could take the edge off.

I stewed over her claim for hours and see myself doing the same again now when I dismiss Fyodor from my office as if his disrespect doesn't warrant further punishment.

He's almost out the door when I hand him the final nail for his coffin. It's up to him what he does with it. "Speaking with my mother behind my back again will see you standing at the end of an unemployment line. Do I make myself clear?"

Guilt colors his tone when he answers, "Profoundly, sir."

18

MARA

*T*hings feel tense when I enter Ark's apartment. The mood is somber, and the air is heavy with sentiment. Anyone would swear the article in the newspaper Darius was reading when Tillie and I slipped into the back of his town car this morning had Ark's approval rating falling instead of steadily rising.

His team should be celebrating, so I'm perplexed about what happened.

Ark didn't have a change of mind, did he?

I didn't hear from him over the weekend, so I assume the schedule a courier handed me Saturday afternoon is still valid. And I'm not late. It only takes fifteen minutes to walk from Tillie's school to the Chrysler building, but since Darius said my collection and drop-off from work includes a detour to Tillie's school, I've arrived for my shift thirty minutes early instead of the usual fifteen.

"Hey, Mara."

A touch of pinkness impinges on my cheeks from the way Rafael greets me. It reminds me of Rio from *Good Girls*, another of Mrs. Lichard's favorite shows. Tillie isn't allowed to watch that one, so Mrs. Lichard saves it for the nights Tillie doesn't beg for a sleepover. Tillie is as obsessed with Mrs. Lichard's cooking as she is with John Pearce.

"How was your weekend?"

"Um. G-good. You?" It is embarrassing how boring my life is, so I won't bore Rafael with the details.

"It wasn't bad. I managed to find that salon you told me about. Got Ark enough stock to get him through at least a week." He smiles at me when heat flashes in my cheeks. "Didn't see you at the restaurant Friday night. Did something more appetizing catch your eye?"

"Ah…" How am I meant to respond to that? Did Ark not tell him what happened? They seem close, so I'm surprised. Though I guess I shouldn't be. Rafael ate dessert with the who's who of Russia. Ark ate me. That isn't close to the same thing. "Where should I s-start?"

Rafael pouts as if disappointed I didn't tumble headfirst into the trap he set before he nudges his head to Ark's third-floor office. "Ark wants you to start in his office." He walks away, rubbing his hands together. "Something about his knob needing polishing." I can barely hear him through his snickers. "Or bookshelves. Perhaps he said his bookshelves need dusting. Whatever it is, he wants you to start in his office." He twists back to face me, his smile blinding. "Do you need me to show you the way, or is Goldilocks okay wandering in the bear's forest unaccompanied?"

I love that he uses Goldilocks as a reference. It is one of the rare few nursery rhymes that aren't about death and despair but more about respecting a person's boundaries and belongings.

"I'll be f-fine. Thank you."

He dips his chin as if my praise is genuine before he disappears down a long corridor. I take a deep breath while heading in the opposite direction.

My steps halve in size when I veer past the bedroom closest to Ark's office. The nasally voice announcing she isn't going anywhere until she gets all the bang for her buck is recognizable even with me only associating with her for mere minutes.

Veronika's voice is as whiny as her words. "He's foolish to give this opportunity up, Fyo. My little minions will vote for whoever I suggest. Our collab could win him the presidency."

A man I've not yet been officially introduced to rakes his eyes down my body when I veer past one of Ark's guest bedrooms. His glare isn't cruel. It is more understanding, which is weird.

After smiling like I have more power than him, he gestures for me to continue before he commences closing the door, blocking a frustrated but determined Veronika from my view.

Her nasally voice can travel miles, though. "I also have a contract. A *legally* binding contract." Disappointment hits me hard when she says, "Arkadiy invited me to a two-week getaway to seduce him. I've not yet had the chance to show him all my tricks, so I'm not going anywhere until I have."

My stomach is still gurgling about her confession when I knock on Ark's office door.

"Come in." Ark's barked order is gruff, and it sends my pulse skyrocketing.

When I enter, my eyes stray to his bulky desk. The first thing I notice is my handbag, neatly packed and sitting on top. The second is Ark. He's standing near a wall-to-wall, floor-to-ceiling window.

His stature emulates the driven businessman he is, but there's something off with his posture. His shoulders are more slumped than sharp, and his breathing is labored.

Since his cell phone is attached to his ear, I wait at his open office door, not wanting to intrude.

Two seconds later, our eyes lock and hold in the reflection of the window. He tells his caller to wait, his tone clipped before he spins to face me. His expression is effortlessly relieved, but his smile is fake. It is rigid and tense, nothing like the one he gave me when he slid my panties to the side mere seconds before sucking on my clit.

When a squawk sounds from his phone, I point to the exit. "I'll w-wait out there."

"No," he shouts, startling me. After lowering his tone and brows, he says, "This isn't anything important."

With his eyes on me, he walks to the servants' entrance door, yanks down the spindle pinning it to the frame, and then pulls it open.

With one exit unblocked, he closes the one I'm standing next to.

The waft of air its closure causes fluffs up my hair. It smells fresh and clean, like I replaced the shampoo he stole.

I haven't, and the remembrance is thrilling.

He is still using my shampoo.

"Yes, Mother, I heard what you said." Ark gives me a sympathetic look at the end of his sentence before he twists back around to face the window.

Since his actions expose his hostility isn't directed at me, instead of fretting, I move into the servants' corridor to collect a cleaning cart and get to work.

Ark's office either had a dust storm roll through it over the weekend, or he's never allowed anyone in the business half of his home to clean the mess. The shelves were coated in dust, the bathroom was poorly stocked and cleaned, and his desk is messy.

Is because I've not yet had a chance to clean it.

Ark's sixth phone call since I started has only recently finished, and although I love that he feels comfortable enough around me to discuss private matters in my presence, I didn't want to disturb him.

I've kept myself as busy as possible, so there is only his desk left to clean before I can move on to other areas of his apartment.

A bottle of surface spray freezes midair when Ark snaps out, "Don't you dare."

I swallow the brick the sternness of his words lodged in my throat, before twisting to face him. His shoulders are still tight, as pinched as his brows, but there are sparks of the man who ate me on the desk hidden behind the stony mask he's wearing.

I try to keep my voice professional. It is virtually impossible with how hot Ark's stare is making me.

"The s-spray won't get anywhere near your paperwork."

"I don't give a fuck about the paperwork." His head tilts, aligning our eyes. "Something far more valuable than paperwork is on that desk." His eyes bounce between my heated cheeks and dilated gaze for several seconds before he asks, "And it reminds me that I haven't asked how you are. Did I...?" His brutal swallow maims my throat. "Are you hurt?"

Hurt?

He answers my silent question by lowering his eyes to the little frilled apron part of my uniform.

Oh.

"Um. No. I'm-I'm fine. Thank you."

I'm more than fine. Even with our exchange ending awkwardly, I used it to stimulate myself—more than once.

That was unheard of only last week. I've never been interested in self-pleasure, but knowing a man as powerful and handsome as Ark self-stimulates made it less daunting.

I made myself come—multiple times. It didn't feel as good as it did when Ark made me climax, but I won't be so quick to turn down the idea if it were the only thing on offer.

Ignoring the grumble of my stomach, which I'm not entirely sure is based on actual hunger, I ask, "Are you okay? Things s-seem a little... *tense.*"

He smiles, wordlessly expressing his gratitude for my concern, before he plucks the surface spray out of my hand and heads for the servants' entrance. "It isn't anything I can't handle." He dumps the bottle onto the cart before spinning to face me. "Have you eaten today?"

His growl when I shake my head forces my thighs together.

"I'm not m-much of a breakfast eater." That's a lie. I tell Tillie a minimum of once a week how important breakfast is. I just skip it when things are tight. Tillie's birthday party made things tight.

Ark folds his arms in front of his chest before asking, "Did you read the employment contract I forwarded with your schedule?"

I nod. "Yes. M-multiple times."

"So you saw that lunch is provided for all employees?"

Again, I nod.

"That term now includes breakfast." I try to interrupt, but he speaks too fast for me to keep up with. "Starting now."

When he flattens his hand on the small of my back and guides me toward the exit, I stammer out, "I've only just s-started. I can't stop for breakfast."

I learn he is watching me more closely than I realize when he says, "Despite popping into Val's office to ask about her weekend, you still arrived thirty minutes before your shift. That's plenty of time to squeeze in some breakfast."

We make it halfway to the kitchen before Ark's long strides halt, and his hand falls from my back like he was scorched from our near touch.

I don't know the woman standing across from us, glaring at me, but Ark most certainly does.

"Mother, what are you doing here?"

19

ARKADIY

"What happened to not judging a book by its cover?" I thrust my hand at my office door as if Mara stands on the other side. Its shake is unmissable. I'm not scared. I am furious about the way my mother ignored Mara's offer of an introduction before dragging me away from her as if she has the plague. "You don't know Mara. She's—"

She cuts me off with the same excuse she gave me multiple times the past forty-eight hours. "Going to ruin your political career. Your campaign for the presidency is just taking off. Being involved with a woman who has a child will complicate things."

"How?" Not needing to hear her answer to know which direction she will take, I issue the poorest excuse in the book. "Mara is an employee. I'm not... *fucking* her."

She looks at me like she knows all my sordid thoughts, her lips pressed into a thin line. "You're not seeing that woman—"

"Mara," I snap out. "Her name is Mara."

She doesn't fold as easily as Veronika. "You're not seeing that woman for who she is. The similarities between her life and Karolina's have distracted you from your objectives." Anger surges through me when she says, "You choose a life of solidarity for a reason, Arkadiy. You know the odds if you were to become a family man, yet you want to play with fire like there's no possibility you will get burned."

I step closer, my voice trembling with fury. "It is a little too late to worry about me getting burned, wouldn't you say, Mother?"

She scoffs as if my anger isn't valid. "People will talk, and they will judge. Then once their curiosity rises to a point they can't ignore as to why you picked her out of all the women in the world you could have settled down with, they will dig and dig and dig until *all* aspects of both of your lives are on display for the world to see. Is that what you want, Arkadiy? Do you want your dirty laundry aired for the masses to sniff?"

Just the prospect of my secrets being shared would usually have me backing away instantly with my hands held in the air, but it isn't as easy to do this time. Mara fascinates me, and every red-blooded man knows obsession is the most potent drug on the market.

As my mother stands, her eyes flashing with determination, I suck in the scent of Mara's shampoo, hopeful it will cool the fire raging inside me when she says, "This is not about your happiness, Arkadiy. It is about the image you agreed to present on behalf of our family when you made the decision you did years ago. Certain things are expected from you. Being involved with a single mother won't fulfill those expectations. It could ruin everything."

She places her hand on my shoulder, her expression softening as she vainly tries to display she cares about me. "I'm not asking you to step back solely for myself. This could destroy Riley as much as it could you. Don't put her through more pain than necessary. She's been through enough."

I pull away from her touch, my heart pounding. I'm not shocked she is placing the entire burden of our family's secrets on my shoulders. She has done it my whole life. But this is the first time she's used Riley to get me on board with her plans.

Usually, she acts as if she doesn't exist.

"Ark—"

"I need time," I interrupt, my tone announcing I'm not making a suggestion. It is a demand.

"Time is not in your favor. Ballots—"

"I. Need. Time," I repeat more forcefully.

"Fine." My mother sighs, her shoulders slumping before she heads for the door. Never one to leave without having the last word, just before she exits, she says, "I just want what is best for you. You're my only child, and I don't want to see everything you've worked so hard for stolen from you because you've forgotten that being the head of the family means you sometimes have to make difficult decisions."

I watch her exit, equally furious and confused. I know what she is asking is too much, but I can't shake the feeling that she is also right.

I'm also super curious to discover why she left Riley out of the equation while referencing how many children she has.

20

MARA

"You should try it on."

Even with my heart racing a million miles an hour from being snuck up on unawares, I keep my balk hidden. I doubt a day will pass when I won't have to suppress the urge to squeal, but the more I work with Ark's team, the more developed my skills are becoming.

I shouldn't be so hard on myself. Even long-term employees struggled to hide their fright when Ark's mother arrived out of nowhere for an impromptu visit at the beginning of the week. They scrambled in all directions, leaving me as the sole employee to officially welcome her.

She didn't accept the hand I held out to her in offering so a woman as refined and influential as her wouldn't be subjected to my annoying stutter. She dismissed my welcome with a gesture nowhere near as friendly and with her chest puffed out like a rooster.

The air stretching the material of her couture blouse deflated like a popped balloon when Ark halted my exit by snatching up my wrist. He gave me no indication I should be fearful of the repercussions of my cowardice when he told me he would meet me in the kitchen, but I must not be competent in his expressions, because I haven't seen hide nor hair of him since Monday morning.

It is now Friday afternoon.

I stuff away my pathetic whine for a more appropriate time when the person who snuck up on me reminds me that they're still present. "The color will contrast beautifully with your skin tone, and it will make your eyes even more dazzling."

I finish taking in a one-of-a-kind Wilfred Iwona gown before spinning to face the voice. I'm not surprised by Riley's arrival considering her high placement on Ark's team, more relieved.

Riley and Rafael were the only two people who didn't glare at me with disdain when I was introduced as the newest member of Ark's team at the commencement of my placement. They smiled with their eyes before joining me in the kitchen for the impromptu brunch Ark had instigated but failed to attend.

Breakfast was plentiful. The spread that morning and each that followed was more than Ark's team could handle. You'd swear Chef is feeding an army of a hundred, not the ten or so guests who float in and out of Ark's apartment throughout the day.

The wastage was heartbreaking until Chef boxed up the leftovers at the end of the day and had Darius load them into the car that drove me home. The residents of my building have been eating like kings, and although it has only been a week, my uniform is already getting a little tight around the midsection.

When Riley arches a brow, impatiently awaiting an answer, I run my hand down the gown she caught me admiring. "It's beautiful, but I don't think it is me."

"Why?" she asks, her tone neither stern nor angry. She's more curious than anything.

"Because..."

I want to say that never in my life would I find it suitable to spend eight thousand dollars on a dress, but the pain in Riley's eyes cuts me off. They're so bright and confident, yet clouding years of hurt—possibly even decades. My stinginess could cut her down further if she mistakes my reply, so I'd rather veer on the side of caution.

"Because today isn't about me." My chest sinks as pain strikes my heart. "It's about her."

Unlike mine, Riley's sigh is vocal when she follows the direction of my gaze. A film crew is documenting Veronika's visit to Wilfred Iwona's invitation-only boutique. Her charm and intelligence have had the crew eating out of her palm for the past three hours and me quickly remembering my place.

I'll be fortunate to carry her purchases, so I don't need to try them on.

My eyes snap to Riley when she says, "This dress wasn't designed for Veronika. Her body type is all wrong for this style. Her hips and ass will ruin it." Her eyes are back on me, heavy and demanding. "You, on the other hand, were made for this dress."

She plucks said dress from the rack like her bank account won't cry processing the surcharge for a gown this pricy before she heads for the changing rooms at the back of the boutique.

"Let's go, Mara. I don't have all day." Her tone is snappy, and it has my thoughts drifting to another resident of the Chrysler building for the umpteenth time today.

I haven't seen Ark in person in almost a week. I'd be a liar if I said I hadn't missed his presence. An aura like his lights up the room when he enters it, so every room in his once glitzy apartment has been bland and uninviting since Monday morning.

I follow Riley like a puppy does an owner when she hits me with a silent demand for obedience. Her "do as I say" stare replicates Ark's to a T.

"Wilfred will have a fit."

Dark hair spills down Riley's back when she cranks her neck back to face me. "Why?"

I wish she were more than a one-word interrogator. I'm the type who requires prompting to initiate a conversation—a lot of it.

Shame slowly chokes me when Riley refuses to accept my many silent rebuffs. "Because I don't have the funds to replace the gown if I w- were to wreck it."

"I'm fine with that." Her shoulder almost touches her ear as her glance at the outfit I changed into before chaperoning Veronika's appointment switches her "so what" expression to brilliance. "It isn't like you don't have the skills to make this gown what it should be."

I look at her as if she has a second head. "That dress is perfect."

A grunt rolls up her chest as she screws up her button nose. "It could be better."

Now I'm certain Wilfred will have a fit. I took only a handful of online fashion courses, but even I know you never diss a designer on their home turf.

This is Wilfred's only brick-and-mortar store. People travel across the globe to gain access to her designs in person. She is hugely successful, so I'm surprised by Riley's level of criticism.

Riley isn't. She looks smug. Calm. She seems so comfortable in her own skin that I wonder if I read the pain in her eyes wrong. Perhaps her true personality only flourishes when surrounded by like-minded people and not the uber-rich she spends most of her time with.

Eager to discover if my findings are true, I nudge my head to a box of tissues outside the changing room. "Grab the tissues."

"What for?" Her gag is audible. "If you think a dressing room is a designer's equivalent of a hairdresser's salon chair, you are poorly mistaken. I don't do crying. Ever." There's a hint of deceit at the end of her reply.

"I'm not going to cry." I can't recall the last time I cried, so I am confident in my assumption. "I just refuse for my pits to get anywhere near that gorgeous material, and I'm sweating s-so much that I'm worried the chicken at lunch was bad."

She smiles, and it eases the swirls of my stomach. I've never had a girlfriend, so I've never learned the difference between banter and gross oversharing.

I feel like my line was a bit of both.

"Oh my god." Tears prick my eyes as I take in the full picture in the floor-to-ceiling mirror in the main changing room.

The gown is a perfect fit. It hugs my breasts and floats over my midsection before pleating at my hips to give my body the ideal hour-glass shape. I'm not yet convinced I can pull off the bulky mermaid tail skirt, but I can't take my eyes off the detailing in the bustier to worry about not showing an ounce of leg.

I feel pretty. Beautiful, even.

I look like I'm worth my weight in gold, and I am not the only one noticing.

"Wow."

That didn't come from Riley, whose mouth hasn't re-hinged since she began dressing me like a Barbie doll almost twenty minutes ago. It is far too deep to belong to Riley and way too possessive.

She also can't make the hairs on my nape stand on end by speaking one word.

Only one man has that skill.

Arkadiy.

The air in my lungs evicts in a hurry when my eyes lock with Ark's in the reflection of the mirror. He wets his lips before adjusting his position so he can rake the front of my body. His hooded gaze is wildly inappropriate for an employer to issue an employee.

His hiss when he reaches the flirty neckline of the gown makes me wet. I've never heard a more carnal noise, and I paid careful attention to every moan he released when he stuffed his fingers deep inside me.

Lust hangs heavy in the air when Ark returns his eyes to my face. His hooded watch infuses the stuffy space with a seductive mix of pheromones and has me fighting not to squirm.

Thank goodness the full length of the dress's skirt can hide the press of my thighs. They're flattened together and pulsating. That's how burning with need I am. I'm tiptoeing on a tightrope from nothing but a stare.

Imagine how explosive the fireworks would be if he touched me again.

When Riley coughs, reminding Ark and me that we're not the only two people in the world, a touch of shyness impinges on my cheeks.

"You look amazing, Mara," Ark says.

I open my mouth to issue a similar compliment. He is dressed similarly to the afternoon he drove Tillie and me home. His dress shirt and suit are both black, but the lightness of his tie makes his outfit more powerful than a funeralgoer. But before a word can seep from my lips, the man of the hour's arrival is sensed by the woman he is here for.

Veronika's voice pierces my ears when she shouts Ark's name. She uses his full name, and despite her naturally high pitch, it rolls out of her mouth as if she is in the middle of ecstasy.

The hem of the dress she's trying on isn't close to decent, but jealousy never surfaces since Ark's eyes don't float down her body.

His top lip furls at one side, and his breathing comes out in a hurry.

His reply mimics Riley's to a T when she realizes the fashion faux pas Veronika is making with one of Wilfred's most iconic pieces.

"That's not how you're meant to wear that gown." Perfume and another smell I can't quite describe fluffs up when she makes a beeline for Veronika, who suddenly looks panicked. "You're wearing it upside down. The hem is beaded, not the bust."

Ark and I stand shoulder to shoulder for several minutes, watching Riley tear Veronika to shreds. I kind of feel bad for Veronika until Ark says, "Designers." His *tsk* adds to the spasms in my pussy. "You'd swear they only create masterpieces for themselves."

It takes me a few seconds to click on to what he is saying. When I do, I'm shocked.

Riley is Wilfred Iwona.

That's why she didn't care if I ruined her gown. It is hers to do with as she pleases.

"Does Veronika kn-know Riley is Wilfred?" I ask Ark, too curious not to snoop.

I feel his eyes on me, hot and heavy and floating over my face, before his breath tickles my ear. "No. Riley likes to keep her pseudonym separate." A touch of a smile graces his lips, and it makes me hot. "When rumors started circulating that she was copycatting Wilfred's style, she placed an ad in a local inquirer announcing herself as Wilfred's newest understudy. Nobody has questioned her since."

"Because she's young," I say before I can stop myself. "People assume anyone under the age of twenty-five is only good at m-making coffee and designing apps." A snippet of bitchiness lowers my tone. "And cleaning up after them."

With all of *Wilfred's* team assisting with the near catastrophe Veronika has caused a priceless gown, I shift on my feet to face Ark. I plan to ask him to lower the zipper I can't reach in the back of the dress, but I take a handful of seconds to admire a bone structure too complex for the world's best sculptor to replicate.

Ark is a beautiful man. It is impossible not to stare. His lips are plump, his nose is perfectly straight, and his eyes are so intensely imposing I swear they can see through to a person's soul.

I'm appalled by my behavior when my stalk is busted. Ark doesn't seem to mind. He only caught my stare because his eyes were conducting their own lengthy gawk of my face.

It is an effort to reel in my shame that I am lusting over a man above my league, but I give it my best shot. I push off my feet and head deep into the underbelly of the boutique while tugging on the zipper in the back of the dress.

"I sh-should get changed. Darius will be here shortly," I say while recalling the new schedule Rafael handed me the morning of my inauguration.

Despite Mrs. Orlov's numerous reminders over the past week that I am a member of Ark's cleaning team, not his private life, there isn't a single cleaning task on my new schedule.

I sneak in a handful of tasks when no one is looking, but for the most part, I've spent my week twiddling my thumbs and chaperoning Veronika to and from appointments.

The remembrance that I am Veronika's equivalent of a lap dog should lower the excitement that slicks my skin when Ark senses my struggle with the zipper.

Regretfully, it doesn't.

My new schedule has kept me off Mrs. Orlov's radar long enough only to catch the occasional berate. It would be ten times worse if I were stuck in the apartment with her day in and day out, and I can't help but wonder if that was Ark's plan when he designed my new schedule.

"Let me."

Ark's full, throaty tone sends goose bumps racing to the surface of my skin. They grow in size the closer he approaches, then augment when the briefest flutter of his fingertips as he pulls my hair to the side of my neck shoots a shiver down my spine.

I hear a zipper lowering before an audible gulp swallows it.

"There you go."

The dress hangs loosely around my frame, but I can't force myself to move. Ark is still clutching the zipper, which now sits near the two dimples in my lower back, and I don't want anything to force it away, not even the perceived hurt our closeness could thrust onto a woman who wants to be more than Ark's friend.

If they're not already more than that.

I overheard Veronika's defense. I know she is refusing to leave until she gets the full shebang out of Ark's invitation. I'm just confused as to why Ark is agreeing with her terms. He's powerful and well-liked. He could have any woman he wants, so why is he bowing at Veronika's feet?

He must want her. That is the only plausible explanation I can find.

"I—"

"Shh," Ark whispers, his word as searingly heated as the look he gives me in the mirror while moving his hand to the shoulder strap of the dress. "We're not doing anything wrong. I'm just ensuring the gown isn't crushed when it floats to the floor." A smile unwillingly tilts one side of my mouth when his following comment floats over my ear. "I know firsthand what Wilfred charges for a custom gown. The dry-cleaning bill she would impose if it were sullied before it is officially purchased would be atrocious." The trickle of desire making me hot turns me into a furnace when he discloses the reason the gown fits so perfectly. "I also want a moment to admire my brilliance. I did well with my measurements considering what I had to work with. This dress fits you like a glove."

Panting, I peer up at him.

Even if I want to act stupid, his eyes won't allow it.

They tell me everything I need to know.

This dress wasn't removed from the sale floor before Veronika could unearth its beauty.

It was never placed there since it is a custom creation.

I'm one hundred percent confident of this, and my assuredness flourishes when Ark says, "It's not the quality of the dressmaker that makes a gown exquisite, Mara, but the qualities of the woman wearing it."

As my breathing tapers, the noise of the film crew and the starlet they're documenting ceases to exist. There is no one else in the world but Ark and me. But even if there were, there's no way I could stop this.

I'm blinded by need and achingly desperate for him to finish what we started in his office last week.

"P-please."

I flick my eyes to the side when he flattens his hand against the rouching in the middle of my gown. He's not saving the gorgeous material from the dirty floor of the boutique. He's ensuring it remains glued to my body while also exposing I'm not the only one incredibly turned on by his closeness.

He's hard, his cock throbbing as brutally as the pounds of my clit.

I lean into him when he buries his nose into my hair, and he inhales deeply. "Fuck, I've missed that smell."

As the velvety serenade of his moan rolls through me, his hand dips lower. He's seconds from touching me again, from making me his, when we're interrupted by a highly likely source since I asked them to meet me here. The boutique is only one block from the bulk-buy grocer we visit once a month.

"Mommy!"

Tillie skips across the room, dragging Mrs. Lichard with her. Her steps are as fast as the one Ark uses to slip through the curtains of the changing room.

Her innocence makes her oblivious to the cause of the redness creeping up my neck.

Mrs. Lichard is nowhere near as fortunate.

Her cheeks are still inflamed from the near-miss when we climb the stairs of our building two hours later and stumble onto a package on my doorstep.

"Who is it for, Mommy?" Tillie asks, her eyes wide like they were when she unwrapped her Nintendo Switch.

"I d-don't know." My stutter is easily excusable. I'm perplexed as to why we have received a gift. It isn't my birthday, and I don't actively give my address to anyone, so no one could have sent Tillie a belated present.

Tillie is so excited that she looks on the verge of peeing her pants. "Open it, Mommy!"

Her elation grows tenfold when I peel back the red ribbon tied around the glossy white box in haste before popping open the lid.

Air whizzes between my teeth when I drink in the dress Ark purchased for me. It looks as regal in the box as I felt while I was wearing it, but Tillie doesn't pay it an ounce of attention. Her eyes are steadfast on the invitation that arrived with the one-of-a-kind custom gown.

It is for Ark's fortieth birthday party, and her name is cited next to mine.

"Can we go, Mommy? *Please.* I'll do all my chores and clean my room." She races inside, prepared to start her promise now if it gives her a chance to attend a celebration I usually decline before she sees the invite. "And you won't even have to buy me a new dress." Her beaming-with-joy eyes lock on to the glossy white box. "There's plenty of material in there for the both of us."

21

ARKADIY

"*W*hat the hell are you doing?"

My eyes shoot to Mara, arched over the top rung of a wooden ladder, to Rafael, watching her daring maneuver from the safety of an armchair in the corner of the room.

"And what the fuck are you doing watching her?"

I don't give him a chance to answer. I enter the den faster than I exited my office when my mother blindsided me for the umpteenth time the past week and stabilize the wobbles of an ancient-looking ladder before Mara can hurt herself.

"Down. Now."

"Ark." Mara starts her defense with a giggle, downplaying my panic as if it is irrational. "The chandeliers are d-dusty, and you have a ton of guests arriving next weekend."

The ladder wobbles in the aftermath of her shudder when I say, "I don't give a fuck if they're covered with cobwebs. I didn't hire you to clean the chandeliers. Down. *Now!*"

With my snapped command leaving no room for arguing, Mara commences climbing down. Her scent gets stronger with each rung she descends—as does the firmness of my cock.

That is the exact smell I seek anytime I shower, and the exact smell my mother is using against me to paint me as an evolving monster. She said it is too innocent for a "real man" to find appealing, and anyone who believes otherwise should seek a psych evaluation.

Halfway down, Mara mumbles, "I don't understand why you hired me, Ark. The toilets, showers, and sinks are cleaned every morning before I arrive, and all the beds are m-made. I've got nothing to do but dust chandeliers and polish silverware."

I'm stolen the chance to relish how fast her stutter is lessening in my presence when Rafael mumbles under his breath, "It isn't the silverware he wants you to polish."

My glare would have more heat if I hadn't noticed how much Mara's confidence thrives from his multiple underhanded comments that I want her. The self-assurance that flourishes in her eyes makes her even more fascinating, and it has me hopeful I can block out my mother's hurtful comments for just an hour.

That's all I want—an hour of peace. Then maybe my head will stop thumping as ruefully as my heart does anytime I force myself to walk away from Mara instead of walking toward her.

My mother hasn't stopped harping in my ear for the past two weeks. I'm at the end of my tether. Her prolonged visit to Myasnikov has put me in such a bad mood everyone is avoiding me—even the woman who has had more impact on my life in weeks than my mother has had in decades.

"What is it? Are you hurt? Did you hurt yourself?" I ask Mara when a hiss follows her final step down from the ladder.

"It's n-nothing."

This woman's ability to lie is as woeful as her ability to sit still. I kept on the cleaning service company Val helms to ensure Mara didn't need to clean toilets and make beds for a living, but it seems as if she would rather be elbow deep in shit than sit around, twiddling her thumbs all day.

I've caught her scrubbing the inside of the wall oven, cleaning the tracks of the windows, and rearranging the linen cupboard this week alone.

Now, she's dusting the damn chandeliers.

If she had the appropriate equipment, she would have scaled the building by now to clean the floor-to-ceiling window of my office from the outside. I do not doubt that.

Mara has work ethics by the bucketload. Veronika—the woman who refused to leave town until she received the whole nine yards for our "date" multiple media agencies ran as front-page news—can't say the same.

She didn't even show up to the etiquette class my mother organized for her, hoping it would have me seeing her in a different light, because it was scheduled to start at 10 a.m.

She stood across from my mother, the very essence of a woman who would sell her soul to the devil for the right amount of coin, and told her she doesn't get out of bed before midday for anything or anyone.

Her lack of interest in bettering herself proves she isn't the woman to stand by my side, but my mother isn't convinced. She's confident that once the "hero complex" fueling my obsession with Mara wears off, I'll be grateful Veronika is in the wings, ready to swoop in and save the day.

Mara entering the kitchen to collect the food I have Chef prepare in excess each meal stole my rebuttal.

Mara thinks Chef is bad with portion control. She has no inkling I ordered him to triple the quantity he usually serves each day to ensure there are leftovers for Mara to take home. I don't care what she does with the food once she leaves here with it. Knowing she can eat when hungry makes me desire to hand-feed her anytime her stomach growls.

When Mara's second hiss is strained through clenched teeth, I guide her toward the armchair Rafael vacated. I don't know where he goes after placing Mara into a situation that demands a response from me, but he disappears if it means Mara and I will be the only two people in the room.

I know what he's doing. He knows I'm not strong enough to withstand the magnetizing pull that forever cracks between Mara and me and is hopeful it will remind me that my mother is not a woman I should take advice from.

It does. Every spasm affects me, but I am stuck between a rock and a hard place. It isn't solely my skeletons I'm fighting to keep hidden. They're not even Mara's, but I have no right to steal her cloak of invisibility any more than the woman I have an unhealthy obsession with.

Partway across the den, Mara says, "I'm fine, Ark. Truly. The arch of my foot is just a little tender from trying to m-maintain a grip on the ladder."

"Grip on the *top* rung of a ladder you should have never been on."

"It is my job to c-clean—"

"It is your job to do whatever the hell I tell you to do," I interrupt, doubling the rise and fall of her chest. "And for now, I am telling you to sit."

She plops onto the armchair, her submissiveness sending a current straight to my cock. It acts as if I didn't find release only hours ago when the hem of her maid's outfit slips high on her thigh from me carefully lifting her foot to inspect her ankle.

I've told Mara numerous times to wear whatever she feels comfortable in, but each day, without fail, she arrives looking like every billionaire's wet dream, and I'm forced to stroke my cock for the second time before midday.

Heat creeps across the back of Mara's knees when I roll down the cuff of her sock. It matches the coloring that hits my cheeks when I notice her ankle is swollen.

"Did you fall? Your ankle looks inflamed. That isn't arch damage from gripping a ladder too firmly."

"It's nothing—"

I flash her a stern glare, stopping her lie before it can be fully issued. I have enough people lying to me and for me. I don't need more.

You'd swear Mara heard my inner thoughts when she confesses, "I wasn't watching where I was going, and I t-tripped over a box in the entryway this morning." The color drains from her face as she glances at the floor. "It was addressed to Veronika."

Her hiss this time is more in jealousy than pain, but I let her play it off as if it is in response to me removing her shoe, because she has no reason to be jealous.

Even weeks after our first meeting, I still can't be in the same room as Veronika for ten minutes without wanting to dig a pen in my ear. There's no way we would have lasted the eight-year term of the contract Fyodor wanted us to sign, and mercifully, both Veronika and my mother are out of time to prove otherwise.

Veronika's "invitation" expired this morning at 8 a.m. sharp.

She is finally out of my hair, leaving me only one gargoyle left to wrangle—and perhaps a heap of guilt I've never truly acknowledged belongs on my shoulders as much as it does everyone else's.

When Mara's chest sinks, disappointed by my lack of reply, I wet my lips before saying, "Apparently, the makeup Veronika left behind when she packed this morning is invaluable to her, so Rafael organized to have it couriered to her hotel."

Needing to keep my focus off the rapid rise and fall of her chest before it forces me to make a similar mistake to the one I made last Friday, I lower my eyes to her foot.

When I saw Mara through the boutique window, my feet moved for her before my head could talk me out of it. That's how hard I have to fight to keep my distance when our exchanges could be eyeballed by a lady threatening to throw more than my career under the bus if I act on my desires.

Annoyance about how close I came to forcing Tillie to walk in on a scene inappropriate for a child grinds my back molars together as I inspect Mara's foot more diligently.

It is swollen, but I don't believe it is broken. She should still seek medical attention, though. Even if she didn't make my dick ache, she is an employee who was hurt on my watch. Seeking medical assistance is the right thing to do.

"Did you have your ankle looked at when you rolled it?"

The shampoo I'm obsessed with wafts into my nostrils when Mara shakes her head. "Rafael offered"—when I growl, she speaks faster— "to take me to the ER, but I told him it wasn't necessary. My foot is fine. Look..."

She rolls her ankle and almost howls.

When I shoot up to my feet, confident I never want to hear her cries of pain again, Mara's watering eyes follow my stalk. "Where are you going?"

"To call a doctor," I answer, not looking back.

"A doctor? Don't be absurd. I rolled m-my ankle. It isn't an emergency s-situation."

"Dr. Morgasten is a resident of the Chrysler building. He'll come straight down. Then you can get back to..." A growl ends my reply when I peer up at the chandelier. It is even more hazardous from this viewpoint. "Home. You can go home as you should have hours ago."

I loosen the tightness of my jaw with a quick grind when the receptionist answers my call. "Good evening, Mr. Orlov. How can I help you?"

"Dr. Morgasten's residence, please," I request through clenched teeth, frustrated by her inability to refer to me by my given name as asked numerous times over the past three weeks.

Apparently, my mother's orders outrank mine.

"Right away, sir," she replies, not missing the sternness of my bark.

A clank sounds before it is swallowed by a noise I never want to hear again. "He-he? Dr. M-Morgasten is a m-man?"

Mara's eyes widen when they meet mine. Although they still stimulate a jolt of excitement to my cock, that isn't the only response they entice.

They announce that she is scared.

My focus momentarily rips away from Mara's whitening cheeks when a gravelly voice sounds down the line. "Arkadiy, what a pleasure it is—"

I hang up before Dr. Morgasten can issue all of his greeting, before twisting to face Mara front on.

I don't need to ask the profession of the man who hurt her.

Her frightened expression tells me everything I need to know.

Medical professionals are meant to save lives.

Her unvoiced confession just cut one of theirs short.

I try to keep my tone neutral. It is a woeful waste of time. It couldn't be more possessive if I tried. "If you don't want to see someone about your foot, you need to ice it."

Mara's chest sinks when she sighs in relief. "I will. The instant I get h-home—"

"No. Now. You will ice it now."

"Now?"

She looks as bewildered as I feel when I stride across the den, pluck her from the armchair, lift her into my arms, and then veer my steps to my bedroom.

22

MARA

I swallow to soothe the dryness of my throat when Ark's long steps veer us past Veronika's room. There wasn't an ounce of deceit in his tone when he said she had left this morning. However, I'm still shocked to see her room is empty. All the designer dresses she picked last week are gone, and the vanity mirror the cleaning staff wipes down every morning doesn't have a speck of the compact powder that gives her skin a luminous shine.

Even the hundreds of boxes of shoes once stacked on the far left of her room have been removed.

For someone who packed in such a hurry that she forgot her favorite makeup, she must have had an army at her beck and call to gather the rest of her belongings. They cleared out the equivalent of a boutique store in under two hours.

That's an impressive record.

My heart flips when Ark's long strides continue until we enter his bedroom. Since it is the furthest from the den and always meticulously cleaned before I arrive for my shift, this is the first time I've been here in over two weeks.

It smells different from what it did back then, more feminine than mannish. The girlie palette would flip my stomach with unease if some of it didn't register as familiar.

Ark is still using my shampoo.

The air that wafts up when he places me on the mattress and stuffs a pillow under my ankle announces this without a doubt, not to mention my quickest peek into his bathroom when he pushes the door wide open to wordlessly assure me there are more exits than people capable of blocking them.

Multiple unused bottles of my favorite shampoo are on the vanity, waiting for him.

As my eyes track Ark to the built-in bar to gather ice in a washcloth, I say, "You don't need to bother. My ankle d-doesn't hurt."

He ignores me. It seems to be his go-to defense mechanism of late.

Silent and brooding are my favorite words to describe his personality over the past two weeks. Teasing is another, but that is reserved for the brief touches he rewards me with when no one is looking, and the longing stares he bombards me with when a dozen people separate us.

I hiss for a completely different reason than pain when Ark places a makeshift ice pack on my ankle. It is freezing, and the coolness of the droplets rolling down my foot and soaking into his bedding makes me yelp.

"Hush," Ark says, his quirked lips softening the snap of his reply. "The colder the compress, the less chance of inflammation. Rest, ice, compression"—he squeezes the washcloth around my ankle during his last word—"and elevation. All standard first-aid treatment for an acute injury."

"I wouldn't say my injury is a-acute."

I unknowingly walk straight into his trap. "But you admit you're injured?"

"That isn't what I meant," I say with a laugh, grateful for the return of his deeply guarded nurturing side. "You're twisting my words."

"Am I, Mara?" I love how he says my name, and not even the tiredness of a long week can conceal that. "Because they sound crystal clear to me."

It takes me a moment to realize what he is saying.

When it clicks, I'm gobsmacked.

I didn't stutter again.

This is only the second time in over a decade my vocals haven't displayed nerves while speaking with the opposite sex.

While grinning about my bewilderment, Ark attempts to cut the invisible rope binding us together. "Rest in here for as long as you need. Once the swelling goes down enough you feel confident putting pressure on your ankle, I'll organize for someone to take you home. You can start fresh again next Monday."

My worried gasp reduces the length of his strides.

"Next Monday?" I don't wait for him to answer me. "I can't take a w-week off."

I'm not stuttering because I am nervous. I am stammering because I fear not having enough funds to pay for the groceries I'll need to purchase since I will miss out on a week of Ark's generosity.

The food he sends home with me each day doesn't solely feed Tillie and me. It also feeds Mrs. Lichard and a handful of elderly residents who can't afford both surging rent prices and food.

I could try to stretch my wages to cover some basic necessities for my neighbors, but I don't want to do that to Mrs. Lichard. For years, she refused payment for watching Tillie before and after school. Supplying her with some groceries is the least I can do for all the help she's given me over the past six years. I don't want to pull back on purchases just as her pantry is starting to look not so empty.

"I c-can work. My ankle is fine."

A sob involuntarily leaves my lips when I slip off Ark's bed. The ice seems to have aggravated my injury, or perhaps the tightness of my one-size-too-small shoe was acting as a compression. My ankle is now swollen like a balloon and extremely tender.

"Sit before you hurt yourself more." Ark's bossy demeanor should scare me senseless, but I find it as endearing as his handsome face. "Bed. Now." He lifts me like a child and places me back onto the mattress before he wedges his pillow under my foot. "If you move again, I'll tie you to the headboard myself."

Heat floods my veins when images Mrs. Orlov assures me that I have no right to conjure roll through my head. Ark's fingers. His tongue. Those chunky, kissable lips. I imagine them in places they have no right to be—*again*—and the furious hotness they trigger have me grateful for the coolness of the ice pack he returns to my ankle.

"Hush," Ark murmurs again, mistaking my whimper as one of pain. "I won't hurt you."

His breath quivers in our shared air since he stands mere inches from me when I whisper, "I know."

As his throat works hard to swallow, his hand lifts a fraction higher. It lingers on a teasing portion of my thigh the immodest hem of my uniform can't conceal before he locks his eyes with mine.

He stares at me for several heart-thrashing seconds, taking in my parted lips, the rosiness of my cheeks, and my dilated eyes before the corner of his mouth hitches.

I suck in a desperate breath, my heart racing, when his spare hand moves for my face. This time, I don't flinch. I don't even blink for fear of giving him the wrong impression. I return his heated stare as he forces a felonious hair back into line before I breathe through the sensation of the back of his fingers trekking down my cheek.

Again, a touch so simple shouldn't cause such a wild response, but there's no denying the inferno raging through my stomach when his fingers' focus shifts to my mouth. The burn makes me squirm and has me wishing he'd move his other hand up a few more inches.

My nipples bud when his head tilts, and then I hold my breath. His closeness is too much to bear. He's so beautiful, so controlled, yet clearly unhinged to mistake me as a precious gem.

Can he not see my cracked insides? His mother is skilled at unearthing them. The way she cornered me today and gave me the dressing down of my life is why I scaled a ladder outside working hours.

She was extremely clear with her message that I am using her son's "childhood hang-ups" to wriggle my way into his life, and that she won't leave Myasnikov until he sees me for who I truly am.

Since Ark has been more stressed since her arrival, I've contemplated telling him everything.

A purge is as good as a vacation, right?

When I gasp for air, my lungs never a willing participant when thoughts of my past creep up on me, Ark says, "Breathe, Mara."

My chest shakes as I draw in a big breath. It thrusts out my breasts and tightens my uniform around my nipples, making their erect state painfully obvious.

A low hum sounds from the back of Ark's throat. I don't know if it is his unvoiced approval of my submissiveness or because he's noticed how firmly my nipples are budded.

I go for the latter when he murmurs, "Good girl."

I lick my lips, the heat his rumble caused too intense to ignore. We're so near that my body feels every delicious thud of his pulse. The heat and hunger radiating between us is the equivalent of a dangerous inferno. I am burning up everywhere.

Needing to center myself, I close my eyes.

With one sense down, the other four take up its slack. I hear Ark's swallow and the movements of his eyes as he drags them over my face, and taste his smell.

God, he smells good.

The femininity of my shampoo does little to regulate the sheer masculinity that bores down on me when I'm no longer capable of fighting the urge to tilt nearer to him.

Just his breaths on my cheek instigate a rush of excitement. I'd give anything to feel the full, throaty rasp of his voice floating over the sensitive regions of my body again.

The thought makes me tremble.

My eyes flutter open when Ark whispers, "It's almost too much. Having you here. In my bed. Smelling like this." Everything outside his room ceases to exist when he adjusts the collar of my uniform, his fingertips floating over my collarbone. "It is almost too much."

My throat is burning so much that it is an effort to get my words out, but I manage—just. "Then I'll go."

"No," he spits out, gently pushing back on my shoulder. His expression is complex, and his eyes are narrow. "My threat is still valid, Mara. I will tie you to my bed if that is the only way you'll learn to sit still for two damn seconds."

"You just said you don't want me here." I've never once in my life snapped at anyone like this, but I can't hold back. "But you won't let me go. You're confusing me, Ark. I don't know w-what you want."

"I want you!" Inky-black hair curtains his face when he shoves his hands into his pockets, and he twists away from me. "But having you could come at a cost greater than anyone could ever imagine." He turns to face me, the fury in his eyes lessening when he notices my bewilderment. "I can't do that to you. I just can't."

"Do what to me?"

I feel the inexplicable pull that forever overwhelms me when he is near growing as intently as the hurt in his eyes when he says, "You're a mother, Mara. You have a child." It isn't hatred for Tillie in his eyes when he continues. It's admiration. "A precious daughter you're meant to protect from the monsters of the world." The animosity I was seeking earlier fills his eyes as he mutters, "From monsters like me."

The sound he makes when he races through his bedroom door is pained, as tormented as the hiss that whistles between my teeth when I try to go after him and fail.

My ankle could bear my weight. I didn't lie when I said it was more uncomfortable than painful. I'm just not brave enough right now to pretend it can.

23

ARKADIY

*R*afael's dark eyes lift to mine when I enter my office at the speed of a bullet being dislodged from a gun. He's nursing a half-consumed glass of whiskey and sniffing a cigar like he doesn't screw up his nose every time he's offered one by a foreign dignitary.

He places down the gift from a Saudi prince when I say, "Call Darius and organize for him to transport Mara home. She'll be out for a week in her condition."

"Fuck her over *that* good?"

His question is a knife to the gut, and I snarl my disapproval.

Rafael grunts before slipping onto the chair across from the desk. "What the fuck did you do, Ark?"

"Nothing," I snap back as I move to the bar, needing something to fill my hands before my nails add to the permanent nicks and scars covering half my body.

Rafael glances at me with his brows pulled, then asks, "What do you mean nothing?"

"How else can I explain it to you, Raf?" I pour a generous serving of whiskey, toss it back, then slam the glass down. "It's pretty self-explanatory."

"You carried her to your room, in your fucking arms. She may not have been clutching your biceps like Ann in *King Kong*, but she sure as fuck had portions of your body brushing against her fingertips." The bewilderment on his face increases. "Yet you did *nothing* the instant you had her alone, in the very far corner of your apartment, away from the prying eyes of the woman who has your head in such a tail-fucking-spin that *I'm* struggling not to puke." Since he isn't asking questions, more summarizing events, he doesn't wait for me to reply. "What the fuck is wrong with you? Why wouldn't you take advantage of that?"

"*Advantage?*" I choke on the whiskey lingering in the back of my throat. "Perhaps therein lies the problem. I don't want to take advantage of her."

"She hurt her ankle, dickwad. She's not intoxicated or strung out on drugs. She knew what she was doing and would have been an *extremely* obliging participant."

I can't deny a single thing he says since it is true. Every inch of Mara's body begged for me to touch her. Her nipples. Her lips. Those fucking eyes. They were all begging, and it took everything I had to walk away.

I did it for one reason and one reason only.

Tillie.

As if he read my silent thoughts, Raf says, "You're an idiot."

"I'm reasonably sure we established just how fucked in the head I am decades ago." I down another three-finger serving of whiskey. It does little to ease the bristling of hesitation prickling my arm hairs. "The fact you're surprised has me hopeful I can pull the wool over more than your eyes in the near future."

Rafael scoffs but remains quiet, the fight not in him.

I slump into my chair and then run my fingers through my hair. The scent my quick rake wafts up worsens my mood. I can smell Mara on me, and it has nothing to do with the number of times I've stroked my cock to the scent of her shampoo.

When she whispered that she trusted me, I stood so close we almost became one.

At that moment, there was no one in the world but us.

Then the quickest whiff of a perfume I will never forget saw me throwing it all away as if our sparks are empty candy wrappers.

I've never felt more ashamed or conflicted.

"So," Rafael starts, pulling my focus back to him, "how do you want to play this?"

I stare at him, lost.

"Mara." He scoffs again. "*Obviously.*"

"She needs to take a few days to heal her ankle." *And to let me get my head screwed on straight before I do something that will monumentally alter her life.* "Once it's good, she can continue with her placement."

He twists the knife in deeper. "You still want her to work for you?"

"Of course I want her to work with me. Why the fuck wouldn't I want her to work with me?"

He snorts. "I don't know... probably because you don't want to torment yourself anymore."

I debate my reply before delivering the weakest one. "You don't know what you're talking about."

Rafael's eye roll is more mature than his tone. "All right. Whatever you say." After hooking his left ankle onto his right knee, he repeats, "So how do you want to play this?" This time, he doesn't wait for me to show my hand. He reveals his royal flush straight out the gate. "Do you want Darius to carry Mara to your town car and up five flights of stairs before showing himself into her apartment she's never let any man in but you? Or are you happy for me to call a random Uber driver and hope he's willing to accept a quick butt grab for additional services rendered?" I straighten, my glare hot enough to scald, but Rafael acts oblivious. "I'd offer, but..." Air whistles between his teeth. "Her maid's outfit does crazy things to my—"

"End that sentence and I will end you."

He stiffens, the smile leaving his face. "Therein lies the *real* problem, Ark. You can't play the game for both sides. That isn't how it works." He stands, straightens his jacket and tie, and heads for the door. "Reel her in or let her go." He grips the doorframe, incapable of leaving without making sure I know I'll never be without his support. "I'll be around for a few hours if you need to borrow a rod."

My hum is low, but he must hear it, as he leaves without so much as a backward glance.

I wait for the stomps of his feet to stop sounding into my office before picking up my phone and calling a frequently called number.

Darius answers two rings later. "Sir..."

I should order him to collect Mara, to continue the avoidance tactic I've been using the past two weeks, but I can't do that anymore. Avoidance isn't the solution. The jolt that darted up my arm when I touched Mara's elbow is proof of this. I want her more than ever, and I've spent the last two weeks being told I'm one wrong move from becoming the demon from my nightmares.

I take a breath before asking, "Were there any mentions of a doctor in Mara's file?"

He's hesitant to answer, aware my fuse is short when it comes to Mara's privacy.

"It is important, Darius." Focusing on finding the man who hurt Mara may be the only thing capable of pulling me out of the bottomless pit swallowing me whole. "I—"

"Mara hasn't seen a doctor since a complication in the third trimester of her pregnancy." Again, my thoughts stray to Tillie when he discloses, "She went into early labor. A training doctor at a women's clinic five clicks out from Myasnikov helped her. She—"

"A woman helped her?"

I sigh in relief when he answers, "Yes."

If he had said no, my reservations would have been worse. Predators come from all walks of life, but Mara's fret only surfaced when she learned Dr. Morgasten is male.

"Was there anything else? Anyone male?"

He waits a beat before answering. "No. But I have no access to her other files." By other files, he means the name she used before she hid her identity.

I denied Fyodor's suggestion of running Mara's DNA through a private security firm. She is hiding for a reason, and I have no right to remove her invisibility cloak until I am confident I can protect her from any downfall its removal could cause.

"Have you changed your mind on Fyodor's suggestion?"

I consider Darius's question for almost a minute before I shake my head like he can see me.

He can't. My office and bedroom aren't wired with surveillance.

They are the only two places where I can be myself, hence me inviting Mara to infiltrate them.

"Cross reference Mara's cleaning schedule with doctors who reside at the Chrysler building. I want to know if there was a doctor she once cleaned for but abruptly stopped, or if she lodged any complaints about any of the residents. She may believe he's a doctor, but he could have falsely presented as one to scare her into not saying anything. People with power think they can get away with anything."

Darius's voice is as rigid as my hands are balled. "I'll have a report on your desk in an hour."

Just before he disconnects our chat, I call his name.

"Yes."

I wait a beat before asking, "Are there any cameras in the servant corridors?"

Suspicion is rife in his voice. "I think so. Why?"

Instead of answering his question, I boss him around like the scent wafting through the air vents of my room doesn't have me on the verge of being sick, and that he is to blame for the churns of my stomach. "I need access to them."

I can hear his brain ticking over, seeking answers to questions he isn't game to ask, but he keeps his tone professional. "I will have them forwarded to you ASAP."

"Thank you."

A second after I end our call, a knock sounds at my office door. I doubt it is my mother. She'll need more than an hour to lick her wounds after our last tussle, though she isn't nicknamed Vicious for no reason.

She doesn't back down even when she's losing.

"Come in."

My hope that Mara is stronger than my mother is making out

wavers when I recognize the tuft of the mustache that enters my office two nanoseconds before the face of its owner.

Rafael's exhaustion of a long week filters through his tone when he announces, "There's someone downstairs asking to speak with you."

I shift my eyes to the test results I was given earlier while saying, "I'm busy."

"I told him that, but the concierge said he's refusing to take no for an answer from anyone but you." When I sit up straighter, he mutters, "It ain't him. I don't care how many years pass. I will *never* forget that fucker's face." He steps deeper into my office like he's suddenly aware of the cause of the change in my scent. It's more feminine than manly, and it makes my blood boil. "He said it is regarding Miskaela."

"Who?" I ask, lost.

Rafael shrugs but remains quiet, leaving the ball on my side of the court.

With how worked up I am, I should take more time to consider my objections. But when a bull wants to charge, he wants to charge. So instead of telling the stranger the appropriate channels to approach me, I jerk up my chin, inviting him into a sanctum nowhere near as calm as it once was since it now smells like the perfume of my abuser.

24

MARA

A squeak pops from my lips when a heavily slurred voice behind me says, "Why are you wandering the dark corridors of the servants' quarters at this time of night, sweetheart?"

This is why I should have listened to my intuition when it cautioned me to leave the conversation Ark and I desperately need to business hours.

After deliberating our exchange for an hour and wishfully hoping Ark would return, I hobbled halfway to the underground parking garage before I allowed my heart to talk over my fears. It told me it was rude to leave without first telling Ark of my plans and that discussing our relationship during work hours was injudicious, considering the basis of my heart's pleas.

It wants Ark as badly as his eyes displayed he wants me when he spoke those exact words.

I also want the chance to prove I can protect my daughter. I've fought for Tillie all my life, from the moment she was conceived, so Ark's fears aren't valid. I will protect my daughter better than my parents protected me, and that shield will grow tenfold with a man like Ark at my side.

The walk down the long corridors that weave throughout this

building wasn't pleasant, but I made it without a twinge crossing my features.

My strengths are greater than I've made out, and it is time for Ark to learn that.

I want him to know the real me. The good and the bad.

I just wish I'd had the courage to use the main access point of his apartment when the slurred voice returns. "Did you hear me, sweetheart?" My pulse is thumping so loudly that I don't realize he is directly behind me until his alcohol-laced breath fans the back of my neck. "I asked what you're doing down here."

He spins me to face him, his grip aggressive. I give him a tight smile when his eyes finally make their way from my breasts to my face, and then square my shoulders, willing myself to look anything but frightened.

"I w-work here."

My bravery is all an act, and the elevator attendant who glared at me weeks ago knows it. "You w-w-work here?" He rolls his bloodshot eyes, making way for maliciousness. "This ain't no fairy tale, princess. And *he* sure as fuck ain't no prince."

I shouldn't know who his last sentence refers to. Over three dozen men are residents of this building, but the way his eyes slit further while looking past my shoulder announces who his disdain belongs to. Ark's office door is only mere feet from where we stand.

I shy away from the unnamed man when he attempts to curl the wayward strand of hair Ark fixed into place earlier around his finger. His expression appears disappointed until he notices my trembling thighs. He looks like the type who prefers his women more scared than satisfied.

"Do you know he got me fired?" A sneer hardens his features, making them even uglier. "Supposedly, he didn't like the way I looked at you."

"No-no, I didn't kn-know that."

He *pffts* me as if I lied. "I'm not surprised he noticed me watching you. You're *really* pretty." He wets his lips, his greasy tongue's slither enough to flip my stomach. "But from what I've heard, he's done with you now. Kicked out with barely a scratch on ya." His eyes are once again on my breasts. "Guess he's nicked up enough for the both of you." I flinch as if he struck me when an evil smile stretches across his face. "Don't worry, sweetheart. I'll keep the marks to a minimum. Why spoil a perfect canvas before the masterpiece is fully unveiled?"

One step and I'm gone. I sprint to Ark's office before pushing through his door as if his privacy is null and void when it comes to me.

When I notice the office is barren of a soul, I race for the main entrance door, my sore ankle a thing of the past.

As my hand circles the antique doorknob, I'm squashed against the door firmly enough for my lungs to squeal. A tattooed hand pins my head to the door while another clamps my thigh just below the hem of my uniform.

"No... pl-please," I beg, thrashing and screaming, mindful silence never wins and having far more to live for this time not to fight.

Ark's greenish eyes pop into my head two seconds after Tillie's baby blues, but the stranger's hand slides higher before I can add them to my defense.

Whiskey puffs from his mouth as his fingers dig into the fleshy part of my thighs. His painful grip flashes up horrible memories and churns my stomach with nausea.

While fighting with everything I have, I plead for him to stop, and scream the words I once held back to reduce the severity of my punishments.

Nothing stops him. He continues to steal the air from my lungs as ruefully as his demoralizing attempts to strip my confidence.

I won't let that happen. I was a child back then. I was half their size and weight. I can't use those excuses this time around.

"No!" I scream, refusing to go down without a fight. "Get off me!"

A mere inch from my panties, his hand is suddenly yanked away, and a breathy grunt emits from his lips.

I'm too shocked my pleas worked this time around to move, but it doesn't take a genius to realize what is happening.

A fist connecting with the bridge of someone's nose over and over again can't be mistaken, much less the stern rumble of a man bristling with fury. "What the fuck do you think you were doing?"

I twist my head toward the snarled voice, gasping when I spot Ark towering over the man who was endeavoring to assault me. Blood is gushing from the ex-elevator attendant's nose, and a dark shadow is already circling his left eye. However, they're not the cause of my shock.

Since Ark is facing away from me and only wearing a towel, I can't miss the mottling of scars covering a majority of his back. They're textured and silver, meaning they were most likely done years ago, but painstakingly extensive. They go from behind his left ear, across his shoulder blade, and down to the waistband of the towel hanging precariously off his waist.

Are they the reason he calls himself a monster?

Is he afraid Tillie will see his scars and believe he is no longer worthy of me?

It dawns on me that we're not the only people in the room when Ark's eyes shoot to the side, and he shouts, "You were meant to keep the building in lockdown!"

"He isn't meant to be here," Rafael replies, his wide eyes bouncing between Ark, my attacker, and me. "Someone must have let him in... He must have..." He stops, shakes his head, and then starts again. "I fucked up. I'll fix it. I will make this right." He tugs the ex-elevator attendant up with a deadly tight grip on his arm and hoists him in my direction, doubling the shake of my thighs. "Apologize."

"For what?" he asks, abhorrently confused. "Getting a little rough with a prostitute he no longer wants?"

Rafael firms his grip, forcing the man to yelp.

"Apologize, Paarth!" he demands again. "Before that pathetic whimper is the last noise you *ever* issue."

Paarth's eyes widen like he is aware Rafael's threats aren't idle before he strays his wet eyes to me. "I'm sorry."

"Louder!" Ark demands, scaring me with his menacing tone. "And say it like you fucking mean it."

Paarth's slur comes out sounding like a sob. "I'm sorry. I thought you were... That he was... I didn't mean to hurt you."

"What the..." Rafael wordlessly urges me to move away from the service entrance door when the wet patch on the front of Paarth's pants dribbles to his feet, wetting his shoes. "Did you seriously just piss yourself?" An accent that isn't solely Russian annunciates parts of his ridicule. "You sure as fuck better hope they can extract your putrid scent from the carpet, or you'll have more than words with Ark's fists this evening..."

I miss the remainder of his reply when he pushes my attacker through the narrow opening of the servants' entrance.

I'm in such a daze several long seconds pass in silence.

The scent of Paarth's urine is overpowering. It has me on the cusp of vomiting. I've only sampled one scent more rancid—my speech therapist's cum.

With my mind too trapped in the throes of my past, I'm confused when Ark asks, "Did he hurt you?"

"Wh-who?"

He hesitates to approach me. He double-guesses his decision a handful of times before he eventually mutters a cussword under his breath and moves closer, his steps fast and with confidence.

After taking in the buttons on my shirt and noticing they're untouched, he lowers his eyes to my thighs.

"The blood." He swallows as if his throat is burning too much to speak. "Is that from..." He can't finalize his question, and I'm glad. My mind is so far from the present I may have given him the wrong answer. "Come. I'll call a doctor."

"No," I shout too loudly. "No do-doctors, please."

"Mara." He sounds genuinely petrified and so incredibly guilty. "You're hurt."

"No, I'm no-not." I drag my hand across my thigh, wiping away the droplet of blood my attacker's nails caused my skin. "It is barely a sc-scratch. I'll be fine."

I wobble unsteadily when memories surface faster than I can shut them down.

Those were similar to the words my father said to my mother when she found the bruises and grab marks Dr. Babkin left behind the first time he raped me.

It isn't that he didn't believe me, more that he was happy to use Dr. Babkin's marks to hide his own felonious acts.

Confident I am seconds from being sick, I issue Ark a weak smile before racing through the exit Rafael used moments ago.

Ark shouts for me to stop, but I can't. I'm too trapped in the horrors of my past to keep my secrets to myself, and I don't want their ugliness to change how he looks at me.

25

ARKADIY

The popped buttons I anticipated seeing in Mara's shirt occur to mine when I dress in a hurry. I stuff the crinkled hem into the trousers I pull on sans underwear before I stuff my sockless feet into the shoes I toed off on my way to the shower.

I wasn't showering to imbed more of Mara's scent into my skin. I was trying to man the fuck up. The only time I ever achieve that is in a bathroom, so I was hopeful a ten-minute head soak would pull my head out of my ass enough to stop me from doing something stupid that would hurt Mara.

Unintentional or not, that was never my aim.

I want to protect her, not cause her more harm.

I may have lost the chance now.

I'm out of the servants' exit in under thirty seconds and racing down the corridor, my feet thumping as much as my fist when I threw it into Paarth's face.

I shouldn't have reacted the way I did. Violence is rarely the solution, but fury engulfed me when I noticed how Paarth was towering over Mara while tears glistened in her eyes and she pleaded for more than her virtue.

Tillie was featured multiple times during her begs.

As was another name I tried to pry from her the night we met.

I don't know the whereabouts of Dr. Babkin, but I do know one thing.

When I find him, he's a dead man.

The anger in Darius's eyes when he notices my approach announces that Paarth's punishment is far from over. The promise in his narrowed gaze frees me to follow the direction of his head nudge. He jerks it toward a pre-war elevator I didn't know this building had until now.

Mara's sniffles quieten when my hand shoots between the steel doors, stopping them from closing. I move to the far left of the elevator almost too small for two before entering, ensuring there is plenty of space for her to exit if she so wishes.

The tightness in my jaw slackens when she doesn't immediately flee. She hogs the panel like one push of a button will pop open the doors, her eyes facing the front.

I hate her shakes when the elevator doors close before it commences its descent. They cut me to pieces, but since they couldn't create one-tenth of the damage already done to my body, I accept them without protest before encouraging more.

"Don't touch me-me," Mara pleads when she hears my steps, the quick return of her stutter doubling my fury.

"I'm not going to touch you." She doesn't respond, but she must believe me, because she doesn't issue another plea for distance for my next steps. "I just want to offer you support."

"I'm okay. I-I'm fine."

"You're not fine. Stop saying you are fine. That man tried to brutalize you." I can barely get the words through my clenched teeth, but I continue since I know she needs to hear this. "That is *not* something you need to be okay with. What he did to you is *not* okay."

"He di-didn't do an-anything."

"He did," I retort, knowing not all our conversation centers on tonight's incident. "And I *believe* you, Mara. I *know* you're telling the truth."

Her sob bounces off the elevator panel before stabbing my heart, fatally wounding it.

It is so familiar, so horrifying, yet so much better than the silence I endured last time.

"Why do you b-believe me?" Sheer bewilderment lengthens her curt reply.

"Because you have no reason to lie. Especially not about something like this. Why would anyone fabricate something like this?" Her chest stops rising and falling when I stand close enough for my breaths to bound off her nape. "Breathe, Mara. I'm not going to touch you. You're okay." My words are as shaky as my hands when I lower them to my sides. "I'll keep my hands balled at my sides the entire time." Her heart rate increases when her eyes shift to the side for the quickest second, and then her shoulders roll forward. "You only need to lean in if you need me. If you don't need me, don't move. I just want to be near so I can catch you if you fall."

A shuddery breath whistles between her teeth when the warmth of my body calms her shivers.

"You're okay," I say, stepping nearer. "I won't let anyone hurt you again." My last word comes out with a soundless sigh when she adjusts her position so her temple rests an inch above my heart.

She isn't falling. Her legs are remarkably strong considering how badly she is shaking.

She is wordlessly accepting my offer.

"I won't touch you," I pledge again, giving her the final push to rest her head on my pectoral muscle.

The flattening of her ear on my chest means there's no chance of hiding my body's response to her closeness, so I don't bother trying to conceal it. I let her hear the panic tearing me in two, hopeful it will announce that this is as hard for me as it is for her.

As she stares up at me with those eyes—those goddamn eyes that talk directly to my soul—she blinks back the tears that are dangerously close to falling.

The longer she stares, the more my anger simmers.

Revenge isn't on my mind right now.

Comfort is.

"You're okay," I promise. "I've got you."

Mental torment is exhausting. I know this firsthand, so I'm not surprised to sense Mara's struggle not to close her eyes when we reach the underground parking level. Her blinking lengthens as her muscles loosen, but instead of tugging her close, forcing contact, I select the floor for the penthouse before jabbing the close door button.

We ride the elevator to the penthouse and back three times before Mara's body finally gives up its fight to stay awake. Her head rolls until her nose buries between my pecs and her legs buckle, leaving me no choice but to wrap my arms around her.

"It's okay," I assure her when she stiffens for the quickest second. "You're okay. You are safe."

Her shoulders remain tight for almost thirty seconds. She isn't the only one struggling. In her fright, she dug her nails into my hip. Their piercings won't produce anything close to the scars years of abuse peppered my skin with, but it takes my fucked-up head a lot longer than thirty seconds to realize that.

My heart hurts from how fast it is beating, and my molars are close to being grinded to shreds.

Needing to sit before I fall, I inch us toward the far wall of the elevator.

"I'll keep my back to the wall," I promise. "The exit will *not* be blocked at any time by anyone." Mara's lashes are touching her some-how-tear-free cheeks again, but I continue talking so she knows she isn't in any danger. "We're going to rest here for a little bit until you're either strong enough to walk or trust me enough to carry you."

A ball lodges in my throat when she whispers for the second time tonight, "I trust you."

She shouldn't.

I don't trust myself, especially not after what I faced today, but the thought of her trust and the ease of its achievement swells my chest with pride.

After pressing my nose to the scent that has kept me captivated from day one and inhaling deeply, I say, "We don't need to go anywhere right now. We can sit here until you feel safe." *And until I've stopped reeling over the fact that someone is touching me and I'm not freaking out.*

The media didn't solely heighten my playboy title to sell magazines. It was because a reporter learned about my requirement for Rafael to bound all my bed companions before I entered the room.

Touch in any way is usually a deal breaker for me. I don't care who you are or how much damage you could inflict on my career, if you break my sole rule, our exchange is immediately ended, and you're bombarded by a team of twenty lawyers who will remind you of the strict non-disclosure agreement you signed before you were invited into my realm.

I can't do that this time around. For one, I removed the NDA from Mara's contract before handing it to Rafael to administer. And two, I instigated the contact.

I need it.

Since I can no longer see her eyes, I need to feel her pulse, to acknowledge it as a sign of life.

I need her touch, even though it scares the living fucking shit out of me.

26

ARKADIY

I don't know how long we stay sitting on the hard tiled elevator floor before Mara locks her glistening eyes with mine. My guess is an hour, but my ass is convinced it is closer to five.

"Will you take me home? P-Please."

I nod without thinking. "Of course."

When I stand, I take her with me. It feels natural to have her in my arms. Right. But as much as I don't want to let her go, it has to be her choice.

"Can you walk, or do you want me to carry you?"

Mara weighs up her options before saying, "I can w-walk."

The light above our heads bounces off her cheeks when I carefully place her on her feet. Astonishingly, they're without a single tearstain.

Her strength is proven tenfold when she exits the elevator at the underground parking level with only the faintest tremble to her thighs. They could have more to do with bearing weight on her ankle than the ordeal she just went through, but I'm not one hundred percent confident in my assumption yet, so I will keep my opinion to myself.

I dip my chin in gratitude to Rafael when he hands me Mara's purse and my cell phone before he sinks into the shadows of an industrial heating unit. He kept the parking lot locked down to ensure Mara is rewarded with the privacy she deserves.

"Corner of Prescott and Twenty-Second Street," I instruct Darius after assisting Mara into the back of my town car and sliding in behind her, my tone pretending I've not directed him to that same address each evening for the past three weeks.

Darius's concern for Mara reflects in his eyes when he locks them with mine in the rearview mirror before he dips his chin. I issue him the same grateful response I gave Rafael before sliding up the privacy partition.

Just because Mara isn't going off the rails like you'd expect a victim of a crime to react doesn't mean she is out of the woods yet.

Her internal battle is the one that needs the most attention.

I take a breath, praying she won't pull away from me, before I curl my hand over her balled one on the seat between us.

She doesn't pull away. She glances down at my hand, smiles softly, and then returns her eyes to the window.

Our trip to her apartment is done in silence. I won't lie. The quiet is killing me. It has me in such turmoil that I forget Mara isn't mine to do with as I like when we arrive at her building. Not thinking, I pull her into my arms and exit the vehicle without seeking permission.

The knot in my stomach that I'm making unforgivable mistakes loosens when Mara's moves mimic the ones Tillie made when I removed her from the cab. She nuzzles into my chest and sucks in my cologne as if it is as addictive as her shampoo.

I don't check if the elevator is functioning. I head straight for the stairwell, bypassing the apartment Rafael and Darius cleared out the weekend Darius's search yielded unfavorable results for Mara's building supervisor.

After entering Mara's apartment like the space is mine as much as it is hers, we go through the motions I imagine every victim undertakes when they arrive home after a crime. We deadbolt all accessible entry points, triple-check the window latches, and switch on almost every light.

Then we head to the bathroom.

Desecration in any form stinks. It clogs your pores and makes you feel dirty, so it is only natural to want to get clean as soon as possible after a violation.

That was another reason I was showering when I felt an incessant need to get to Mara.

Thank fuck I listened to my intuition.

Who knows what that sick fuck would have done to her if I hadn't.

Though I'd give anything to stay, I issue Mara the privacy she deserves.

"I'll wait for you in the kitchen."

I'm partway out of the bathroom when she whispers my name.

She waits for our eyes to meet before saying, "Th-thank you."

I don't know why she is thanking me. Paarth was at the bottom of the Chrysler's employee pyramid, but if he weren't angry at me for looking deeper into his personal life, he wouldn't have had a bone to pick with Mara.

I didn't introduce him to her life, but I am the reason he forced her to relive her nightmares.

That means I am not the man she should be thanking. But once a coward, always a coward.

I dip my chin before reiterating that I'll wait for her in the kitchen.

I go through the same motions there as I did anytime screams ripped through my mother's bedroom. I put the kettle on the stovetop and fetch two mugs from a shelf above the freestanding oven before collecting teabags from a container in the pantry.

My routine is so familiar that only the compact design of Mara's kitchen stops me from believing I am back in my youth, striving to be the "good boy" *she* wanted me to be when I acted out in rebellion.

I knew what was happening to me wasn't the norm, but my mother never queried while I misbehaved. She said I was jealous that she paid more attention to my new stepfather than me and that I'd have more than a handful of "minor" injuries to contend with if I ruined the best thing that had ever happened to her.

I'm so deep into wading through the throes of my past that I don't realize the kettle is whistling loud enough to wake Mara's neighbors until she leans over me to switch off the gas implement.

I jump when the frilly edge of her dressing gown brushes past my back, and I fucking hate myself for it.

This isn't about me. It wasn't back then, and it isn't now. Not in the slightest.

I put a stop to my self-loathing when Mara whispers, "S-sorry," before she removes the kettle from the stovetop, fills the mugs, and then fetches the milk from the refrigerator.

"Your hair is wet," I murmur when the invigorating scent of her shampoo pulls me out of my nightmare. "You'll catch pneumonia if you let it dry naturally. Let me dry it for you." My last sentence leaves my mouth before I can stop myself, and it pummels me with shock.

My bewilderment is understandable. The faintest whiff of a feminine product only hours ago gave me hives. Now, I'm convinced one sniff of Mara's hair could calm the wildest storm.

Mara's wet hair swishes against her back when she twists to face me. "Um..."

"Please," I plead, not above begging for the chance to fix my mistakes.

Her eyes dance between mine for several heart-thrashing seconds before she whispers, "O-okay."

With our teas discarded before they're touched, Mara helms our walk back to the bathroom for a towel. It dawns on me that her shampoo comes in a range of bathing products when my cock stirs at the scent clinging to the steam of a scorching-hot shower.

"We can go back to the kitchen," I say when Mara's hand shakes as she passes me a semi-damp towel. "I don't mind."

"He-here is fine." Her tone is confident despite the shake of her words. "They will keep winning if-if we don't take the occasional leap of faith."

With the strength of a tigress, and before I can acknowledge that she said "they," she turns her back on the only exit and tugs out the elastic keeping her drenched locks hostage.

27

MARA

*A*ir leaves my mouth in a hurry when the faintest creak of the bathroom floor sounds through my ears. I'm not scared. Well, not for me. This is as big a deal for Ark as it is for me. I just have no clue why.

Does he know all the right things to say because he's dealt with sexual abuse before or because I shared too many secrets while endeavoring to escape the clutches of a predator?

I'm terrified it could be a combination of both, but I can't hide from the truth any longer. We must be honest if we want any chance of being a "we."

With Ark's wide and tormented eyes locked on my reflection in the vanity mirror, he brings the towel to my hair and carefully commences drying it. He sections off pieces and squeezes them with the towel before he scrunches the ends to encourage their natural waves.

It's clear he's done this before, and it piques my curiosity to a point I can't hold back.

"You've d-done this before?"

His ghostlike grin frees me from the worry that I've made a mistake interrogating him while he's comforting me.

"I have. Many times." He shakes his head as if disgusted, but his tone is anything but. "My older sister was extremely demanding when we were younger, and seemingly blind to my assigned gender." His smile dips. "I dried and brushed her hair every night for years."

He rolls his eyes as I suspect he did anytime his sister demanded access to his hair-wrangling skills before he switches the towel for a brush. He drags the bristles through the knots his thorough drying caused, his brushstrokes neither painful nor angry.

He's so deep in thought I assume our conversation is over, so I'm shocked when he says, "I stopped pretty much any type of nurturing when Karolina died. It seemed pointless." Something in his eyes alters their coloring. They appear more blue now than green. "The reason for her strict shower routine no longer existed, so my skills were no longer needed." He swallows harshly before he murmurs, "Or so I thought. Riley took up Karolina's vacancy only a few short years later."

I have so many questions, tons of them, but my intuition is begging for me to go slow. Since I'm trying to trust it as much as I am the man blocking the only exit of the bathroom with his bulky shoulders, I listen to its pleas.

"Riley is your s-sister?"

Unease flares through his eyes before he dips his chin.

"*The* Riley Valentine? Or are we discussing a random Riley I've yet to m-meet?"

His fingertips tickle my nape when he gathers my hair in his hands so he can plait it. "*The* Riley Valentine. Though we should probably stop saying it like that or she'll get a big head."

A puff of air escapes his lips when I murmur, "Too late."

I'm so grateful that some of my stupor is lifting. Paarth's attempted attack scared me, but I've faced far worse, so I don't want it to waste the opportunity it's presented me with.

I've learned more about Ark in the past ten minutes than I have in the past three weeks.

"She is quite the force," Ark whispers as he ties an elastic at the bottom of my twisted locks. "She'll need to be to survive this." He sucks in a sharp breath, conscious he said too much, before he places the brush on the vanity and nudges his head to the hallway. "Come. It's late. We should get you to bed."

I don't recognize my voice when I ask, "W-will you stay?"

Again, I'm not scared. I just have a feeling Ark shouldn't be alone right now, and since I'm just as desperate for him to stay, why not kill two birds with one stone?

Ark freezes for the quickest second before his eyes shoot to the paper heart collage Tillie and I made last week.

Just knowing he's concerned about his influence in her life eases my hesitation by a ton.

"Tillie is having a sleepover with a neighbor. She won't be home until tomorrow afternoon."

When he cranks his neck back, the worried gleam in his eyes shrinks the bathroom. "I should go. It will be safer if I go."

He thinks he's taking advantage of me.

I'm not close to reaching the same verdict.

"I d-disagree." His hand shoots out to grip the doorframe when I whisper, "You will wash away his scent better than any bodywash will."

"Mara..." His chest heaves as he drags in a shuddering breath. "Fuck..."

I'm diving deep, headfirst into dark waters, but for some reason, I feel more free now than ever.

Knowing his struggle, sensing how much he wants to protect me, and witnessing it only hours ago rewards me with more strength than I thought possible.

He fought for me.

He protected me.

He made me feel like I was worth something.

Now I want to do the same for him.

"Please."

Rejection hits hard and fast when he murmurs, "I can't." The brutal sting is nowhere near as bad when he adds, "I can't do touch. I don't like to be touched...It's... I..."

When he struggles to be honest about the reason he has a phobia of touch, I say, "It's okay. I d-don't need to touch you." The invisible wings

I'm attempting to fan out should wilt from the weakness of my reply, but they don't. They expand to their full girth, meaning my voice is without a quiver when I address my needs for the first time. "I just want you to continue teaching me that fear isn't the first emotion you should experience when you want someone to touch you."

"Mar..." He's so torn he can't get my full name out, not even with its shortness. "I don't want to hurt you."

"You won't." When his eyes sling back to Tillie's bedroom door, I murmur, "You won't hurt either of us."

"How do you know that?" Sheer bewilderment colors his tone.

"A mother knows these things. They know wh-who to trust with their children and who to steer them clear of. It isn't intuition, more that a mother knows. She *knows* who her children are safe with. I can't put it simpler than that."

The pain in his eyes triples as he thinks over my words, and then the truth smacks into me.

Oh god. His mother knew he was being hurt, and she did nothing to stop it.

Like all victims of abuse, Ark tries to shift the focus off himself. "Do you think she also knows the body is designed to endure more pain than anyone could comprehend?"

"Probably," I reply, nodding. When his eyes squeeze tightly shut, like my confession pains him to hear, I push out, "Some say birth is the equivalent of breaking every bone in your body. If that isn't proof of what one can endure, I don't know what is."

My throat tightens when he asks, "And you did that when you were...?"

"Fifteen," I fill in, too exposed and raw to lie.

A low sound leaves him as some of his remorse shifts to anger. "Fifteen?"

I don't want to add to the absolute agony in his eyes, but since I genuinely don't believe they can harness more hurt, I nod.

"Fuck, Mara. You were just a kid."

"I was," I agree, stepping closer. The threads holding him together are as worn as mine. They're mere seconds from snapping, but I tug on them ruefully instead of leaving the fragile frays untouched. "As were you when you were hurt."

"Don't," Ark snaps out. "This isn't about me. This is about that fuck" —he points to the door as if Dr. Babkin is on the other side—"and what he did to you that made you so scared you can't speak without a stutter."

The thread I mentioned earlier wholly unravels, and in all honesty, it's freeing not having it flap between us anymore.

"He raped me," I confess, stealing the air from Ark's lungs. "The first time was when I was—"

"*First?*" He's enraged with anger, filled with hate, yet there's something hauntingly beautiful about the protectiveness beaming from him. "He did it more than once?"

I look at my feet and then nod, the memories too hard to bring up without a dip in confidence.

Ark takes a moment to compose himself before asking, "Did you tell anyone? Did you report him to the medical board?"

Again, I nod. This one is weaker than my previous one.

My chest heaves for air when the softest touch lifts my chin. Ark stares at me after aligning our eyes. His spine is rigid and his jaw is tight, but there's no hate in his eyes. No pity.

Not for me, anyway.

"You told?" His voice is a whisper, full of disbelief.

I nod before brushing away the tear the bob forced from my eye.

"Did it stop?"

I'm torn on how to reply. Speaking up saved me from Dr. Babkin for a couple of weeks, but it also thrust me into a nightmare far darker and more depraved.

Ark takes my silence as an outright denial. He bristles with anger, his fury hot enough to scald. "I'm going to track down that fuck and make him regret the day he laid eyes on you. I'm going to kill him."

I follow him out of the bathroom and down the hallway, my strides remarkably strong for how hard I am shaking.

Ark grips the handle of my front door when I say, "It's too late." A shiver moves through me as flashbacks of my past rear their ugly heads. "He's already d-dead." I stray my eyes to the floor to hide the deceit in them before saying, "There's no one left for you to punish... *except me.*"

"Punish you?" He spits the two words as if disgusted. "I don't want to punish you, Mara."

"You may not want to, but you are."

"How?" he bites out.

"By not trusting me to do what is best for me and my daughter. By letting me believe my st-stutter makes me weak." I fold my arms over my chest to ward off the chill rolling down my spine. "By taking what he did to me and using it against me."

"That's not what I am doing." His voice quickens with fury. "I just found out, so how could I have already used it against you?"

"You knew," I whisper, my chest rattling as I strive to hold back a sob. "You knew because a victim knows a victim."

He tries to *pfft* off my underhanded claim that he is an abuse survivor. It rumbles in the back of his throat and tightens the firmness of his jaw, but not a waft leaves his lips when I stare at him, pleading for him to be truthful.

A relationship doesn't need to be perfect.

It just needs to be honest.

Desperate for him to open up to me, I push past the barriers he is erecting between us. "Was it your mother?"

"No!" he denies in a hurry, the rebuttal cracking from his mouth like a whip.

My stomach gurgles when I say, "Your father?"

"No. It wasn't anybody, so stop asking!"

His anger should scare me; it should have me backing away with my hands held in the air, but the nurturing side he pulled out of the trenches in the elevator only hours ago refuses to surrender. I need him as open and raw as me. I need his heart unguarded if I want any chance of infiltrating it.

"Intra-familiar sexual abuse—"

My knees weaken when he shouts, "It wasn't sexual."

I'd give anything to hug him, to lessen his shakes with some form of contact, but I keep my hands at my side, rewarding him with the same respect he offered me only hours ago.

My dedication is rewarded tenfold when he mutters a short time later, "If she had to pick between maiming me and touching me, she mostly picked the former."

Mostly? God.

I take a conscious breath to lessen the nerves in my voice before asking, "She?"

As Ark's eyes float down the hallway, he breathes out so heavily his chest sinks. "My step-grandmother." I learn this goes way deeper than the occasional whack on the bottom when he murmurs, "She hurt him as a child, so he hurt them."

My lips quiver when I speak. "Your sisters?"

He nods almost robotically, and it breaks my heart. I was able to leave my abusive home because there was no one there to protect but myself, and I only built the courage when I found out I was pregnant with Tillie. I doubt I would have ever left if I had siblings, particularly a younger one. I struggled to leave my mother, and she was an adult.

"Ark... I'm s-so sorry."

He shakes violently, but since the lid has been lifted on years of secrets, he can't reseal it. "I didn't know about any of it until just before Karolina couldn't handle the shame *he* forced on her for a second longer. I assumed *his* mother hated me because he hated her. I had no clue he was hurting my sisters because she had hurt him. I swear to you, I didn't know. I would have stopped it if I had known." It is a fight not to wrap my arms around him and hold him tight when his voice dips with shame. "I should have known. It's rare for the abused not to become abusers."

"That isn't true." When he grunts as if he doesn't believe me, I speak loud and clear. "The rate of abuse amongst individuals with a history is approximately s-six times higher than the base rate for abuse in the general population." I talk even faster so he can't interrupt me. "But that's because those figures don't include the choices—"

"Choices? What choices? They take them all away."

I allow his snapped comment to affect my vocal cords for only the quickest second. "Th-that's the point I'm trying to make. *They* chose to abuse. *They* chose to act on their delusions. *They* chose to ignore consent and a person's God-given right to give it. *They* chose, Ark. Just like *we* choose to do the opposite." It hurt to hear him say he believes all survivors turn into abusers, but I know in my heart he doesn't honestly believe I am capable of hurting Tillie. "We know the pain, so we would never..." My words fade to silence as my eyes slide to Tillie's bedroom door. "I would *never* do that to her."

I choke back a sob when Ark mutters my name in vain. "Mara... *Fuck*. That wasn't what I meant. You would *never* hurt Tillie." He steps closer, the honesty in his eyes bursting through the protective bubble into which I'm trying to fold myself. "I know that."

He stops just before he reaches me when I reply, "Just like I know you would never harm her either." I dance my eyes between his, the pain in them weakening with each bounce. "What happened to us doesn't make us monsters, Ark. It makes us strong. We survived. We *survived* them."

My eyes stop stinging with tears when Ark snatches up my wrist and pulls me into his chest. They stream down my cheeks and soak into his shirt until there are no more left to shed.

28

ARKADIY

A creak discloses Mara's tiptoe into the kitchen half a second before her scent. I take a moment to gather my thoughts before placing a dollop of milk into a freshly brewed coffee and then spinning to face her.

My breath catches when our eyes lock. She should be looking at me in horror, disgusted by the ugliness of the skeletons in my closet.

Her expression isn't anything close to appalled.

She looks radiant and relaxed. I'd even go as far as saying free. She doesn't look close to a woman who fell asleep on my lap for two hours with her hands knotted in her dressing gown so her fight to touch me would never be defeated.

A shiver racks through me when I recall how desperately I wanted her to lose her battle. Our stumble from the entryway of her apartment to the sofa in the living room presented the perfect excuse, but she was as scared to touch me as I am to admit I want her hands on me.

I'm not scared because I believe she is capable of physically hurting me. It is wondering how she will react to a quirk I obtained from years of abuse, and if it will change the headrush that bombards me every time she looks at me.

The crinkle between my brows smooths a smidge when Mara asks, "Have you eaten this evening?"

It is a struggle for her not to stutter. It is only achieved with conscious effort, but I appreciate how far she will go to hide her fear from me. She is determined to prove I am trustworthy, and I honestly don't know what I did to deserve her faith.

Her smile when I shake my head shoots a rush of desire through me, soothing some of the agitation our nap on the couch didn't take care of. "Are you hungry?"

Her smile doubles when I murmur, "More like starving."

"Shall we eat in or out?" Her nose screws up when she floats into the kitchen to check her cupboards and refrigerator for supplies. Her act of having guests over is so natural that it feels like we've been living together for years. "I have enough s-supplies to whip up a quick stir-fry, but that's about it."

"Stir-fry sounds great." I join her by the refrigerator before peering at the limited supplies inside. "Though I wouldn't recommend using that chicken breast. It is looking a little funky."

The expression I was expecting earlier jumps onto Mara's face when she sniffs the chicken breast I purchased to make Tillie soup. "That's bad."

I fetch my wallet from the hallway table and stuff it into the back pocket of my trousers, happy to use a three-block walk to get my head screwed on straight and to check in with my team on Paarth's choice of punishment. "I'll run down to the grocer. Is there anything else you need bar chicken?"

A dark lock not secured by Mara's loose braid falls into her face when she shakes her head. It barely flaps in the briskness of her shake before she says, "Can I come with you?" When suspicion highlights my features, she adds, "I often don't realize I need something until I s-see it on the shelf."

I know what she is doing, but I don't hate her inability to give a man space when he needs it as much as I do Rafael's clinginess.

"Okay. If you think your ankle is up to it, I'm fine with you joining me." I lower my eyes down her body in a long, dedicated sweep.

"Though you should probably get dressed first. You still have another fifty-plus years before you're close to the age where you'll get away with wearing a dressing gown in public. I'm considering a change-up next week."

I'm hinting at the obvious difference in our ages, but she acts oblivious.

"I'm allergic to cats, so if dressing gowns are your thing, go for it." She smiles at me in a way that gets my heart racing before she exits the kitchen. "I'll be back in a minute."

For several long minutes, I watch the direction she went before I pull my cell phone out of my pocket and send a quick text.

ME:

We're heading to the grocer in ten.

As expected, Darius answers without delay, proving he is as on alert to answer my every whim during ungodly hours as he is during the day.

DARIUS:

Understood. I am out front when you're ready.

I read his reply three times before I go off script.

ME:

It seems like a nice night for a walk, so why don't you check in with Rafael before calling it a night.

It takes him a lot longer to reply, so I anticipate more than a one-word text.

DARIUS:

Understood.

You shouldn't be able to hear someone's worry in a text, but I can.

ME:

I will reach out when I need you.

DARIUS:

Copy that.

After I store my phone, I move to one of the windows I opened when I learned my culinary skills aren't as proficient as I believed. I keep my gawk of the taillights of a blacked-out SUV hidden by raggedy but meticulously clean curtains.

It takes Darius almost ten minutes to obey my order, and I'm highly skeptical it wouldn't have occurred if he hadn't received Rafael's approval first.

Their defiant personalities are infuriating, but I guess it could be worse.

They could not care at all.

"Is everything okay?" Mara asks upon returning to the kitchen and spotting me by the window.

She looks up at me with captivating eyes, her watch weakening my hesitation for every second she stares. She's wearing a long-sleeved blouse and a skirt that teasingly flaps against the glossy skin just above her knee. Her heels are strappy, and the kinks my bad hairstyling skills added to her locks make them extra voluptuous. Her makeup is demure in a way a woman as beautiful as her could never pull off, and her lips are glossy.

She is stunning, and my inability not to stare doubles the electricity firing between us. It seems so natural to stand across from her that I forgot she forced the resurrection of my ghosts only hours ago.

I should hate her for making me so vulnerable, but deep down, I know the purge will inevitably strengthen me. I just need the shame to fully disperse first.

"I thought we were eating in?" I murmur when I realize Mara will turn the head of every man in the five-star restaurant she should be dining at, not to mention a handful of women.

Mara's eyes flare like she heard my private thoughts before she says, "We are. This old thing is nothing." She spins, fanning out the hem of her skirt. Her happiness is infectious. If I could bottle it up, I would be an extremely wealthy man. Her eyes glisten with joy when she stops spinning. "It was once a tablecloth."

"A tablecloth?" A low hum escapes her before she nods. "Then perhaps we should lay it back on the table?"

The innuendo in my question can't be hidden, and I don't regret it. Our mini therapy session did little to ease the intensity of the sparks firing between us.

If anything, it's made them more potent.

My cock hardens when Mara whispers, "If you play your c-cards right, that could be a possibility." Her stutter isn't in fear or because it would be foreign for her to speak without stammering. It is from the unbelievable heat in her kitchen.

How do I know this? My throat feels just as scratchy when she hits me with a playful wink before she helms our exit from her apartment.

The direction of her eyes when she deadbolts her front door announces the neighbor watching Tillie for the night. If I remember correctly, Mrs. Lichard is a sixty-four-year-old widow with two grown sons. Her eldest is an investment banker, and her youngest is serving in the military. Barring a broken wrist from a motorbike accident, her children's medical records hint at a normal upbringing.

Their medical files are too thin to measure. Mara's are several inches thick.

Yes. *Files.* She has more than one.

Mara stuffs her keys into her purse as she says, "The elevator is back in order, but..."

I save her from finding a reason not to enter another small box by saying, "It is a nice night for a walk."

Even with the hour late, as suspected, Mara turns heads as we undertake the three-block walk to a local grocer. We dodge alley cats and a group of young men with too much time on their hands before we reach a twenty-four-hour grocer that doubles as a liquor store.

Mara seemed more at ease with the boys who wrongly believe they run the streets than the store attendant who peers at her over a folded-up newspaper. The shake of her knees as she collects a basket at the front of the store sees me floating toward the back, faking an interest in an article a journalist requested to interview me about yesterday.

Since Dr. Babkin is dead, I have a bone to pick and no one to take it out on. A highly fabricated article that makes it seem like I am only days from popping the question to Veronika would make you believe an ill-informed journalist would be the first on my hit list, but that isn't true.

Words can't hurt Mara. Store attendants who lower their newspapers for an uninterrupted view of her ass, though. They sure could.

I snap the attendant's picture before forwarding it to Rafael.

While approaching the counter, the thud of my shoes stealing the cashier's focus from Mara's ass, Rafael replies.

RAFAEL:

Babkin?

My back molars smash together.

If he heard Mara's pleas for help, why did it take him so long to assist?

I press on the brakes when I recall how Mara's fight bellowed through the bathroom of my office. She gave it everything she had: nails, voice, and grit.

Half the Chrysler building probably heard her.

As the cashier's throat works hard to swallow from catching my imprudent stare, I punch out a reply to Rafael.

ME:

No. But I want everything you have on them both by the a.m.

RAFAEL:

On it.

I pull a black Amex out of my wallet and toss it onto the counter. "Put the number on file. Anything she wants"—I nudge my head to Mara, who's digging through prepackaged chicken breasts on the bottom shelf of a refrigerator at the back of the store—"is to be placed on this card. Do you understand?"

His throat bob mollifies my frustration enough to end Rafael's wild goose chase before it truly begins.

> ME:
>
> This probably isn't news to you, but if it will keep you out of my hair long enough for me to see Mara through the second wave, I'll share it. Babkin is dead.

The cashier processes my card and hands it back to me as Rafael's reply pops up.

> RAFAEL:
>
> Not soon enough, as far as I'm concerned.

Since I agree with him, I steer our conversation toward a threat much closer to home.

> ME:
>
> Paarth?

I'm not surprised by Rafael's reply, more disappointed. I have an excess amount of rage to let go of and still no one to take it out on.

> RAFAEL:
>
> He chose to hand himself in to the authorities.
> He's been remanded until Monday.

After a quick grind of my jaw, I end our conversation the same way I did with Darius.

> ME:
>
> I'll reach out when I need you.

I've only just stored my wallet when I recall not all the heat in my veins is from Paarth's injudicious mistake.

> ME:
>
> Keep my whereabouts off my mother's and Fyodor's radar until I'm back on deck.

A smirk tugs my lips at one side when I read his response.

RAFAEL:

Already done.

It fades when another message pops up.

RAFAEL:

They think you're deliberating on *their* top picks for the future First Lady.

I picture his disgruntled moan when I send a thumbs-up emoji before storing away my phone.

Although I could leave the store attendant's fate in my team's hands as I did both the building supervisor of Mara's building and Paarth, I'm too bristling with annoyance to let his demoralizing gawk slide.

"You like her." I'm not asking a question, so it doesn't sound like one.

He tries to play it safe. "Who?"

I stare him dead set in the eyes while lying through my teeth. "My wife."

"Wife?" He chokes on the word I struggled to express without cringing only last month. Now it rolls off my tongue as natural as I breathe air. "I didn't know she was married."

"She is," I lie again, stepping closer. "And I don't appreciate people looking at what is *mine*. Especially men undeserving of her time." There's no missing the possessiveness in my tone. It is full of warning and silent threats. "So anytime you see her, I suggest you look the other way." He stiffens abruptly when I add in Russian, "Or lose the ability to see entirely. The choice is yours."

The color in his cheeks drains as his smile vanishes. "Of course. I meant no harm."

He loses the chance to add more assurance to his reply when Mara's scent tickles my senses. She places her minimal purchases on the counter before digging through her purse for some bills.

"I've got it."

She tries to stop me from grabbing my wallet. When she is unsuccessful, she uses words. "It's fine, Ark. I can't invite you to eat and expect you to pay. That isn't how hosting works."

She can speak without a stutter because the cashier isn't game to lift his eyes from the register. He punches her purchases into a dated cash register before bagging them and handing them to her.

I accept them on Mara's behalf before placing my hand on the small of her back and guiding her outside. She doesn't stiffen from my hands being on her. It is from the cashier's clamber for a morsel of power.

"Congratulations on your recent nuptials."

29

MARA

*N*uptials?

I glance at Ark, who looks gorgeous in a crisp midnight-blue business shirt, minus the stuffy tie he's rarely without, and designer slacks that cost more than I make a month.

He's glaring at the cashier.

If looks could kill, the cashier would be on his knees, clutching his chest.

The cause of their tension dawns on me when the butterflies in my stomach augment. They're not fluttering with the fear that usually shakes my vocal cords. They're too low for that. They love the protectiveness beaming out of Ark and how sharing some of my secrets with him didn't change his obsession with my safety.

The knowledge frees my voice from encumbrances when I say, "Thanks. It's new but amazing."

My *husband*'s mouth curves egotistically when I shift my eyes back to him, and I hit him with an animated wink. It reduces the scowl between his brows and hovers his hand so close to my back that goose bumps prickle on my nape.

I arch into his embrace, craving his touch, before I guide our walk back to my apartment building.

Something as simple as being guided down an isolated street shouldn't instigate a fiery response, but I feel like I am on fire. My thighs ache from the number of times I press them together, and my panties feel damp.

The responses of my body grow more uncontrollable the longer we walk. Our attraction is intense. Burning. And his closeness is the drug my body desperately needs to fully wash away the haunted memories clinging to my skin.

Icy winds announce winter is only a hair's breadth away, but I feel so toasty when we enter my apartment ten minutes later that I sag against the door, needing its coolness to subdue the inferno burning me from the inside out.

The fire is upgraded to catastrophic when Ark spins to face me. He radiates power and authority, but I pay the most attention to the hunger in his eyes.

He craves me as badly as I crave his touch, and it's reached a point where I can no longer hide the truth. "Kiss me. *Please.* Wash it away."

The lack of fear in my voice is shocking, but it has nothing to do with how fast Ark jumps to my command. I scarcely register the groceries being dumped onto the entryway table before his hands are in my hair, and his mouth narrows toward my parted lips.

As we breathe as one, our eyes locked and silently devouring, he tugs on sweat-damp strands, forcing my head back before his eyes seek permission to kiss me like I didn't beg for him to do precisely that.

When I nod, he leans in deeper before spearing his tongue between my lips. My fingernails scratch at the varnish on my door when he strokes his tongue along mine, tasting every inch of my mouth.

I'm desperate to lose my fingers in his dark mane, to drag my nails over his scalp while returning his confident embrace, but the consciousness that not all the thudding of his heart is from our heated kiss stops me.

If I want him to shift my thoughts of sex from painful to pleasurable, I need him to exert the authority he did during our previous exchanges. To do that, he needs to feel comfortable and confident.

Touching him won't allow that.

When I balance on my tippy-toes, stealing the last ounce of air between our bodies, Ark growls into my mouth before he deepens our kiss. I'm pinned between him and the door, hungrily aware of his desires as well as I am mine. He's hard, his cock thick and strained against my damp panties that are seconds from being exposed by the unladylike thrusts of my hips.

With my palms flat on the door, I return his kiss with as much eagerness as he is displaying. I stroke my tongue along the roof of his mouth and nip at his lips while grinding myself against the impressive bulge in the crotch of his pants.

My clit throbs for attention, as thunderous as my heart. I want his mouth on me again, down there, but I'm too scared to ask.

Before our exchange on his desk, I'd never been pleased orally before.

Actually, I'd never been pleased. Period.

I was assaulted and discarded. That was as far as my sexual experiences went.

You wouldn't know that, though, from the deep moan that emits from Ark's mouth when the shimmers of an orgasm wrack through my body from grinding my clit against his crotch.

"Fuck, Mara..." Ark growls over my lips, doubling the searing ache coursing through me. "I want you so bad it hurts." He kisses my mouth, nose, and neck before he pinches my chin with his thumb and forefinger to align our eyes. "But I will stop this now if that's what you want. I will walk away without—"

I roll my hips upward, ending his worry.

Then I re-lock our lips.

In minutes, our exchange moves from the foyer to the living room. The pillows Tillie picked from a thrift store flatten against my back when Ark lays me on the couch before he plants a knee between my legs.

I continue grinding, the image of him splayed between my legs too much not to respond. I squirm so much that my skirt becomes a belt, and my damp underwear take care of the final divot between Ark's prominent brows.

Hunger beams from him, and it makes his words husky. "If you need me to stop—"

"Don't stop. *Please.* Never stop."

A low rumble rolls up my chest when he smiles. It is both wicked and devilish.

"I need to fasten your hands." I nod before all his question leaves his mouth. "Are you okay with that?"

I'm breathing so hard that my breasts thrust forward with every desperate gasp.

My face is too hot, flushed with lust, and the situation worsens when Ark unbuttons his business shirt. His body is divine, a powerhouse vessel of sex and seduction.

I pant into a smattering of his chest hairs when he leans over me to tie my hands above my head with the sleeves of his business shirt.

He binds my hands together firm enough to double the throbs of my clit but loose enough that panic is the last thought to enter my head.

"If it's too much—"

"I'll tell you." Our eyes collide, and sparks ignite when I say, "You can trust me, Ark."

I had hoped he would have realized that by now.

After a brief nod, his gaze slides down my body. His breath hitches when he stops at the apex of my pussy. "You're already wet for me."

My shoulder blades meet when the back of his fingers flutter down the lines of my pussy. Pleasure sizzles in my veins as the desire to thrust my head back and moan overwhelms me when he asks, "I want to taste you here again. Can I?"

The fact he seeks consent already drives me wild with need, so I won't mention how burning the urge becomes when he spots my nod.

The heaviness of my breasts is unmissable when the pad of his thumb slides over my clit. I almost vault off the couch, the intensity of the zap his touch instigates pushing me insanely close to the finish line.

"You're so sensitive." He massages my clit with slow, timed circles, his eyes unmoving from my face. "Could you get off like this? With only my hands on you?"

I nod, unashamed. I'm so desperate for him that my hips churn restlessly as my eyes coach him to lose control.

He makes true on my wordless beg with a soft yet still menacing grin. He massages my clit with his thumb until a rhythmic, terrifying pull draws energy from my body and makes me shake.

My core clenches as tiny shivers roll through me. My orgasm isn't as intense as envisioned by the firmness of my shakes, nor emotionally cathartic, but it still feels fantastic.

I writhe against Ark's hand as tears prick my eyes, regions of my body as sensitive as my heart.

As he slows the strokes bombarding my clit, he says, "That was to ease you into the plethora of pleasure I'm about to bombard you with." The velvety rasp of his voice coerces me to flutter my eyes open. "Now the real fun can begin."

My wrists strain against their bindings when he slips my panties to the side, and he nuzzles the cleft of my pussy with his mouth. Air leaves my lungs in a hurry when his impatience to taste me again sees his tongue circling the nervy bud aching for his attention two seconds later.

God, that feels good.

His five o'clock shadow chafes the sensitive skin between my pussy and my ass when he eats me with an expertise that has my thighs shuddering like I plunged into an ice bath.

I rock against his mouth and whisper his name while his tongue tirelessly focuses on my clit.

He strokes it, licks it, and sucks it into his mouth until I can't ignore the flutters making me a sticky mess.

I scream his name as I climax, my entire body shaking.

This orgasm is all-encompassing. Blinding. It turns me into a blubbering, shaky mess, yet I can't get enough. I roll my hips and grind against his mouth until the sizzle of back-to-back climaxes slick my skin with sweat.

Ark's pursuit doesn't relent, either. He continues licking, moaning, and eating. He fucks me with his mouth until another orgasm churns through me like a tornado.

My hands pull against the restraints as I thrash violently. Then I still, the prompts of my body no longer mine to command.

The knowledge should scare me.

It doesn't.

It's freeing to hand the burden of my body's protection to someone else and entrust him to take care of its every whim.

"That's it." Ark glides a finger through my pussy lips as his thumb rolls over my oversensitive clit. "Let all that tension go."

He parts me with his fingers and then slowly slips one inside me.

"You have such a pretty pussy, Mara."

I can't take my eyes off him as he stretches me with his fingers. He starts with one and quickly moves it to two before he eventually increases the burn by squashing three fingers inside me.

"I need to get you ready for me, but if it's too much—"

"It feels great."

A low hum vibrates from his chest as his fingers go deep. I pulsate around them, lost to the sensation tightening my chest with the rope that was once knotted in my stomach.

My fingers curl around the shirt holding them hostage when Ark's palm places a perfect amount of pressure on my clit. I'm almost too sensitive, too enamored. I am being hammered by emotions but incapable of allowing them to be heard. The wish to climax again is too strong, the drive too urgent.

When Ark's mouth returns to my pussy, my toes curl as my hips lift from the couch. I collide my pussy with his mouth before moaning through the rumbles of his growl as he loses control.

His tongue drives me insane, poking and protruding, but his fingers take all the control. They slide in and out of me at a frantic pace, dotting my body with as much wetness as the perfect furl of his fingers.

I'm so lost to him that another climax crashes into me without warning.

My nails scour Ark's shirt as I quiver through a blistering of stars and fireworks. Sweat mists my skin as my lungs hunt for air while I fight to breathe. To think. I can't do anything but surrender to the madness of a powerful tsunami.

There's the hysteria I thought I'd only ever imagine.

My orgasm is so vicious that it leaves me as violently as it overwhelmed me. I sink against the sofa and draw in desperate breaths, my body ravaged by a beautifully brutal climax.

When Ark's fingers slide out of my pussy and he climbs up my quivering body, I smile at the achievement on his face. He deserves more rapacious applause, but I'm too exhausted to do anything but stare.

"You still with me?"

His smile augments the wave in my stomach when I reply, "Just."

"One more." He adjusts the tilt of my hips, giving himself room to settle between my thighs before he lowers his hand to his belt. "Then you can rest."

"One more...?" My arched brow announces my confusion on my behalf.

Heat creeps across my neck when Ark angles his head and stares at me like a hunter would look down the scope of a rifle.

"Oh."

An intense current surges through me when his cock settles between my legs. We're still mostly clothed, but since my hands are bound above my head, I missed the strip tease that removed his impressive manhood from his trousers.

I'd be a liar if I said I wasn't disappointed.

My heart thumps when Ark reminds me of his mind-reading capabilities. "Next time." I assume he means the show he unknowingly puts on anytime he breathes, but I am proven wrong when he locks his eyes with his homemade restraint and says, "Maybe next time I can remove the restraints."

"Maybe," I murmur, too focused on the wild need in his eyes to care about anything but our current exchange.

Dark hair curtains his face when he tears open a condom before he rolls it down his thick shaft. I don't know where he got the condom, but I'm glad he came prepared. I may have strangled myself if we had to stop this now.

I squirm more from the intensity of Ark's watch than the heaviness of his cock when he braces it at the opening of my pussy. He coats the tip with the slickness of my multiple arousals before he lifts his eyes to my face.

"I'll go slow." His words are a promise, not a suggestion. The thudding of the vein in his neck proves this, not to mention the glint of fear in his eyes that he's about to hurt me. "Are you ready?"

When I nod, his soundless groan vibrates against my swollen flesh.

He massages my clit with his thumb as he slowly enters me. The burn is excruciating, as scourged as the expression that crosses his face when pain is the first emotion my body registers.

"No," I murmur when he inches back, removing the first handful of inches he fed in. "It feels good. You f-feel good. You're just so... *big.*"

Heated delight rolls through me when he places more pressure on my clit. He doesn't move. He remains perfectly still, but within a handful of rotations, the tightness between my legs slackens, and his expression becomes less devastated.

"That's it, baby." I clench around him as he returns the handful of inches he stole. His muscles flex when he takes in how intimately our bodies are joined. "Accept me inside you. You're taking me so well."

As tremors of an orgasm surface again, I swivel my hips, riveted that something so painful can also be enjoyable. Our exchange isn't rough and impatient. It's slow and rhythmic, a perfectly timed embrace that shows you can lose control and still be gentle.

Ark's control is mesmerizing. I love how he stares at me with fire in his eyes that reveals he wants to ravish me, but he will hold back his desires to ensure I am comfortable.

That proves what I've known since day one.

Ark is not a sexual predator.

Sex offenders are delusional with their thoughts. Their inability to self-regulate and control their impulses means they often believe they're more important than the person they are abusing. They think their abuse isn't harmful and that they're entitled to whatever they want, so consent doesn't need to be sought.

Ark isn't doing any of those things. He's in control; he sought consent, and instead of exploiting my vulnerabilities, he's ensured I know I have all the power.

If I want this exchange to stop, it will happen immediately.

The unvoiced acknowledgment of that is addictive. I've never felt more powerful, and the confidence it rewards me with can't be missed when I beg, "Fuck me."

I'm almost blindsided by an orgasm when I hear the rawness of Ark's throat in his reply. "No."

It's taking everything he has to hold back the urge to claim me like he's desired since the night we met. He wants to possess me, fuck me. He wants to claim every inch of me, and I want the same. I want to give that part of me to him, and solely him.

"Please."

My pussy ripples around him when his cock flexes before he shakes his head. Although he is denying me, his body is announcing he wants this as much as I do.

"I want to experience s-sex. True sex. I want to feel desired and wholly wanted. I want to be fucked like you dreamed about fucking me the night we met." His pumps quicken as the air gets humid with lust. "Don't let him take that away from me, Ark. Don't let him win—"

My eyes roll into the back of my head when he rams into me, sinking fully inside with one fierce thrust. He's so deep I gasp, the burn both unbearable and delicious.

"Mara," Ark moans, driving in deeper, pushing just past the threshold of pleasure to pain. "You feel so good. So tight. You take my dick so well."

Every muscle in my body tenses as he pumps his fat cock in and out of me in a steady yet timed rhythm.

Over the next several minutes, I can't look away, captivated by how he knows exactly which buttons to push to take full control of my body.

I'm mindless with need when he hooks one of my legs over his back so he can both take me deeper and rejoin our mouths. He spears his tongue inside me, its plunge as deep and exploring as his thick cock. I'm sore from how deep he is taking me but fascinated that it isn't a painful ache.

Nothing this good could ever be classed as painful.

Pleasure spreads through me as I moan into his mouth. I'm covered in a slippery layer of sweat. Even Ark's shirt is damp, and my vision is hazy.

I am on the cusp of another orgasm and unashamed to admit it. "I'm... I'm..."

While rolling his hips in a way that drives me crazy, Ark says, "I know." I cry out when he grinds his hips against mine, loving the spasms it rewards my clit with. "You get tighter when you are about to come. You're strangling my cock." His lust-strained voice is capable of making me come. "Look..."

When I struggle to lift my dog-tired head, Ark slips a hand under my ass and raises my hips. I mewl at the visual of his big cock thrusting in and out of me. The condom is slick with lubricant, both inside and out, so there is no resistance to his pumps.

I writhe with pleasure, my core clenching when I'm too overcome by the visual not to respond. As my back arches, heat throbs through me, and my lungs saw in and out.

Every part of me is pulsating, but I can't get enough.

Neither can Ark.

He draws out the length of my pleasure with timed thrusts and body-quaking moans.

We groan together when my orgasm refuses to relent. It lasts forever, its roll through my body so violent that the wall I erected to keep my emotions at bay shatters.

I try to force my sobs to sound like moans, not wanting our connection altered by a pocket of emotions I'd rather work through alone than with company.

My efforts are woeful.

The first tear only careens halfway down my cheek when Ark notices it.

"Fuck."

30

ARKADIY

*P*ain spreads across my chest when I dab at a blob on Mara's cheek. I'm hopeful it is sweat, even with my heart knowing that isn't the case. I pushed her too hard, too fast, and now I'll regret it for the rest of my days.

Remorse clings to my skin when my pointer finger and thumb absorb the salty droplet. Sweat and tears are of similar denseness, so I can't confirm its origin by touch, but I don't need confirmation to authenticate its derivation. The horror in Mara's eyes tells me everything I need to know.

I fucked up.

"No," Mara pleads when I remove my semi-erect cock from her snug pussy in one quick maneuver.

It should be fully deflated. The thought of hurting anyone usually has it shrinking like a punctured tire, a slow yet controlled deflation. But this is Mara, a woman who has been hurt in unimaginable ways. It shouldn't be close to erect.

"Ark..."

Mara's wet eyes bounce between mine when I arch over her to free her hands.

That's where I fucked up. It wasn't the first mistake I've made, and it most likely won't be the last, but there's no doubt in my mind that I should have never restrained her.

You can't encounter what she did and not have phobias.

Limited control is probably a massive trigger for her.

Probably? She was raped, dickhead. Of course she'd be fearful of being pinned down.

"I shouldn't have... I..." I cuss again before unknotting my shirt in a hurry, needing to untie her and cover up the reasons I know how horrific the repercussions of abuse can be. "I shouldn't have bound you."

"It's okay," Mara assures me, confident and without quivering.

When she tries to secure my wandering gaze and fails, she tries with words. "Look at me."

I can't. I'm too ashamed.

My sister would roll in her grave if she learned how I treated a victim of sexual assault.

"Ark... *please*," Mara tries again.

When her plea doesn't reward her my attention, she touches my face.

That gains her my utmost devotion, but this time, it isn't with a viciousness founded on hate. Astonishment is the main instigator, followed by need. I can smell myself on her skin, and it is as intoxicating as the delicious palette of her pussy.

Her eyes—those fucking eyes—sear through to my soul and smooth the shakes shuddering my body.

"It's okay," she assures me again, gently nodding.

With her hand on my face and her thumb stroking my brow, I can't help but respond.

It isn't as expected.

I lean into her embrace and breathe in her scent, accepting her comfort even though I know I don't deserve it.

Her smell comforts me. It's different since it is a combination of our scents, but it is extremely cleansing.

I drink it in until my muscles relax enough to unclench my fists, and then I lower my eyes to her face. She looks fuckable and sweet at the same time, and it has me torn on how to move forward. Usually, I flee before sending in a team of lawyers when I fuck up.

I don't want to do that this time around.

"Why?" I ask, ignoring the hard rock in the back of my throat that's slowly killing me.

Mara chews on her bottom lip as she contemplates my question. Her delay in responding gives me plenty of time to prepare for the onslaught her answer will no doubt hit me with, so I'm caught off guard when she once again displays her strength.

"I didn't realize it could feel so good. I was overwhelmed. I..." There's a length of silence and then a sigh. "I let go." As she scoots up the couch, her shaky hands lower the hem of her skirt. "Now I feel embarrassed. I don't know how I'm meant to act, Ark. I've never..." She stops again and breathes out heavily. "It never felt good. Not once. So I let my emotions get away on me."

My knuckles pop as the truth smacks into me.

She's never been with anyone but the predator who assaulted her.

Dr. Babkin is the only man she has slept with.

And you went and fucked it up by making her true first time all about you.

"Mara... I'm sor—"

She squashes her finger to my lips as the fire in her eyes re-ignites. "I don't need an apology. I also don't want one." Her eyes bounce between mine for several seconds before she says, "I just want your trust."

"I trust you." My pledge leaves my mouth before I can stop it, and it is as honest as the day is long.

Her smile sends a current through my body, changing my temperament from hostile to blazing in under a second. "Then you should know that I would tell you if it were ever too much..." A fire blazes through her eyes as she licks her lips. "As I am sure you will me."

When her eyes lower to my crotch, I'm hard again in an instant. Her eyes give away her every intention, and within seconds, the air fills with the scent of her re-forming excitement.

She doesn't move forward as per the silent pleas of her body, though. She waits for approval, the anticipation of my endorsement adding to the misting of sweat on her flawless skin.

My heart rate rises. It isn't in fear. My abuser's kink was pain. My pleasure was never at the forefront of her mind. It is contemplating the shift of power Mara is initiating and how I will handle the imbalance.

It is easy to feel in control when you're the master of someone else's pleasure. Receiving it, though, is an entirely different kettle of fish.

I need the control, the reins.

I've not handed them over in almost three decades.

This will be a challenge for me, but a challenge I am willing to face if it returns Mara's confidence to what it was before I made her uncomfortable.

After straightening my spine, I pull off the condom covered with evidence of Mara's multiple orgasms before I rake my fingers through her hair.

She hums her approval of my grapple for the reins as she wets her fuckable lips.

Shockingly, excitement is the first spasm to roll down my spine when her wet and delectable mouth arrows toward the engorged crown of my cock.

Mara has a mouth designed to be fucked, and my dick is raring for the chance to prove my theory right.

I've never been harder.

"I won't touch you." Her whispered words float over the crest of my cock, thickening me more. "And you can stop this at any time."

The possibility of that is nonexistent when she circles her lips around the tip and gently suckles. I'm barely an inch in her mouth, but it feels good. *So fucking good.*

Muscles bunch when she swivels her tongue on the underside of my cock while lowering her lips down my twitching shaft. She takes me to the back of her throat, her mouth hot and inviting.

"Yes," I hiss like a snake, confident I could die now and not feel like I've missed a worthwhile experience.

There's only one way this could be better—if Mara's hands were pumping my shaft in beat to the hearty sucks of her mouth.

But I'm too scared to ask, too scared I may react badly, so I close my eyes and get lost in the sensation of her velvety tongue absorbing the beady drops of pre-cum on the crown of my cock.

Her lips glide up and down my shaft nonstop over the next several minutes, doubling the urge to thrust my hips forward. The wish to fuck her mouth claws at me in desperation. I want to come, to surrender to the madness stealing my smarts for the past hour, but I hold back. I fight to issue Mara the respect she is deeply craving.

It is a fucking hard feat.

Inches upon inches of Mara's luscious skin is on display, and although her hair is a tangled mess and her face is void of makeup, she is still the most beautiful woman I've ever laid eyes on.

My thigh muscles clench when she greedily takes me to the back of her throat, stimulating me as I've never experienced. Tingles race down my spine, and my balls pull in close to my body.

"God... Mara. That feels so good."

When she moans her approval of the lustiness of my voice, I rock my hips forward, stuffing more of my cock inside her mouth. Her moans vibrate on my crown, sending spasms of pleasure rolling down my spine.

Air sucks from my lungs when her eagerness to please me has her gagging on my cock. I bite on the inside of my cheek when she runs her tongue down the vein feeding my monster dick.

"Fuck..."

I breathe through my nose, struggling to push past the intense reaction making me as desperate for her touch as I am to come. She can't take all of me, but I'm not disappointed. The sections she's working feel fucking amazing.

"You're going to make me come so hard."

I'm gripping her hair too painfully, jerking my hips too wildly. I fuck her mouth like I paid for the privilege, but Mara can't seem to get enough.

Her nails claw at the sofa as her moans vibrate my crown.

"Keep going... Just like that... Take the lead."

Her noises are feral, and they have me losing all sense of control.

I still as the most animalistic growl rolls up my chest.

Then I come into Mara's mouth, spurting hot, salty cum onto her tongue and down her throat.

I'm so fucking spent that before I can consider the consequences of my actions, I flop onto the sofa next to Mara, then pull her over until she is straddling my lap. My heart is thrashing too wildly for her to miss, but it feels right having her in my arms, nuzzling my chest.

It feels like home.

A short time later, when I have some sense of control over my lungs, I peel back a wisp of hair stuck to her sweaty cheek before lifting her eyes to mine.

I smile, relieved that there isn't an ounce of fear in her eyes.

She looks happy. Accomplished.

She looks like she knows her skills at sucking dick are sky high.

I'd be jealous if I believed that was true. Even with what we're establishing as fresh as a baby, I know her expression isn't egotistical.

She's content, and although it won't last, her fear is forgotten.

I gave that to her, and she did the same for me.

Even now, sexually and emotionally exhausted, and the urge for her to touch me overwhelming me, I feel fearless enough to say, "She told me I was dirty. That since I was born a bastard, I'd have to work harder to wash away the sins my out-of-wedlock birth caused." I stop to swallow the anger bubbling in my throat and heating my face. "The water was hot... *hot enough to burn...* yet I still felt dirty even after she scrubbed my skin raw."

A memory flashes up, momentarily stilling me, before the softness of a delicate hand pulls me out of the trenches before I'm wholly buried.

Mara's thumb is scarcely stroking mine, but the disbelief it smacks me with sees even more secrets being shared. "Just the briefest touch would instigate hives because I knew she would use it as an excuse to say I was dirty again. Then she would have to bathe me, and the routine I did everything to avoid would start all over again." Anger echoes in my tone. "I did everything I could to stay clean. I went to the library during breaks at school. I ate my lunch with gloves I stole from the cafeteria. I didn't touch anyone, and I sure as hell didn't allow anyone to touch me. I did everything I could, but the abuse didn't end. I—" I stop when I choke, and then I fiercely shake my head.

These are my secrets to share, but I don't want to share them. I never have with anyone. Not even Rafael knows how dark they go.

And I will do everything I can to make it stay that way.

Air leaves Mara's mouth in a hurry when I stroke the pad of my thumb over her erect nipple. I don't want to use her to get over my anguish. I want her to help me forget.

The burn at the back of my throat feels nowhere near as scalding when she leans into my embrace instead of repelling from it.

Although appreciative of her wave of the white flag, she is a fighter more than first perceived. "Abusers target children because they're the most vulnerable."

She almost yelps when I tug her nipple firmly. This is not a discussion I want to have while my cock is poking into her ass. It should be as flat as a tack, not digging into her curves.

My lips thin when she persists. "They are inappropriate in front of a family member to s-see if they will get away with it." I freeze, curious to see where she's going with this. "When they do, they become more risqué. They groom you in front of the people who are meant to protect you because they know they won't do anything about it since they're just as abusive."

Fuck. Fuck. Fuck!

I thought I deserved to be abused because I was too scared to speak up.

Only now am I realizing that isn't the case.

Even when you're brave enough to push back, you can still get hurt.

I stroke Mara's back, hopeful my simplest touch will weaken the rise and fall of her chest, before asking, "How long?" Her eyes bounce between mine like she is confused. I know she isn't, but I act stupid. "How long did it take for the abuse to stop?"

"Um..." I hate the shake of her thighs. "It d-didn't... until I left."

My voice is calm even though I'm anything but. "Because you were pregnant with Tillie?"

Shock registers on her beautiful face for half a second before understanding settles it.

She nods. "I had hoped he would s-stop since I was pregnant." Her hands knot into her skirt. "But it made him worse."

"Because she was proof that he was a pedophile."

She doesn't try to hide her disgust from me. She simply nods before breathing out slowly. "I think th-that's why he was so rough the last time. He wanted me to miscarry." Wetness glosses her eyes, but her cheeks remain tear-free. "I didn't want that. I wanted Ti—"

"I know," I interrupt, stilling her fidgeting hands. "You don't need to tell me, Mara. I know." I take a deep breath, then hold her gaze while sharing a secret I had planned to take to the grave. "I am sure it was the same for Karolina with Riley. Even knowing how she was conceived and the hate associated with it, I'm confident she wanted her from the moment she knew of her existence."

31

MARA

*M*y chest grows tight and hot while waiting for Ark to expand on his reply, to explain how his baby sister is actually his niece. If I were holding my breath, I would have been asphyxiated by now. He isn't exactly skirting, more not ready to be totally upfront with me.

I understand why. We were strangers only weeks ago.

It feels weird admitting that, particularly because I can still taste his cum on my tongue.

The reminder of how delicious he tastes has me squirming on his lap. Fortunately for me, my grumbling stomach frees me from looking like a heartless sex fiend.

"Hungry?" Ark asks, deliberately ignoring the elephant he left sitting in the corner of the room.

I want to push him some more, to reopen the lines of communication he's endeavoring to shut down, but I also need a minute to wrap my head around the fact I shared the source of Tillie's conception without hyperventilating.

Tillie wasn't planned, but she is very much wanted. She gave me the will to live when I wanted to die and the strength to fight only yesterday when I thought my life had rewound a decade, where I was in Dr. Babkin's office, striving not to die.

I am terrified about Tillie learning the method of her conception. It has nothing to do with who she is. She is much more than a byproduct of rape. She is my world, and I won't allow anyone to make her believe differently.

But since I need time to work out how I can ensure that remains the case, instead of pushing, I say, "More like starved."

I accept a soapy bowl from Ark before rinsing and drying it and placing it and two wine glasses into the kitchen cabinet. We've worked side by side for the past two hours cooking, eating, and talking.

It's early. I don't know the exact time since I haven't been able to take my eyes off Ark for a single second. My guess is sometime in the a.m.

Despite the hour, I'd give anything for our exchange to continue. Our conversations rarely veered beyond meal prep and our mutual hunger, but a lack of conversational skills isn't to blame. Another mutual craving has kept our word count at a minimum. It is very much sexually based.

You'd swear there's a timer above our heads, ticking down too fast for us to keep up with, so we're rushing through the stages most couples take months to achieve in hours.

The haste of our gathering would be scary if it didn't feel so right.

It's rushed but undeniably beautiful.

I shouldn't be surprised. The shock of still being wanted after showing so much of my ugly side is addictive. I crave it as much as the sneaky glances Ark has hit my thighs with in the past two hours. His hooded watch has my hunger at a pinnacle, and I'm once again lost on how to ignore the elephant in the room.

I close my eyes and breathe in deep, inhaling the scent of Ark's heated skin.

God, he smells good.

His cologne is pricy, and his choice of shampoo makes me feel safe, but I pay the most attention to our combined scents. I can smell my arousal on his skin and see the crinkles our heated exchange caused to his once pristine dress shirt.

I moan, incapable of denying the tension for a second longer before I pop open my eyes.

Ark is facing the same torturous battle. The front of his pants is extended, and he's opening and closing his hands like he's fighting the urge to delve them back into my hair.

"Ark..."

He saves me from making a fool of myself. In three quick strides, he takes my mouth hard and fast, the urgency of his touch sending sparks straight to my clit.

He kisses me desperately, tasting the spices that flavored our shared meal and distributing a taste that is uniquely him.

I respond to the urgency of his embrace with just as much rigor. I match the strokes of his tongue and moan into his mouth when his kiss makes my thighs shake.

The effortless strokes of his tongue and the playful nips of his teeth make me so legless that I stumble backward, needing something to brace against.

The moment my backside lands against the kitchen cabinet with a thud, Ark lifts me to sit on it and then yanks up my skirt. His tug when he shreds off my panties chafes my skin, but I'm lost in a sensation too perfect to convey panic.

I gasp into his mouth, loving how greedy he is to please me again when he wedges himself between my splayed thighs before he plays with the wetness between my legs.

"Mara... *Christ.* You're drenched for me."

I should be ashamed by how wet I am, embarrassed I've barely sat still over the past several hours, but I'm not.

Being desired is a drug I don't see myself quitting anytime soon.

Ark groans when I rock against him, desperate for friction. I'm frantic for him to touch me, to make me scream his name, but since I can't remove his cock and guide it between the folds of my pussy without touching him, I must wait.

Patience is not my strong point when it comes to this man.

"I need to get you ready for me. I don't want to tear you—"

"I'm ready," I interrupt, squirming. "I'm wet. You s-said so yourself."

I may have gotten away with my lie if I hadn't stammered. Since I did, Ark curls my toes by running his thumb down the opening of my pussy before slowly pushing it inside me.

"Christ," he murmurs again, talking through the lust curled around his throat.

"See. I told you I was ready."

Every sentence I speak without a stutter takes a mammoth effort, but the dividends it pays are phenomenal.

In less than a nanosecond, Ark pulls his massive cock out of his trousers and lines it up with my pussy.

"Ready?"

Air hisses between my teeth when one nod sees him lurching forward and ramming into me.

He's so profoundly seated that my cervix spasms violently and my thighs shudder.

"*Yesss.*"

My hands seek something to grip as my body fights not to protest the sudden intrusion. It burns taking so much of him so fast, but it also feels good.

My nails find something to clutch when Ark pulls my hands behind my back before he pins them to the kitchen cabinet. They stab into the opposite hand, and the burn their scratching causes adds to the tingles racing through my core.

With my arms used as an A-frame brace, Ark tugs me forward until my backside is suspended off the edge of the counter and my hips are free to swing.

Desire shivers through me when he says, "Open wider for me, baby. If you want me to take you hard and fast, you need to open up for me."

My immediate compliance sees his cock sinking into me, stretching me, and making me gasp.

With one hand clamping my arms behind my back and the other supporting my hips, he thrusts into me again and again and again.

I grow slicker and hotter with every grind, and our combined moans make the humidity in my poky kitchen unbearable.

But I can't get enough.

I grunt and groan, dying for that feeling I doubt I'll ever experience without him. It feels too surreal to imagine it with anyone else. Too good. I can't picture anything rating as high as the euphoria I feel when Ark makes me come.

"Oh god." I pant through the coils retightening in my lower stomach. "You're so deep."

"Because I want you to take all of me." As he slams his hips upward, his face hard with lust, the veins in his neck work overtime. "To feel *all* of me."

My head falls back when I take the last inch of him. He's fully seated now, owning and commanding every inch of my pussy.

"Mm," I moan, the urgency of our exchange relieving.

I was worried pushing him out of his comfort zone would alter things between us.

I had no reason to fret.

The more we share, the closer we become.

I've never trusted a man as much as I do Ark right now, and it is proven without fault when he adjusts my position, and it removes the only exit from my view.

Panic should be slicking my skin.

Fear should be present.

They're not.

I'm seconds from climax, and I am not the only one aware of that.

Ark takes me harder and faster. He fucks like a machine, and within minutes, I'm overwhelmed for the umpteenth time this evening.

This time, Ark falls into orgasmic bliss with me.

The squeezes of my vagina as it fights through a brutal orgasm set him off, and the heat of his cum when he releases inside me prolongs the length of my climax.

We shiver and shake as we ride the tidal wave threatening to swallow us whole until it subsides enough for me to realize not all of Ark's tremors are from his release.

Some are from my fingertips brushing the scars on his back.

32

ARKADIY

I let go.

I freed her hands.

And then I came when her spiral into climax saw her desperate enough to stop the unrelenting pummels of my hips with her hands.

I came while being touched.

That's unheard of.

I've not once achieved that before, and I was with women not on the cusp of learning not all my abuse was nonsexual.

Jesus fucking Christ.

What is this woman doing to me?

33

MARA

My throat feels hoarse when I peer down at Ark's hips. Our eagerness means his pants and boxers are huddled around his knees, and his cock is still buried deep inside me, but try as I may, I can't miss how the whiteness of my thumb contrasts with the pinkness of an old scar.

I didn't notice this one earlier because Ark's business shirt hung over his cropped but still manly pubic hairs. It isn't as mottled as the scars on his back, but it still displays the torment a child was forced to endure against his wishes—torment I added to since I'm clearly incapable of keeping my hands to myself when blindsided by a ferocious climax.

"I'm s-so sorry."

I snatch my hands away, mortified I broke his trust the instant he rewarded me with a snippet of it before shuffling back far enough to remove his semi-firm cock from my pussy.

"I d-didn't mean to to-touch you without p-permission."

Ark looks horrified, and since it doesn't seem to have anything to do with our combined releases glistening on his cock, it doubles the gurgles of my stomach.

"I'm-I'm not on birth c-control, but I can get the m-morning after pill." His horrid expression augments. It matches mine to a T when his cum dribbles down my thigh. "I-I'll go get it n-now."

I don't get a step away before Ark snatches up my wrist and pulls me back. He doesn't speak. He leaves the ball in my court. Again.

Sheepishly, I raise my head, aligning our eyes. He looks at me like he hates me, so you can picture my shock when he does the last thing I expect.

He kisses me senseless.

It is unmistakably possessive and makes me feel like I am the most delicious thing he's ever tasted.

By the time he pulls back, I can't remember the reason for the wetness pricking my eyes, much less the ache in my chest. There's too much throbbing in an area several inches lower to give a little heartache an ounce of attention.

"But..." I stop, too confused to continue.

Ark smiles, seemingly pleased by my bewilderment, before asking, "What was your preference for dessert again? Ice cream or...?"

He leaves his question open for me to answer how I see fit.

I follow along nicely.

"Mousse. Mousse was my pick."

His smile makes me so hot that you'd swear I didn't recently climax.

"Did we remember to get mousse?"

I stare at him as if he is daft. It is all an act. A man as brilliant and motivated as him wouldn't be mindless. I, on the other hand, wouldn't remember the name of the cleaner I've used every day for the past six years if asked right now. Nothing but working out how I can keep Ark's smile planted on his face is on my mind.

"We didn't buy any because I already had some," I answer when Ark patiently waits. "Chef made way too much Thursday night."

"Ah. Yes. That's right. I forgot." He's lying. Don't ask me how I know. I just do. "Dessert?"

He doesn't wait for me to answer. He moseys to the fridge and rifles through the limited items inside like he's lived here as long as me.

It takes a few moments for my bewilderment to clear enough for lucidity to take hold.

His reaction wasn't in response to me touching him.

Horror only filled his face when I stuttered.

Gosh. Does that mean what I think it does? Does he fear me stuttering in his presence more than he does me touching him?

This is horrible for me to admit, but I hope that is the case.

Trust is one of the greatest gifts you can give someone, second only to love.

34

ARKADIY

*I*cy barbs pierce through the scars on my back when I bury my head under the water pumping from Mara's showerhead. I can't face scorching-hot showers. I haven't since I was a child. It is either cold or freezing. It will never be close to warm.

As I work my jaw from side to side, I step under the spray more. I'm meant to be prepping to officially meet Mara's daughter, not fighting to rid my skin of sweat that plagues it anytime I consider becoming someone's stepfather.

My stepfather was a monster, a reincarnation of the woman who birthed him. He did terrible, horrible things, and although I'd give anything to pledge that I am nothing like him, my mother's concerns have my mood circling the drain any time Mara brings up Tillie.

I want to protect her. I'd never do anything to hurt Mara, and hurting Tillie would do that. But how do you protect someone if you're the one they could need sheltering from the most?

It is seriously fucking with my head, and every time I think I'm getting a hold of it, I get bombarded by a severe case of anxiety.

As my mother has said numerous times over the past two weeks, I didn't marry and have kids in my prime for a reason. Yet now, right at the pinnacle of my career, I'm minutes away from playing house like a family was always on the agenda.

Ugh.

Why the fuck, out of all the men in the world, did my mother choose him? I could have had close to a normal existence if he hadn't been introduced to Karolina's life and mine when we weren't old enough to take care of ourselves.

I bang my fist on the tile, too worked up to discount all the signs our mother ignored not to respond. They were right in front of her, flashing in neon lights, yet she let them happen.

She let them continue.

She ruined our chance of normalcy, and now my insecurities are doing the same.

A chill runs down my spine when I sense I am being watched two seconds before Mara's shampoo fills the air. There isn't enough heat in the water to produce steam, but the tension that forever fires between Mara and me could cause an inferno. I heat up in an instant, and the incineration is quick since Mara refuses to enter the bathroom without an invitation.

After drenching my hair, making it sit flat enough to curl around my ears, I peer at her from beneath a curtain of water.

Fuck, she is beautiful. Her shoulder is propped against the door-jamb, and her arms are hanging loosely down her svelte frame. With our antics running late into the morning, dark circles are ringing her eyes, and her lips are chapped from how many times we've kissed, but she is still the most beautiful woman I've ever laid eyes on. The silky gown she placed on when we stumbled to bed in the wee hours of this morning hugs her curves, and her hair is down and curtaining her gorgeous face.

She is a sight for sore eyes, and she makes my dick ache.

If I were a good man, a decent man, I'd tell her I would meet her in the kitchen once I'd finished my shower and then sneak out the fire exit.

Since I'm not, I hold out my hand, inviting her to join me.

She doesn't hesitate for even a second.

Her trust loosens the noose clutching my neck while desire takes care of the unease slicking my skin with sweat.

It completely clears away when I twist in enough time to watch her remove her silky sleeping gown. It falls off her shoulders with a soundless whoosh, exposing her lush tits, smooth stomach, and lean body.

She was built to be fucked, but fierce enough to bring the strongest man to his knees.

I don't see vulnerability when I look at her.

I see strength.

Admiration.

I see the woman I want to make my wife.

"We should get married."

Mara balks before her throat works hard to swallow. "Sorry... what did you say?"

She heard me. The thudding of her pulse in her neck is a surefire indicator. She just wants to give me a chance to back out of my suggestion.

I refuse.

"Married. We should get married."

When her face pales, I catch her by the wrist and pull her under the spray. She yelps when the freezing temperature takes care of the wildfire raging through her stomach from my suggestion, but she doesn't attempt to adjust the faucet.

Between brief touches, kisses, and mind-blowing sex, we spoke so much last night, even if she hadn't seen my back when I'd yanked Paarth away from her, she'd know the scars are from burns.

The water *she* bathed me in was hotter than hell, and I've been submersed in its fiery depths for over thirty years.

That's all done with now. Mara flipped my universe on its head in less than twenty-four hours, and I couldn't be happier.

Or scared.

I'm so fucking scared.

And Mara knows that. "NDAs are cheaper and a whole heap less complicated than marriage."

She slaps away my hand when I veer it toward her nipple, already versed that I'll use sex as a tactic to get my way. Our relationship is moving at a breakneck speed, but aren't all the best ones? We stripped our cloaks before uniting in a way only couples do. We scaled the hurdles, so it is only up from here.

A legally binding commitment seems like the next logical step.

Once her nipples are safe, Mara lifts her eyes to my face. "That is what this is about, isn't it? You're worried you've shared too much so you want to protect your privacy."

"No," I lie, equally peeved she's denying me the drug I plan to use to get over my neurosis until I take my last breath, while also in awe about her hitting the nail on the fucking head. "It isn't just my privacy I want to protect. It is yours as well... and Tillie's." My voice is barely a whisper when I add another name to the short list of people I am desperate to protect. "And Riley's."

When Mara arches a brow, confused, I reward her with a level of trust I've never given anyone. "I found out recently that my stepfather groomed Karolina so well she believed it was possible for a forty-year-old man to fall in love with a ten-year-old child. She only learned differently when she walked in on him bathing Riley, *their* two-year-old daughter."

Mara's calculations are quicker than the ones I undertook when my mother exploded this bombshell on me earlier this week, but instead of them fettering her face with worry, they fill it with remorse. "Ark... I'm so sorry."

I continue before I lose the nerve. "The horrified look on Karolina's face when she told our mother what *he* had done to her is still burned in my retinas. She left no stone unturned during her confession. Years of abuse was spilled in under an hour."

A sigh sinks my chest when Mara displays she is both beautiful and smart. "And your mother didn't believe her."

Even though she isn't asking a question, I nod, too ashamed to speak.

The rope around my neck loosens enough for me to breathe when Mara moves closer, her eyes sympathetic. "But you did. You knew because a victim knows a victim."

Again, I nod.

The way she can read me is astonishing.

She truly does have eyes that can see through to my soul.

"Who did you tell, Ark?"

Shockingly, I smile before breathing out slowly. "Rafael. And since I was too scared to tell, he told a lie that saw my stepfather sentenced to twenty years behind bars." She smiles with me, making me believe I'm not insane when I confess, "Karolina hated us for it."

"No, Ark." Her brisk headshake fluffs up the scent I'm obsessed with. "She wouldn't have. I promise you."

I wish I could believe her, but I can't. "She killed herself the day he was sentenced."

I suck in a sharp, desperate breath when Mara says with the utmost confidence, "Because she thought it was the only way she could free Riley as unapologetically as you and Raf had freed her." I shake my head. She either sees it and ignores it or misses it. "When a child is conceived from rape, you never stop worrying that you will push your hate onto them. That you will never love them how they deserve to be loved." I'm shocked when she confesses, "That's why I had originally planned to put Tillie up for adoption. I didn't believe love could be bred from hate." A pained huff parts her lips. "Then I almost lost her in my third trimester. I've never looked back since, and I've loved her from the moment I laid eyes on her."

Her story shows her strength.

Mine reveals I am a coward.

"I didn't see love when I looked at Riley. I saw the pain in Karolina's eyes when our mother slapped her and heard the words our mother screamed while accusing her of seducing her husband. I saw the evil I assumed they had bred into Riley because I was too busy hiding my own shame to do the math." A mixture of sadness and anger bombards me. "Why didn't Karolina tell me Riley was her daughter? Why did she keep that from me by pretending she attended an out-of-school art program?"

I'm not expecting an answer. How could someone outside my

family give me one? But Mara hits the nail on the head for the second time today. "Because you believed the lies of your abuser."

She isn't speaking about the pedophile who raped my sister or the lady who scarred my skin and stole the hearing in my left ear. She is speaking about my mother. My heart knows this as well as my brain.

Too fearful that I'll choke on a sob if I were to speak, I nod instead.

"I took so long to confess to someone outside the circle of my abuse because I believed their warnings of shame. They said I'd be ousted by my family and hated by everyone in the community." There's nothing but honesty in her tone. "If I had a brother, I probably would have kept my secret even longer than I did. Kids are meant to disappoint their parents. We're meant to rebel. It is different for siblings. They don't want to envy each other, but they do." I *pfft* off her factual comment as if it is a lie. "I see it in Riley's eyes every time she looks at you."

God, I want to believe her. Even before I learned the truth, I was never the brother Riley deserved. I encouraged my mother to enroll her in boarding school and hid her from the world because it was easier to hide from the truth than contemplate its consequences.

I was an adult during Riley's formative years. I should have been there for her as I was Karolina.

Mara leans deeper under the spray like the temperature isn't freezing before asking, "Does Riley know Karolina is her mother?"

Even the shortness of my reply can't hide how furious it makes me. "No."

She smiles, thankful for my honesty, before asking, "Are you going to tell her?"

I don't contemplate as long as I thought I would if asked this question. "Yes. *Eventually.* I just need to stop jumping through fiery hoops first. I've taken steps to do that, but they don't seem like enough."

The confused crinkle between Mara's brows is back, and it makes her expression too cute to remember the seriousness of our conversation.

She slaps away my hand for the second time this morning before arching a brow, silently demanding for me to continue.

I do, albeit begrudgingly.

"Our mother"—I cough before correcting myself—"*my* mother is threatening to make it a public announcement if I don't..."

"Stay away from me?" Mara fills in when my anger has words eluding me.

I nod, the fury pumping out of me turning the icy water to lukewarm.

Mara looks like she hates herself more than my mother when she suggests, "Then why don't we keep this between us for now?"

"No," I immediately respond. "I'm not playing by her terms anymore. I can't ask you to be my wife, then hide you away like a dirty secret. I want you at my side."

She looks torn between kissing me and slapping me. I learn why when she whispers, "I'm not asking solely for Riley, Ark." The love her eyes have been rarely without the past twenty-four hours lowers a smidge when she says, "I'm not ready to tell Tillie just yet. I need m-more time."

Her stutter breaks my heart.

I did that. I brought that edge of desperation to her voice. The panic.

My insecurities brought her down to my level, and it is the last thing I want.

I lift her downcast head, re-aligning our eyes. "You have time."

"Not after I stand at your side." I realize my effort to keep her as far away from my mother as possible was fraudulent when she says, "They'll want to know why you picked me, and the stuff they will find could tear our relationship apart."

Her words echo cautions my mother made numerous times over the past two weeks, but I'm not worried. I've done my research. I know what I'm getting into. The journalist who met with me yesterday afternoon knows how hard I will persecute anyone stupid enough to strip the privacy of a minor or a victim of a crime.

I've also never been more honest with anyone in my life. Mara knows all my secrets, yet she is still here, peering up at me in awe. Nothing they could unearth will change how I feel right now, holding her in my arms.

"Trust me when I say I will destroy any media outlet stupid enough to run Tillie's story or yours. Tillie is a child, and her rights are protected by a law I will uphold to its full degree on anyone who dares to test me."

My cock turns to stone when she says, "I trust you."

I hear a but, so I vocalize it. "But..."

Her words are like a punch to the gut and remind me again of how selfish I am being. "Riley is an adult. Her privacy will be nowhere near as sheltered as Tillie's. She deserves to find out how she was conceived with dignity and respect." Her wet eyes bounce between mine. "And she needs it to come from someone she trusts. It needs to come from you, Ark."

Since I don't disagree with her, I remain quiet.

The silence should aggravate the tension hanging thickly in the air. It doesn't. It doubles the chemistry my greatest fears couldn't hold back and has me remembering the question I asked her when she entered the bathroom.

"I am willing to consider keeping things on the down-low on the agreement you become my wife the instant *they* know the truth." I say "they" in a manner she can't mistake. This is for both Tillie and Riley.

Mara's smile... *fuck.* I've never seen such an exotic image.

"Can I think about it?"

Her lips part to make way for a giggle when I say all caveman-like, "No. You cannot. That's not how marriage proposals work. I ask, you say yes."

There's no heat to my tone, no malice. It is as cool as the water I guide her under before I reacquaint our lips, certain I will never take a full breath again without her mouth on mine.

35

ARKADIY

I stop admiring the rosy glow Mara's cheeks get after multiple orgasms when my cell phone rings. I have every intention of ignoring it until it buzzes immediately after it stops ringing.

Only my direct team has my number, and they know not to contact me unless it is urgent.

This must be urgent.

"Stay," I demand when my steps to my phone have Mara's automatically veering toward the bathroom. "Anything my team needs to say to me, they can say in front of you. It isn't like you haven't already sniffed my dirty laundry."

My breath catches when she smiles before she slips her hand into the one I'm holding out in offering.

Being touched and not balking is still extremely fresh, but I can see it becoming addictive if it is done by Mara.

After tightening my grip, forcing firmer contact, I slide my finger on my spare hand across my phone screen, unlocking it. My missed call was from Rafael's private cell. The follow-up buzz is a message from the same number. It displays the urgency of his contact.

RAFAEL:

112

Raf doesn't use that code for anything but a dire emergency, and it instantly rears up my guards.

With his message seen as delivered, Rafael sends another one.

RAFAEL:

I'm downstairs.

It is the fight of my life not to kiss the living hell out of Mara for her understanding of my friendship with Rafael. "Go. Tillie is usually in a carbohydrate fog for a week after a sleepover at Mrs. Lichard's. She'll be cranky if I don't give her the chance to put her best foot forward before meeting you. That won't be until sometime in the p.m."

Her strength flourishes the more time we spend together, but I am still hesitant to leave. She was only attacked yesterday. Leaving her alone now is unwise. The second wave hasn't even hit yet.

I mutter for her to get out of my head when she says, "I am *perfectly* fine being left alone." Her shoulders rise as predominately as the assurance in her tone. "And it isn't like you're going to order Darius away from my apartment anytime soon."

She isn't peeved I have a security detail on her apartment.

She's pleased.

Her screwed-up nose assures me of this, not to mention the loved-up expression brightening her diamond eyes when she says, "I'm safe here." The tilt of her kissable mouth speaks the rest of her reply. *I'm safe with you.*

"Are you sure you want me to go? I can stay."

Again, she smiles and nods before she gathers up my clothes and hands them to me.

I pull her in close and breathe in her scent, confident it is the only way I'll be able to leave guilt-free, before getting dressed.

"I'll be back as soon as I can."

"Take all the time you need," she replies, walking me to the door. "We're not going anywhere."

Her "we're" isn't solely referencing her and Tillie. I'm included in that dynamic as well. The sentiment in her eyes announces this, much less the way she brushes her thumb ever so slightly over the crinkle in my brow.

She is more fearful about touching me than wondering if I will return.

That's how solid our connection has become.

Her breath fans my cheek when she gasps from me leaning into her embrace instead of repelling from it. She'll probably think it's a ploy to get my way when I ask for her hand in marriage again, but the words leave my mouth before I can stop them. "You know we could skip half the shit about to be flung at us if you'd accept my proposal."

I'm not meaning to pressure her. I just want her to be my wife more than my lungs crave air. I feel like I will be able to protect her better being her husband than her boyfriend. There are more privileges with a legally bound relationship than a casual one.

"I won't have a job if there aren't any messes to clean."

I growl at her. It makes her giggle. It is as breathless as she makes me feel when she presses her lips to my mouth to kiss me goodbye.

We kiss in the doorway of her apartment until the ache that I'm leaving lessens. I am still disinclined, but since I am hopeful my departure now will reduce the likelihood of future ones, my strides aren't as short as you'd suspect.

As I reach the sidewalk of Mara's building, I crank my neck back and peer at the ominous clouds above my head. A storm is on the horizon, but for once, I'm going to remember the rainbow we're meant to be rewarded with after the deluge.

"Sir," Darius greets when he spots me approaching an idling SUV at the front of Mara's building.

He's no longer behind the wheel of my main town car because I removed him from my security detail the afternoon he drove me home from this exact location. His contract now only has one objective—protect Mara and Tillie at all costs—so I'm somewhat curious as to why he's left his post today.

He deemed the rear entry point of Mara's building as the highest threat, so he shouldn't be manning an area monitored by employees of his security firm. His priority is Mara's safety, which can only mean one thing.

He is here in regard to something that affects her.

After slipping through the door Darius is holding open for me, I twist to face Rafael. His cheeks are gaunt, his lips are cracked, and he looks like he hasn't slept.

Something is very wrong with this picture. Although it feels similar to the tornado we instigated when Rafael falsified claims of sexual abuse against my stepfather, the tension this time feels capable of swallowing me whole.

"What's going on? I thought you said Paarth handed himself in."

"He did," Rafael answers. "This isn't about him."

My eyes bounce between Rafael and Darius when Darius joins us inside the unmanned car. The driver has been removed to ensure privacy, and the knowledge roils my stomach.

"Who is it about, then?" I ask Rafael, conscious his fists don't ball unless he's already fighting.

A rock lands in my stomach with a splash when Rafael signals for Darius to hand me a single photograph. It boils my veins more ruefully than the oil-ladened bathwater that melted my skin off my back and stole my hearing, and it has me ready to go to war.

"Where did you get this?"

Dr. Babkin doesn't look close to the evilly unethical pedophile I was picturing him as. He was an average-looking schmuck who most likely donated to charities once yearly to lower his tax bill and drove an eco-friendly car.

The only thing that gives away his evil insides is the person he is pictured with. She is young, too young, and her age in the image exposes that her daughter took her genes more than her abuser's.

"Where *the fuck* did you get this?" I ask again, my temper too obliterated to speak cordially.

Rafael works his jaw side to side before answering my question. "It isn't where we got it from you should be worried about. It is *who* gave it to us you need to pay the most attention to."

36

MARA

"They look amazing. You've done such a great job."

I don't hide the pride beaming out of me for the umpteenth time today when Tillie tilts her head to critique her cookie decorating skills. She is her own worst critic. "They're not quite *Master-Chef* worthy, but I think he will still like them."

"He?" I query, acting daft.

She hits me with a look that says more than it should before she digs an air-tight container out of the back of the pantry to store her creations. "I just hope he comes back before they go stale."

"I'm sure he will." I've never sounded more confident. It replicates how I feel.

Ark and I sailed over a lot of bumps during our record-breaking and extremely healing twenty-four-hour reprieve from the world, but the look Ark hit me with when he hinted at marriage for the third time has me confident he will return sooner rather than later.

Tillie stops loading her cookies into the container as her eyes light up. "Maybe you should take them to him so he can taste them while they're super fresh."

Stealing my chance to reply, she races into the entryway to fetch my tattered jacket before she assists me with placing it on.

I love her enthusiasm, but it doesn't alter the facts. "I can't go now. It's almost dinnertime, and I promised Ark we would be waiting here for him when he returns."

"But Mrs. Lichard invited me over for a roast." Before I can portray my excitement of sampling one of Mrs. Lichard's famous baked dinners, Tillie adds, "She only has enough food for two people."

"Oh."

I grow worried about how thin the walls of our apartment are, my stomach roiling for a completely different reason than disappointment, when she says, "So there's no reason you can't deliver Ark his cookies now. I'm sure he'd love a sugary dessert after his supper."

Ark and I ate our dessert without spoons, and our bodies were the bowls.

"Tillie, I—"

She interrupts me, saving me from a horrifically embarrassing conversation. "Toadie is currently on his fourth marriage. Mrs. Lichard said he could have stopped at one if he'd given his wife a little bit of sugar every now and then."

"Toadie?" I ask, confused by the whiplash of our conversation.

"From *Neighbours*." I don't know how she can roll her eyes and cock her brow at the same time, but she does it like a pro. "He's one of my favorites. Mrs. Lichard said I shouldn't get attached, because there are rumors that he's leaving the show."

Here I was thinking she was ditching the chance to meet Ark for roast beef. It's worse than that. We're being pushed aside for a fictional character.

"Can I have dinner with Mrs. Lichard? Please, Mom? We only have seven seasons left."

"Seven seasons! How long has the show been running?"

Tillie's mouth twitches in preparation to reply, but she's interrupted by my ringing cell phone.

"Don't move an inch," I demand to Tillie, my tone feigning bossiness. "If you're going to ditch me for endless slices of juicy roast beef, the least you can do is smother my cheek with kisses before you leave."

Unease burns my esophagus when I peer down at my phone. The

number flashing across the screen registers as familiar. It is from inside the Chrysler building.

I swallow to soothe unexpected nerves fluttering in my stomach before sliding my thumb across my phone screen and squashing it to my ear. "This is Mara. How c-can I help you?"

"Mara, it's Riley. I'm sorry to bother you." She sounds like she's been crying, like Ark went straight to her door after mine to release her skeletons from the closet as ruefully as I forced ours out.

I know that can't be true. Ark is hard on himself for factors outside of his control, but he would never hurt Riley unnecessarily. He was barely a teen when Riley was born, so the decisions made back then are not his to carry, but he still understands how delicate the situation is. He would never just blurt it out.

When Riley sniffles, I return my focus to our conversation.

"It's no bother." We're almost the same age, so I try not to mother her, but worry has words shooting from my mouth before I can stop them. "Are you okay? You sound upset."

"It's Arkadiy."

Another sniffle.

Another length of silence.

Another near heart attack.

"He's not good."

"As in?" I hate that I'm snapping at her, but I am panicked out of my mind. "Was he in an accident? Is he hurt?"

"No. Nothing like that. I'm not explaining myself well. Communication isn't a strong point of my family."

"Try taking a deep breath." I breathe with her, my lungs in desperate need of air while twisting away from the door, conscious of little ears listening in.

When the whistle of Riley's exhale sounds down the line, I ask, "Where is Ark?"

"He's at his apartment... I think. I don't know. He was here, and he'd been drinking. Nothing he said made much sense, but you came up a lot, so I thought I should call you." Her tone switches from worried to desperate. "Can you check on him? I'm worried about him."

Even though I am digging through the entryway table for my purse, I act as if I'm not already halfway out the door. "Did you call Rafael?"

Her snivel breaks my heart. "Yes. He said I should give Ark some time."

"That's probably a good idea." My words are for me as much as they are for her. I stomped all over Ark's privacy yesterday. I don't know if I have a second wave of intruding in me. I am emotionally and physically drained, but also desperate to help.

"I would but I have a bad feeling, Mara. I'm worried he's going to hurt himself."

"He won't. I promise you he won't." While recalling her mother's passing, I snatch my apartment keys out of the empty fruit bowl before heading for Tillie, my mind made up. I forced the resurrection of Ark's ghosts, so the least I can do is comfort him while he tries to wrangle them back into submission. "But I'll check on him. I will make this right."

Riley exhales in relief. "Will you ask him to call me, please? I won't stop stressing until I've heard from him."

"Of course."

My heart gains a new nick when she murmurs, "And tell him that I don't blame him for anything that happened. That I've *never* blamed him."

My heartache for what she went through, and still has to go through, comes across in my tone. "I will. I promise."

She murmurs a thank you before she disconnects our call.

Just as fast, Tillie pushes me toward the exit stairs of our building.

"I won't leave Mrs. Lichard's apartment for any reason or anyone."

She tries her darndest to act ignorant to the fear in my voice when I remind her to brush her teeth before bed. She shouldn't bother. She wears panic as obviously as me.

It feels like I'm walking into a tornado without a raincoat.

I'm about to get drenched, but unlike yesterday morning, my pussy isn't facing the deluge.

37

MARA

"*I*'m arriving at the Chrysler building now," I say down the line, assuming Mrs. Lichard is calling me to make sure I made it across town safely. She's a worrywart. It is one of the things I love about her the most. That, and how madly she adores Tillie.

I smile down the camera when Mrs. Lichard twists her phone to show Tillie sitting on a knitted blanket, watching *Home and Away*.

"It's not my favorite Australian show, but it makes her happy, so I put up with the injustice." A doorbell rings, and Mrs. Lichard's face lights up. "That will be the roast."

"You ordered roast for dinner?" I ask, my voice rife with suspicion.

That would cost a fortune, and Mrs. Lichard is on a pension. She can't afford takeout.

She *pffts* me like my shock isn't warranted. "No." A touch of heat graces her rheumy cheeks when she admits, "I sent the ingredients to Mr. Gordon from 4A and ordered him to make us a roast for dinner."

The redness of my cheeks is more from memories of how Mr. Gordon cornered Mrs. Lichard under mistletoe last Christmas than the unbelievable heat in the servants' elevator I've just entered.

It's super stuffy tonight, and not all the heat is from remembrance of the last time I rode this elevator. Most of it is worry.

I haven't stopped replaying my conversation with Riley through my head on repeat since I left home. That was almost two hours ago since I had to take four different bus lines to get here.

The bus schedules were designed for nine-to-five workers, which is ridiculous considering people who work those hours generally have their own mode of transport. Adding that to the fact Darius wasn't stationed where he usually is when I leave my building has catapulted my panic.

Something is wrong—very wrong.

I tune back into my conversation when Mrs. Lichard says, "You shouldn't have brought so much, Mara. I won't need to go shopping for a year."

I stare at her, dumbfounded. Barring the bulk rice, flour, and pasta we divide from the food wholesaler one block from Wilfred's boutique, I haven't been grocery shopping yet. The list is on my refrigerator, waiting for the day Chef stops overcooking.

When I say that to Mrs. Lichard, shock leaps onto her face. "But... it's all here... Months of supplies were delivered an hour ago."

She spins her phone again, and I gasp. Her little kitchen is overrun with pantry food, condiments, and enough fresh produce to last her until next Christmas.

I've never seen so much food.

I stagger back when she discloses, "Your kitchen is just as brimming. Tillie thought it was Christmas when she helped me take it inside." Since my shock can't be dismissed, she asks, "If it wasn't you, who was it?"

I swallow the brick in my throat before flinging my eyes to the apartment I'm approaching. "I think I know who it might have been."

I would sound more confident if I weren't so lost.

Why would Ark organize groceries when I'm reasonably sure he ordered Chef to overcook on the days I work?

My pride wouldn't allow me to ask Chef directly if my theory was true, but Chef is blunter than his favorite knives. When I dropped hints about my assumption, he told me it is impolite to question someone's generosity, and that doing so was an insult to both the gift giver and the cook.

"Oh..." Mrs. Lichard's reply is way too lusty for my liking. It makes my gills a little green. "Tillie is right. Ark is perfect for you. Perhaps she is right about Mr. Gordan as well." Stealing my chance to reply, she shouts at Mr. Gordan that she's coming before she tells me to message her before I leave so she can make sure I've gotten home safely.

I promise her I will before ending our call and storing my phone.

After a quick breather, I knock on the service entrance of Ark's living room and impatiently wait.

Mercifully, I'm not left hanging for long.

Regretfully, the person who answers isn't who I am expecting.

"Ms. Malenkov," Fyodor greets, his gaze stony and cold. "I was just about to contact you." He waves his hand across his body, inviting me in. "Please, come in."

My legs are already wobbly, but their shakes worsen when my entrance into the living room announces there are more bodies than exits.

The person I'm seeking, though, is nowhere to be seen.

After smiling a greeting to Mrs. Whitten and Val, and struggling to hold back the snarl I'd give anything to issue Ark's mother, I sit on the chair Fyodor gestures at. I trust Val enough to know she'd never place me in danger. I can't issue the same guarantee for the other three.

I'm on the verge of being sick, but since I am desperate for answers, I fight to speak through the clump of vomit in my throat. "Is Ark okay?"

"Yes," Fyodor answers, immediately halving my angst. "He's fine."

"You, however," Mrs. Whitten joins in, "are balancing on a very thin wire, young lady."

Her anger shocks me... until I recall how stringent she is about the rules.

I once cherished her nonfraternization policy.

Now, I loathe it.

"I had no s-sexual contact with Ark—"

"You will address him as Mr. Orlov or not at all."

I grit my teeth before shifting my eyes to the person snapping at me like my cat shit in her prize-winning garden.

Even if Ark's confessions didn't disclose her as a monster, I'd still declare with utmost certainty that Mrs. Orlov is a bully. She looks down at those she believes are below her and will stomp on people beside her for an inch more leverage.

"No, I will not refer to him by *that* name." Orlov is Ark's abuser's surname. He didn't change it when he was legally old enough to do so because he didn't want Riley to be the only one lumped with the name of her abuser.

Even having his blood didn't stop her father from hurting her.

It was the same for me.

Mrs. Orlov gasps, shocked and appalled by the sternness of my tone, before she seeks assistance from Fyodor. "Are you going to allow her to speak to me in such a manner? Do something, Fyodor!"

He looks torn. I understand why. I thought he was Ark's employee, not his mother's.

After a quick breather, Fyodor says, "We are all here for the same reason. Arkadiy's well-being."

Everyone nods, agreeing with him, except Mrs. Orlov. "He wouldn't be guzzling whiskey as if it were water if this wretched witch hadn't brainwashed him."

"Nora, please," Fyodor retaliates before I can. "If you can't be quiet, you will need to leave."

Mrs. Orlov's face lines with anger as words are spat from her hard-lined mouth. "I'm not going anywhere." Her eyes are back on me, narrowed and glaring. "Unlike you."

Another tense stretch of silence passes before Fyodor breaks it. "I was requested this afternoon to organize you a severance package."

My eyes widen to the size of saucers. "By wh-whom?"

He continues as if I didn't speak. "The package is extremely generous. You will receive full wages for the term of your contract and an additional twenty-five percent for any leave you may have accrued during your contract period."

Before I can get over my shock that I'm being offered two years' worth of salary for two weeks' worth of work, Mrs. Orlov's whispered snarl steals my focus. "Veronika suggested he fuck her out of his system, not pay for the disservice. This is absurd."

I agree with her, but Val will never allow personal feelings to enter a business discussion. "As Mara previously stated, any association between her and Mr. Orlov was *after* her employment contract with Chrysler Holdings had ended. If her new contract did not include a nonfraternization policy, she is well within her rights to refuse the severance package on offer and seek legal counsel before progressing further with negotiations."

"I don't want Ark's money," I add on, "so I deny the offer of s-severance."

"Regretfully," Fyodor starts, his tone more respectful, "your contract had a nonfraternization policy for both you and your employer."

"Then she retains her right to seek legal guidance for a breach in contract by *both* parties."

Val flashes me an apologetic grin when Mrs. Orlov takes her wave of the white flag in the wrong manner. "I knew it. You don't want my son. You want his money!"

I shake my head, but she surges forward with her plans to derail me with a viciousness everyone is shocked about.

She slaps me.

"Nora!" Fyodor shouts when she gets up in my face and screams, "If it isn't true, if you truly care for him, sign the severance package, then leave without causing a scene. Let him live his life how he wants!"

As I nurse my stinging cheek, I say, "This isn't the life he wants. He told me so only yesterday."

My fight loses steam when the last person I thought would go against my relationship with Ark sides with the opposition. "It's what he wants, Mara." Rafael enters the living room, looking tired and with-drawn. "He told me so himself this morning."

My heart is breaking, but I try to save face. "Then he will have no trouble telling *me* the s-same."

After removing the knife Nora stabbed into my stomach by ordering for her to be removed from Ark's apartment, he twists it back in deep. "He doesn't want to see you." His eyes plead with me to listen as he steps closer, blocking out the frantic thrusts of Ark's mother as she tries to free herself from the security guard's grip with his broad frame. "Sign the contract. Don't let pride prevent you from providing the life your daughter deserves."

"N-no. I refuse."

"Please," he pleads, his words barely a whisper. "He won't survive this without knowing you're okay, Mara. He needs *you* to do this for him. He needs you to *save* him."

His words make no sense. How can pushing me away help Ark? But the sheer actuality he delivers them with spears an arrow into my heart so effectively I nod before I fully understand what I am doing.

"Okay. I'll sign it."

38

MARA

Seconds after I scribble my name across a document terminating my contract with Orlov & Associates, I'm handed a printout of the ridiculous amount of money Ark paid to get rid of me.

It burns a hole in my purse when I shove it inside, too embarrassed to look at it.

I sold my soul to the devil only hours after encouraging Ark to do the opposite.

I've never felt more ashamed.

As Fyodor stores my severance paperwork into a leather briefcase, Rafael helps me to my feet. "I'll show you out."

"It's fine. I know the w-way."

"Mara," he pleads when I pull away from him, the thought of being touched after being so perversely violated too sickening to ignore.

When I enter the servants' corridor, I veer left instead of the usual right. With Mrs. Whitten and Ark's mother deep in conversation at my right, there's no way I can confront either of them in my current head-space. I'm so mad that I'd be tempted to physically assault her as she did me.

The further I walk, the angrier I become. This goes against every-thing I believe in. The railroading, the bullying. I swore when Tillie was born that I would never place myself in a predicament like that again, yet here I am, nursing a stinging cheek and a broken heart from people I didn't allow in.

I'm so mad at my cowardice it takes me longer than I care to admit to realize which door I've stopped next to.

I'm outside Ark's third-floor office.

Although I shouldn't, I knock instead of walking away.

I signed the severance papers as requested. That should reward me some morsel of respect.

"Not now!" growls a voice from inside—a voice full of pain and torment.

"Ark, it's me." I hate how weak my voice sounds when I say, "It's M-Mara," but your confidence can't be smashed to smithereens and not have it affect your vocal cords.

There's a cuss closely followed by a thump.

"Are you okay?"

Now I understand why Ark loathes silence.

It hurts the same as fists when issued by certain people.

I press my hand to the door to steady my legs as well as I endeavor to steady my words. "I'm not leaving until you talk to me."

My teeth grit when he snaps at me in the same tone he used the night we met. "Go home, Mara."

His words are so slurred that I'm more fretful than upset.

The last time I confronted a drunk man, I found out my father isn't the God-fearing man he makes out he is to the parishioners of his church.

He is the devil in sheep's clothing.

After another quick breath to ensure fear doesn't jangle my vocal cords, I say, "I want to make sure you're okay. Riley called me. She's worried about you."

I hear another cuss before a crash and a scrape like the thick wooden legs of his bed being bumped firm enough to move them.

"Ark?" I shout when another bang sounds through the door. This one is louder than the fist he threw into the tiles in my bathroom. It's defeated and possibly life-altering. "Please let me in."

Silence.

More painful silence.

That is the only reply I get.

No longer caring about the consequences of my actions or his right of privacy, I dig through my purse for the master keys for his apartment.

I fumble for the key to Ark's bedroom when another bang sounds before it is closely followed by a tyrant of hateful words. "Stupid fucking lies. Stupid fucking people. Stupid fucking *him*!"

Something smashing against a wall booms out of his bedroom during his last sentence.

In a flurry, I find the right key, push it into the lock, and then throw open the servants' entrance door.

The strong scent of alcohol hits me first.

It is closely followed by an overpowering floral perfume. It smells too dated to belong to anyone under the age of sixty, and it seems to be coming from the air vents.

I sense Ark's presence half a second before he scares the living daylights out of me. "I told you to go home."

His hot breaths fan my cheek and add to the whiskey scent making me nauseous.

That was *his* favorite liquor to drown his sins with.

"I don't want you here."

He chugs down a three-finger serving of brown liquid from a glass he's barely grasping before he stumbles to the bar. His clothes are as disheveled as his face, hanging limply like they weren't perfectly tailored for his body, and his shoulders are hanging as low as his head.

I picture a teen struggling to speak up when he whispers, "I don't want your last memory of me to be this. I don't want you to know the monster I can be."

Horrid memories of similar words scream at me to leave, but when he fills his whiskey glass to the rim, my heart refuses to listen to a single plea.

He is hurting badly, and I care about him too much to pretend he isn't.

"I think you've had enough," I say, pulling the whiskey bottle out of his grasp and putting it back on the bar.

He laughs in my face. "I think you're wrong." He downs half the glass in one gulp before turning to face me, spilling numerous droplets on the way. "I'm not surprised. You don't know a damn thing about me or the horrors I am capable of."

"I know you're hurting so you're lashing out." He *tsks* me, so I talk faster. "Riley will understand, Ark. She—"

"Hates me. The only part of my sister I have left fucking *hates* me."

I shake my head, but he doesn't see it.

"And I deserve it. I hid her away because all I saw when I looked at her was *him*. I made her self-respect nonexistent." Shame and hurt fill his eyes. "I was the only male role model she had, and I fucked it up because I was more concerned about hiding my secrets than wondering what hers were."

His anger firms so fast that he cracks his glass.

"Don't," he shouts when I instinctively respond to the droplet of blood rolling down his palm. "You can't fix this." My heart breaks when he murmurs, "You can't fix me. It was stupid of me to ever believe you could."

"I don't want to fix you. I want you to let me in, to be honest with me. I want you to trust me and the process you need to face to move past this."

"I tried!" he yells so loud that any residents sleeping no longer are. "I fucking tried and look where it got me. You're scared of me."

"No, I'm n-not."

His voice is calm although he is anything but. "Then why did you stutter? Just now, why did you stutter?"

"Because... Because..." My heart knows the words I want to yell— *because you're not meant to fall in love on sight*—but my mouth refuses to speak them.

Instead, I try to put the focus back on the cause of his mini melt-down. "I shouldn't have pushed so hard. I'm sorry if it was too much too fast, but you need to remember that it's okay to fall. As long as you get back up, falling is an option."

"What if it isn't? What if there is no possibility you can get back up?"

"You can get back up, Ark. You just have to fight."

I fall into his trap, and I have no clue how to get out of it when he commences kicking in the dirt he dug out to ensure I fall. "What if I don't want to fight anymore? What happens then? What if you've realized what you thought was worth fighting for isn't actually worth anything?"

I pushed because I thought unshackling him from his demons would help him.

Instead, I pushed him away.

"I promised to tell you when it became too much." My heart breaks when he looks straight into my eyes and says, "It's too much." There's no one he hates more than himself right now, but he hides it well with another guzzle of whiskey. "I can't do this, Mara. I can't put you through *this*." He bangs his chest during his last word.

My heart is frozen from the desolate look he hits me with, but it does little to weaken the pleas I toss his way when he flicks his blood-shot eyes to the side of the room and says, "Take her home, Raf."

Rafael emerges from his hiding spot, his angst as palpable as mine. "I'm not sure you should be alone right now, Ark."

"Take. Her. Home!" Ark repeats, his words as violent as the hate that roars from him when he says, "Or I'll void the agreement we made today without a single iota of remorse."

His confidence of his threat is undeniable when he enters the bathroom without so much as a backward glance, and he slams the door behind him.

"I wouldn't," Rafael cautions when I attempt to follow him.

"We can't leave him like this. He's..." *Upset. Hurt. Breaking my goddamn heart.*

Rafael sighs like he heard my private thoughts before he curls his arm around my shoulders and guides me through the servants' entrance. "He'll be all right. He just needs a couple of minutes to calm down."

39

MARA

*R*afael lied.

Things didn't calm down. They got worse. And they continue getting worse.

"I'm so sorry, Mara. I wish I had more to offer you."

I smile to assure Val I know she had my back before I hand her the keys she requested I return this morning.

Although I officially resigned from my position with Chrysler Holdings two weeks ago, I was removed from the cleaning roster only this morning.

Val went to bat for me. She reminded Mrs. Whitten that I am in favor to Maksim Ivanov, and that he wouldn't take kindly to the removal of my position at a building he predominately owns.

Her underhanded threat saw Mrs. Whitten offering me a cleaning roster consisting of the toilets in the staff locker room, the service elevator, a small handful of offices on the lower floor, and any silverware Val's full-time team can't keep up with.

The hours won't be close to what they once were, but since I can't stomach the idea of spending Ark's money, I'm considering accepting them.

"Can I give you an answer tomorrow?"

If I learned anything from my brief relationship with Ark, it is that living life in the fast lane doubles your odds of crashing.

"Of course." Val gathers up the documents from our meeting before heading for the door.

Since Mrs. Whitten didn't want to encourage other employees to break the nonfraternization policy with the hope of a "massive payout," our meeting this morning was held in one of the communal offices in the lobby. This one is poky, and the ventilation is horrid, but since it is surrounded by two-way mirrors, my second dressing-down was done without witnesses.

I fling my eyes to Val when she asks, "Do you need a ride home?"

"No," I reply, shaking my head. "I was just going to hang around until Tillie finishes school. It'll save an extra bus fare."

When a shameful sigh rumbles in my chest, Val smiles at me like I'm not pathetic. "Take all the time you need, both now and with the job offer."

She strays her eyes around three of the rooms circling the surveillance-type pod. Numerous cleaning staff are polishing silverware for an upcoming event. My heart wants to pretend it is clueless who is hosting the first gala in the Chrysler building in over a decade, but my head is cruel and vindictive. It has reminded my heart a hundred times already about Ark's upcoming birthday celebration, and it has been barely seventy-two hours since I last saw him.

"You're better than this, Mara," Val says, forcing my focus back to her. "You always have been."

After a second smile, she leaves me alone to ponder.

I watch my once-coworkers for several minutes while considering Mrs. Whitten's new job offer. The delivery Ark must have organized before he decided I wasn't worth his time anymore will keep our tummies full for months, but it won't help with the rent and utilities for my apartment.

Without stable income, I'll go under in less than a month, so I have no choice. I have to stuff my tail between my legs and accept Mrs. Whitten's scraps until I find something more suitable.

It isn't ideal, but again, I am still better off than some people.

I could have to buy votes instead of achieving them in a respectful way.

I sigh heavily, hating my vindictiveness.

I know Ark's game plan. He spelled it out in black and white only days ago, but it hurt like hell when I saw a news article this morning about his rekindling relationship with Veronika.

Val was quick to snatch up records I am no longer privy to see, but she wasn't fast enough for me to miss Veronika's name back on the guest register of Ark's apartment.

Since I am no longer a part of that team, I'm clueless as to whether her room is still the one on the opposite side of Ark's apartment, or if she shifted her things into the main room.

Just contemplating them being cozy has me reconsidering my intent to work in this building. It hurt reading a headline. I wouldn't survive witnessing it in person.

I'm so worked up that I tear my jacket while stuffing my arms into the openings. My coat is old and from several seasons ago, but I'm on the verge of crying while taking in the unrepairable tear, and the probability worsens when the hairs on my nape suddenly stand to attention.

A shadowed figure is blocking the entryway of the only room not taken up by cleaning staff. Although my body shouldn't know who the figure is, it identifies him two seconds before a light flicking on reveals a face I've missed ogling the past three days.

Ark enters the conference room from the entrance I used to serve him coffee. He isn't alone. Veronika is at his side, wearing a dress similar to the one I saw her pictured in earlier today. It clings to her curves, and with its coloring pairing with Ark's swanky tie, they represent the perfect powerhouse couple Ark wants the media to believe they are.

My molars grind when Veronika cozies into Ark's side like she's afraid of entering a room without a big, strong man at her side.

Her damsel-in-distress routine is cut short when Ark thanks her for her assistance before freeing himself from her clutch. "I'll have Rafael organize a car for you."

She pouts at him. "Are you sure you don't want me to stay?" Her voice is irritating, and I'm glad I don't need to hide my grimace like Ark. The two-way mirror I'm camped behind hides it on my behalf.

I hear Ark's frustration in his tone, but the velvety rasp of his voice still scalds my skin like UVs on a hot summer's day when he says, "I'm sure. This should only take a minute. Then we can..."

A current zaps through me when his eyes suddenly snap to the two-way mirror. The sparks his stare instigate are electric, sending heat roaring through me.

I'm burning at the stake, but since Ark would rather his incineration occur without an audience member who could potentially ruin his campaign for office, he guides Veronika back toward the exit.

Fury burns hotter than the lust scorching my veins when Veronika swoops in for a quick peck when Ark holds open the door for her. Her puckered lips display their desperateness to touch him in any way, not to mention the lusty gleam in her eyes.

I fight like hell to keep my feet rooted to the floor when a door closing harshly draws my eyes back to Ark. We're alone, as the magnetizing pull trying to draw us together announces, and although there is a two-way mirror separating us, Ark stares straight at me as if there isn't.

I return his watch, confused, angry, and incredibly aroused.

There's still so much tension, so much energy. I feel seconds from combusting, and the flames aren't solely from my half of the room.

Ark shoves his hands in his pockets, striving to convey unity between his head and his heart.

He can't fool me.

Mutual attraction drew us together, but something much more profound pulled us under.

I'm dangerously close to forcing Ark to admit that with me, but I lose the chance when the door opposite him pops open and Rafael enters with an equally attractive brunette.

She races to Ark's side with her hand held out in offering, her footing almost a stumble. "Mr. Orlov, thank you for agreeing to meet with me. I am aware your time is extremely stretched, so I won't keep you long."

Ark accepts her hand before he steals her focus with a smile. It is so breathtaking she misses the head nudge he issues Rafael, oblivious that he wouldn't have accepted her handshake if it didn't service his needs.

He wants me removed from a meeting that seems more important to him than I ever was, and I have enough self-respect not to pretend otherwise.

I'm halfway out the door before Rafael can acknowledge Ark's silent demand to remove me from the premises, and heartbroken enough to make a pledge to never return.

40

ARKADIY

*T*he instant Rafael walks through the door concealing Mara from me, I yank my hand out of Detective Pascall's grasp and stuff it into my pocket. I didn't accept her offer of a handshake to facilitate the suspicious groove between her brows. I did it so I could announce to Rafael that the interview I organized was being witnessed by the last person I want to know about my crimes.

Rafael must be able to read minds. I barely nudged my head to the two-way mirror I was seconds from squashing Mara up against and kissing her silly when his arrival broke the spell Mara's presence forever places on me. But he understood the urgency on my face within a second and implemented immediate actions to ratify the injustice.

He's done the same multiple times over the past three days.

I would have folded by now if he hadn't.

I can't be in the same room with Mara and not itch to touch her. It is an impossible task. Even drunk and belligerent, I could barely hold back the urge Friday night. I remained holed up in the bathroom for not even thirty seconds before I sprinted for the exit.

If the elevator had made it to the underground garage fast enough, I would have stopped Mara from leaving that night. Then I would have fallen to my knees and begged for forgiveness, and all the work my team has been undertaking for the past several days would have been pointless.

This has nothing to do with my political campaign, and everything to do with the woman I fell in love with on sight.

Needing to get my head into game mode, I gesture, with the hand not stuffed in my pocket, for Detective Pascall to sit at one of the chairs around the conference room table.

"Please, call me Sanya."

She flashes me credentials to assure me that I'm speaking with a professional before she takes a seat and removes a notepad from the breast pocket of her jacket.

"Water?" I ask, attempting to display I'm not the slightest bit nervous about our meeting.

When she shakes her head, I fill one glass before taking a seat opposite her.

"If this is in regard to an increase in media presence over the past three weeks, I can assure you my department is implementing measures to reduce the disruption to residents in the building as we speak."

"It isn't regarding that." I speak with a professional edge that gives no indication I am affiliated with gangsters. "But I'll be sure to pass your message on to Mr. Ivanov the next time I speak with him."

Maksim Ivanov is a gangster in every meaning of the word. He also owns a majority of the apartments in my building. We met once, but it was too brief to determine how indebted he is to Mara, and if that debt would transfer to me if it were in Mara's best interests. But I'm not opposed to tossing his name into the ring if it'll make the flames less scorching.

"Then what is our meeting regarding?" It is an effort for her to keep disdain from her voice when she says, "I have criminals to catch."

Her innuendo has a double meaning, and I'm done pretending it doesn't.

"I am a private man, Ms. Pascall. If someone wants to know something about me, I prefer a direct approach."

Unwillingly, my eyes stray to the two-way mirror.

Mara thinks our downfall is because she pushed for answers. I know that isn't close to the truth. Her ability to disarm me is one of her greatest assets.

"I do not appreciate when my privacy and the privacy of those closest to me are blatantly disrespected." I was standing in front of a large contingency of media, preparing to announce my forfeit of the presidential race, when Darius announced there was a detective snooping around the premises, asking questions about Mara.

"It is *Detective* Pascall," Sanya snaps out, impressing me with her gall. "And I've been trying to approach you for almost two weeks now. My calls have been left unanswered, hence me needing to dig a little deeper."

She has me there, but I act coy. "I will be sure to have a word with my secretary."

"Thank you." She smiles evilly before flipping her interrogation on its head. "What is your involvement with Miskaela Palkova?"

"Who?" I reply, acting daft.

It is all an act. Dr. Babkin's name was revealed by Mara an hour after I was handed a list of his victims' names by a reporter who had been sold information on Mara's previous name. He couldn't run the story because Mara was underage when she was abused and, as such, is protected by strict victim laws.

The reporter's intel suggested there could be recordings of Dr. Babkin's "sessions" with his victims, but confirmation was only achieved when I left Mara's apartment with the full intention of returning as soon as possible.

Mara wasn't much older than Tillie when her speech therapist added a hands-on approach to their twice-weekly sessions. At the start, it was an innocent finger slip while showing Mara how to hold her tongue while speaking. It took a couple of years for him to progress to more risqué moves.

As Mara hinted last week, the abuse didn't truly start until Dr. Babkin approached her family outside of office hours.

In the footage I watched, he was quick to assure Mara what they were doing was approved by her father whenever she questioned him.

"Remember, your father gave me permission to do *anything* necessary to stop your silly stutter."

I stopped watching from then. The damage to my psyche had already been done, but some good came from the travesty. I no longer need proof that Mara can trust me with Tillie. The evidence was right in front of me.

I didn't see Mara in that footage. I saw Tillie, and every sly look Dr. Babkin hit her with had me desperate to dig him up and revive him just so I could kill him again.

I've never wanted to hurt a man as much as I did in the seconds leading to Rafael switching off the footage and sending Darius's laptop sailing across the cab of my town car, and I was given the chance to do precisely that only hours later.

I'm drawn from dangerous thoughts when Detective Pascall repeats, "Miskaela Palkova?"

My anger that she is endeavoring to drag Mara into a fight she doesn't belong in makes my reply dry and full of deceit. "I don't know who that is."

"Oh..." She can't pull off a daft expression. She looks constipated. "Then why were you seen getting in a cab with her last month?"

My jaw flexes when she pulls out the image that forced me to keep my desires on the back burner for two weeks. Not once has this image worked in my favor. It has slapped me in the face time and time again, and I see it doing the same now as well.

"This is you, isn't it?" She taps on the image of me sliding in the back of a cab on Mara and Tillie's heels. "It sure looks like you."

"It is me," I agree, lost as to where she is going with this, but confident I won't like the direction she takes. "But I still don't know who Miskaela Palkova is."

"She"—she points to Mara—"is Miskaela Palkova."

"Oh." My daft expression is far more convincing than hers. "Then why didn't you just say that?" I pick up the image of Mara, Tillie, and me like my heart isn't racing before inspecting it with more diligence. "Ah. Yes. That is the woman who promised to dry clean the suit jacket her daughter had vomited on—"

"Daughter?" she interrupts. "Miskaela's child is a girl?"

I shrug, hopeful it will hide my wish to cringe. This is why I got into politics. I'm a shit actor. "Or perhaps she was her nanny. I didn't ask for details. I followed her to make sure she upheld her pledge." I scoff like it isn't absurd to ask something of someone with nothing. "My jacket was from a limited collection. I didn't want to be lumped with an excessive dry-cleaning bill when I wasn't responsible for the mess."

Detective Pascall glares at me as if I am a pig. Since I've felt nothing close to clean in the past three days, I don't display my disdain. "You followed her into a cab to make sure she paid the dry-cleaning bill of a sick child?"

"Yes."

I take a mental note to increase the pays of my security team when she flicks to a fresh page of her notepad before asking, "Do you recall the address she recited to the driver?"

I take a moment, pretending to think, before shaking my head. "No."

Sanya huffs, aware I am lying.

I hit her with a snarl like I don't appreciate being unfairly interrogated when I was of the belief that was the reason for her visit. "I followed her into the cab to ensure her offer was sincere. I exited two blocks later when she handed me enough funds to cover my dry-cleaning fee."

"She paid you with cash?" She jots down a note when I dip my chin. "Did you see her wallet? Did she have enough funds to pay for a long or short fare?"

"I don't recall." A spark of brilliance hits me. "Though I do remember her saying something about motion sickness tablets being a waste of money." I stare her dead set in the eyes. "Perhaps she was heading to the airport?"

"Perhaps," she mimics through clenched teeth before announcing I have every right to have my defenses up. "Murderers are known to skip town after committing a crime. They rarely stay to clean up their mess."

I swallow harshly. "Murderer?" When she nods, I laugh as if death is humorous. "I can assure you, Detective Pascall, there wasn't a single droplet of blood on Ms. Palkova." When suspicion hardens her features, I add, "I am a man, and she is a gorgeous woman. Of course I looked."

"Was this... *look* long enough to spot stains over six years old?"

Her question deposits me into the middle of the Amazon without a life vest in sight. I can't speak, swallow, or move. I can't do anything but stare in bewilderment.

While smirking smugly, loving my frozen status, Detective Pascall stores away her notepad before filling her empty hand with a business card. "If you hear anything about Ms. Palkova's whereabouts or think of anything that may come in handy with my investigation, you can reach me here." She drags her finger under her cell phone number scribbled on the back of her card.

After a final smirk, she leaves without so much as a backward glance.

Just as fast, I race to the elevator and select the floor below the penthouse. I'm swimming in waters outside of my depth, and Mara taught me it is better to stretch for a life jacket than unnecessarily drown.

"That isn't wise," a voice sounds from a speaker above my head. "Doc worked the nightshift, and Maksim is paranoid as fuck about her sleep schedule. If you wake her, you'll be a dead man."

I raise my eyes to the blinking contraption above my head before saying, "This isn't about me. It is for Mara."

A chair creaking into place booms around the elevator before, "I'm gonna need more information. Mara is in favor to the Ivanovs"—the possessiveness in his tone pisses me off—"but you'll need more than being on Maksim's good side if you fuck with his wife's sleeping schedule." Humor highlights his tone more than anger during his next sentence. "Forcing him to pull out mid-nap will fuck with her sleeping schedule."

I'm lost, and it is heard in my tone. "It's urgent."

When he hums like he handles fabricated murder charges on the daily, I push out, "Detective Pascall was meant to take my confession for a murder charge, not pin one on Mara."

He cusses before the button I selected almost a minute ago finally illuminates.

41

MARA

"*O*ur relationship has been a whirlwind, but gosh..." A quick stab of jealousy ripples the air as Veronika locks her loved-up eyes with the camera and says, "When you know, you know."

"And you know?" I have mad respect for the reporter when she murmurs, "*Already.*"

Veronika's eyes narrow into thin slits. "Whatever do you mean? We've been dating for almost a month."

"A month?" The entertainment reporter doing live interviews with the attendees of Ark's fortieth birthday checks a notepad before saying, "My calculations are closer to a week."

"That's just silly," Veronika replies, her voice suddenly not so chipper. "We had a slight bump at the start of our courtship, but Ark took care of *that* in less than a weekend. It's been smooth sailing ever since." She leans in close like there aren't millions of viewers hanging off her every word. "Between you and me, you'll find out just how serious things are later tonight."

When she wiggles her fingers to highlight the only one missing a ring is her engagement finger, I switch off the television and dump the remote on my scratched coffee table.

My decision to turn down Mrs. Whitten's position was challenging, but the footage broadcast across the globe tonight exposes that staying would have been more difficult.

It hurt standing across from Ark for five minutes, so I wouldn't have survived being under the same roof as him day in and day out. I would have continually wondered about the reason behind his decision to pull on the reins and possibly take responsibility for issues not solely mine to bear.

I pushed Ark to open up to me, but it seems as if there are more significant issues beyond revealed secrets keeping us apart.

If I had the courage, I would seek answers.

Since I don't, I shoot my hands up to my hair and groan.

I'm close to pulling my hair out when a little voice reminds me that I'm not alone to sulk in my misery as I have been for the past week. "He doesn't love her."

I drag my eyes away from the black television screen to Tillie, who is sitting on the floor, making fan-cast collages from the glossy magazines Mrs. Lichard devours every week.

Tillie continues cutting Veronika out of an image of her and Ark at a charity dinner earlier this week. "I don't even think he likes her."

"Of course he likes her," I deny. "He wouldn't date her if he didn't like her."

"Then why won't he let her touch him?"

My heart thumps into my ears when she places down the magazine she's dismantling to find one under a stack of many. She flicks to a two-page spread of Ark and Veronika's courtship before highlighting an image not even a photoshop expert could piece together.

The sign at the back of Ark's and Veronika's heads don't match since several words are missing from the middle of the slogan.

"It's the same in every photo." My heart slowly crawls out of the hole it was buried in last week when she flicks through endless articles printed about Ark over the last few days. "He won't touch her. He refuses."

The image at the top of the stack shows Ark's hand hovering inches from Veronika's back. Even if she suddenly stopped walking down the red carpet she was commanding like a model does a catwalk, his hand wouldn't have gotten close to making contact.

"Then there's this image." My heart launches into my throat when she thrusts a magazine to within an inch of my face. "He had no trouble touching *this* woman."

Tears prick my eyes when I remove the magazine from her grasp to drink in an image I had no clue had been taken. The reporter of the story is claiming the headless, almost X-rated photograph is of Ark and Veronika seeking outfits for their alleged upcoming engagement party. I know that isn't true.

The person photographed with Ark isn't Veronika. It's me. My heart knows this, and so does Tillie, because if she hadn't barged into the changing room where Ark was assisting me with removing the dress he had purchased for me, the paparazzo's shot would have been far more risqué.

"That's you," Tillie announces, unashamed. She licks her lips before locking her too-worldly-for-her-age eyes with mine. "He won't touch her"—she growls, baring teeth while lowering her eyes to Veronika's photo—"but he had no trouble touching you. That has to mean something."

There's too much hope firing through me not to try to downplay it. "Touching someone without permission isn't kosher. Perhaps he's trying to be respectful of Veronika's boundaries."

Her brows furrow. "So he asked you if he could kiss you before he did?"

I cough to smooth out the scratchiness impinging my throat from her question before acting daft. "I beg your pardon?" I say with a laugh, stupidly nervous.

"When Ark kissed you in the doorway of our home, did he ask first?"

I'm tempted to lie, but I can't. "No, he didn't."

Tillie smiles in gratitude for my honesty. "Because you wanted him to kiss you as much as he wanted to kiss you."

"Til—"

"Just say it, Mom. Admit he wanted to touch you."

"I... I..." I've got nothing, so I revert to a tactic I will always use to get my way. I remind her that I am her mother before anything else. "It is almost bedtime. Have you brushed your teeth yet?"

"No, but—"

"No buts, young lady. Oral health is important." I stack her magazines into a pile, announcing the end of her collaging for today, before nudging my head to the bathroom. "I will join you in a minute."

She huffs, but that is as far as her protest goes.

As her stomps sound down the hallway, I rub at the kink my neck hasn't been without the past week. It's only been seven days since Ark pressed on the brakes, but it honestly feels like ten years.

I'm angry and hormonal and not fit for visitors, so why the hell is someone banging on my door like they're about to conduct a raid?

I try not to let Tillie's assumption that Ark dislikes Veronika so much he refuses to touch her quicken my steps, but I race for the door so fast I almost trip over my feet.

As my heart is hoping, an Orlov stands on the other side of my door. It isn't the one I want, but thankfully, it isn't the one who could give Veronika's claim that I was just a bump in Ark's path validity.

"Riley... what are you doing here?" I peer past her to make sure she is alone before opening my door further, wordlessly inviting her inside.

She enters slowly, her footing unsteady. "Is Tillie here?"

Her concern for my daughter reminds me that the actions of others should never be placed on the shoulders of a victim.

I nod before gesturing my head to the bathroom. "She's brushing her teeth."

"Okay. Good." She takes a deep breath before blurting out a ton of words without stopping for air. "Everything happening is my fault. When Ark came to see me, I pushed him to admit the truth and used you as an example about how telling isn't always a bad thing. I thought I got through to him. The way he spoke about you and the things he said made me hopeful your relationship would get better, and then..." She stops, more to hold back a sob than breathe. "I ruined everything, and I don't know how to make it right."

"It isn't your job to make it right."

"Yes, it is," she counters, her eyes wet and pleading. "He loves you, Mara, but instead of living his happily-ever-after with you, he's going to propose to that witch to protect you."

It hurts to hear that he's planning to propose to Veronika, but I'm too confused to dwell on jealousy. "How will that protect me?"

For someone seemingly capable of talking underwater, it takes Riley several long seconds to whisper, "From what I overheard, Veronika is as bad as our mother..." Lines burrow in her forehead. "My grandmother." She nudges her head to the door barely concealing the faint hum of a child brushing her teeth. "She has images and is threatening to expose the nature of Tillie's conception to her millions of followers."

I'm disgusted at the lengths some women will go. "She can't do that. There are laws against naming underage victims of a crime."

"Veronika doesn't care. She thinks she's untouchable."

I almost *pfft* until I recall how much power she is currently yielding. She has a man as powerful and wealthy as Ark bowing at her feet. I'd feel above the law as well if I were her.

Riley's hands shake when she gathers mine and squeezes them tight. "Please come to the party with me. You're the only person capable of getting through to Ark. He will listen to you."

"I can't." I want to believe her theory that I have more power over Ark than Veronika does, but I would be foolish to do that. "If I go and Veronika does as she's threatening, it will hurt Tillie. She doesn't know about her father—"

I choke back a sob when a faint voice from behind whispers, "Yes, I do." As my wet eyes bounce between a pair almost identical, Tillie slowly exits the bathroom. "You named me Matilda because that's the team you wanted to play for when you went pro. You said they were the cream of the crop when you attended an international comp just shy of your fourteenth birthday." A tear plops down my cheek when she says, "There was only one time a Russian female soccer team played in an international tournament. It was just shy of your fourteenth birthday." She switches some of my sad tears to tears of happiness. "We look so alike Mrs. Lichard thought I had forgotten to tell her I had started playing soccer when she saw the article I searched up on my Nintendo." She looks remorseful for my tears, and I hate myself for it. "I'm sorry, Mom. I shouldn't have snooped. I just wanted to know who my dad was and why you never spoke about him."

"Oh, baby. It's okay. I should have never kept it from you." I pull her into my chest so my shirt can catch her tears. "You didn't do anything wrong. I need you to know that, okay? I should have been honest. Then you wouldn't have needed to snoop."

God. I hate myself. The name on her birth certificate is heavily associated with charges filed against Dr. Babkin in the months following his death. Although he was dead, there was plenty of evidence for a civil suit.

His victims were awarded a majority of his multimillion-dollar estate two years after his death. I didn't come forward to claim my share because I had already been given my reward for years of hurt.

I had a daughter with a smile brighter than the sun.

My heart pains wondering how Tillie handled such harsh news without any support.

It must have torn her to shreds.

As I walk her toward the couch, I ask, "Are you okay? Do you want to talk about anything you saw? You can ask me anything you want, and I will tell you the truth. I promise."

Her strength shocks me when she lifts her head to peer up at me. Her cheeks are tear-free. "I have a handful of questions."

With her reply seemingly unfinished, I say, "But..."

"But..." It isn't time for dramatics, but Tillie wouldn't be Tillie if she didn't test out her acting skills at any given opportunity. "They can wait until after we come back."

I stare at her with my brows pulled together. *We're going somewhere?*

The truth hits me hard and fast when she nudges her head to the left. I was so focused on making sure my secrets didn't irrefutably scar my daughter that I forgot we have a guest.

"Riley..." *Gosh.* She knows exactly what Tillie is going through and what she could possibly go through in the future, and I'm grateful she was here for this.

I doubt she will ever hear the words I spoke to Tillie from her "mother," but I need her to know that Mrs. Orlov's response will never be the norm.

She is also the best person to help me guide Tillie through this, second only to the man who commenced fighting for her before he had even officially met her.

My heart rate soars when it dawns on me what I must do.

I need to make this right.

I need Tillie, Ark, and Riley to know that they didn't do anything wrong, and I know exactly where to start my campaign to make things right.

While pulling an invitation out of the drawer I stuffed it in last week, I say, "You are to stay by mine or Riley's side the entire time. No questions asked."

Tillie fights not to mentally high-five herself.

Riley's eyes widen to the size of saucers.

"Me? You want to leave her under my care?" When I nod, Riley scoffs. "I don't think that's a good idea."

I lessen the terror hardening her features with ten short words. "A mother knows who she can leave her children with."

"Yeah, but I'm... *different*. I'm—"

Her eyes snap to mine when I interrupt. "Trustworthy. I trust you, Riley."

With her shock too high to communicate, Tillie rejoins our conversation. "And she really hates trashy teen dramas, so it is the perfect time for us to binge-watch *Heartbreak High* on my Nintendo while she gets her man."

Determined to get her way, Tillie snatches up her Nintendo and drags Riley out of our apartment before a single protest can leave her lips.

Our plan hits a snag when we exit my building. "I can't let you do whatever you're planning to do, Ms. Malenkov. Ark—"

"Isn't giving orders tonight, Darius. So how about you either step aside and let us hail a cab, or drive us to where we need to go."

"Riley—"

"It's Ms. Orlov," Riley snaps out, her sass giving Tillie's a run for its money. "And the last time I checked, *Orlov* & Associates pays your wages."

I thought Ark was bossy. He's got nothing on Darius's stubbornness. "I have orders—"

"That have now changed." Rafael left me to drown only days ago, but I'll take any life vest he throws out now if it gets me to Ark's birthday party before he nosedives his career for someone unworthy of his time. "Take them wherever they need to go, Darius."

"Thank you," I mouth to Rafael before slipping into the back of the SUV Darius is holding open for us.

42

ARKADIY

"How long will you need?" I twist to face a full-length mirror like I didn't ask a question before fixing my tie.

Maksim's lead hacker, Easton, peers up at me before replying, "An hour. Two at most."

I shift on my feet to face Maksim when he asks, "Do you think you will be able to keep her occupied that long?" He holds out his hands like my gang affiliations are as notable as his when I snarl at him. "I'm just asking. I've seen the way you look at her. You look like you need to shower every time she's near."

"*Because I do*," I murmur to myself. I take a quick swallow before getting back down to business. "What will happen when you get the footage?"

"It will be corrupted before it spreads a virus through any server that has previously played it or stored it." Easton's southern twang gets a pinch of unease to it. "Are you sure you don't want a copy for safe-keeping?"

I swallow the brick his question lodged in my throat before jerking up my chin. "I'm sure." I've seen it once. I don't need to see it again. I need it destroyed. "Get word to me once it's done."

Not looking up from a bank of monitors, Easton nods.

I hold out my hand in offer to Maksim. I don't do touch. I can't stand it from anyone but Mara, but since his assistance will help her as much as it will me, I push aside my neurosis and man up as I should have decades ago.

Maksim accepts my offer of a handshake, his lips tugging at one side. "Still think you should take my advice. Marry her and then fess up. It worked for me."

I laugh like I haven't given his advice some serious consideration over the past few days. The only reason I haven't taken it is because it is the easy way out, the cheat's way. I've skirted my obligations for almost thirty years. It is time to be the man Mara deserves.

I just wish I didn't have to give her up to achieve that.

43

MARA

*B*ulbs flash and reporters shout when Darius pulls our blacked-out SUV to the curb at the front of the Chrysler building.

"Go down the side. We can enter via the service entrance."

He nods his approval of Riley's suggestion before slowly maneuvering us through a swarm of paparazzi striving to capture the arrival of Ark's guests.

Regretfully, over half a dozen follow us down the alleyway.

I cuss softly when Darius says, "They recognize the tags."

"I'll distract them."

I try to stop Riley from exiting, panicked about the questions she could face, but she slips out before I can.

As expected, the press swarms her like bees at a hive. Mercifully, they question her about her connection to Wilfred Iwona and her prediction about her brother's impending engagement more than her personal life.

The hard-hitting questions don't come until after Tillie and I have slipped out the back of the SUV and snuck through the heavily guarded side entrance door.

"Stay with Riley," I order Darius, bossing him around as if he works for me.

He follows my command without protest. "Yes, ma'am."

With the party occurring in the ballroom in the left half of the building, our walk to the elevator is relatively quiet. We encounter only one person, and she seems to know me better than Arkadiy.

My pulse thumps in my ears when the middle-aged woman we just bypassed asks, "Miskaela, is that you?"

After tugging Tillie under my arm, I continue for the elevator, my steps more a jog.

"I haven't seen you in years," my accoster continues, incapable of backing down even with me making it obvious I am not who she thinks I am.

Miskaela died years ago.

I am now Mara, a woman who will do anything to protect her child.

As I struggle to breathe through my panic, the stranger continues her trip down memory lane while I jab at the elevator call button, praying for it to hurry up. "What was it? Your twelfth birthday party, right? You had the jumping castle and a magician. All the children in the street were in awe."

"You had a jumping castle for your twelfth birthday?" Tillie whispers, doubling the output of my heart. "I thought you said you didn't have any parties when you were a child."

With my cover blown and the thudding steps of my haggler announcing she will follow us to the end of Earth if it is the only way she will get answers, I lower my eyes to Tillie and murmur, "I said I didn't have any *memorable* parties. That's different from not having one."

Dr. Babkin's grooming commenced at my tenth birthday party. My father blocked the only exit of his office two short years later.

I hit Tillie with a pleading look for us to leave our conversation until we're not under scrutiny of someone who could irreparably scar her before I spin to face the voice surfacing the skeletons of my past faster than I forced Ark's out of their hiding spot last week.

My scold is nowhere near as burning when I recognize the kind eyes of the lady approaching us. Mrs. Bombae was the neighborhood grandmother. If it wasn't for her guidance and understanding, I doubt I would have ever had the courage to pack my bags and run.

I confessed to her before anyone else that I thought I might have been pregnant, and although the next person I told handed me a ton of repercussions I could have never anticipated, Mrs. Bombae was not at fault for that. She thought my parents were the good Christian people her and her husband were.

No one could have predicted how evil their blood runs.

My voice rattles with nerves when I say, "Mrs. Bombae... H-hello."

She smiles, pleased I remember her, before her glistening eyes lower to Tillie. "Hello, dear. Who do we have here?"

"This is Matilda." I tug Tillie in close like we're not almost the same height before finalizing my introduction. "My-my daughter."

"Daughter?" Shock registers but she is quick to mask it with delight. "How lovely. She looks just like you, Miskaela." She bobs down to meet Tillie eye-to-eye like she did when I was her age. "Do you think you might play soccer like your mother? Did she tell you how she was almost scouted by a famous team all the way from Australia?"

"She did." Tillie nods so fast that she makes me dizzy and almost sends the wetness in her eyes toppling down her cheeks. "That's where she got my name from. She said since she couldn't play for the Matildas, she'd raise one."

Mrs. Bombae giggles. "That's such a lovely story, Matilda. Thank you so much for sharing it with me."

She stares and stares and stares until my stomach's grumble pulls her from her thoughts.

"The Palkova genes are strong with this one, Miskaela... *extremely* strong." After another lengthy stare, she returns her focus to Tillie. "How old are you, dear?"

"I'm t—"

"She just t-turned eight." I pull Tillie in tighter, my clutch almost cruel. "She often f-forgets she just had a birthday, so she says sh-she's turning eight. But she's eight now. Just turned eight."

I'm blubbering, but it can't be helped. I know the look she is giving me. It is the same one my mother gave me after taking in the positive pregnancy test she bought me.

She thinks she is looking at my father's child instead of his grandchild.

"We ne-need to go. It was lovely seeing you again," I lie.

We make it four steps away before a confused whisper stops me. "If Matilda and you are the reason your father is visiting Myasnikov, why wouldn't he just say that?"

Bile burns the back of my throat as I force words through the fear caked there. "My father is here?"

She nods gently. Confusion is all over her face. "I saw him last week. Friday afternoon in this very lobby. I assumed he was here on business, but when I approached him, he said his visit was personal and that he would appreciate it if I kept my knowledge of it on the down-low."

I feel sick, incredibly ill. The Chrysler building is only blocks from Tillie's school.

The monster from my childhood was within walking distance of my daughter.

Oh my god, how could I have been so reckless?

I swore to protect my daughter, and I failed.

Mrs. Bombae's dainty laugh pulls me from my alarmed state. "He was so secretive he made me promise that I wouldn't tell your mother that I had seen him. I told him he'd have to buy me an extremely expensive steak for me to even consider his request." Her pinched brows make her wrinkles more noticeable. "I was meant to have dinner with him on Monday. He never showed up."

"Because he's missing. Presumed dead."

The brunette who rushed to Ark's side last week joins our conversation. She seems to know me, and she doesn't appear to be a fan of mine.

"The circumstances of his disappearance are eerily similar to the disappearance of a man six years ago." Her eyes drop to Tillie for half a second before they return to my face. They're not as cruel now but extremely unhinged. "Perhaps you've heard of him." There's no remorse in her eyes, no hesitation on her face. With two short sentences, she hacks my confidence down to a penance like I'm the criminal. "Luba Babkin. Does his name ring a bell?"

Tillie attempts to bite at the bait she's dangling in front of me, so I speak quickly and clearly. "I have heard of him, but I am under no obligation to announce the reason as to why my name is associated with his, Ms..."

"Detective." She flashes her credentials too fast for me to take in. "Detective Sanya Pascall from Trudny PD."

The fact she is a police officer strips the last of my understanding. She knows my rights as a victim, yet she is attempting to exploit them in public.

"If you have questions in regard to my relationship with Dr. Babkin, I suggest you contact a victim advocacy lawyer before approaching me again."

My steps are thwarted for the second time when she says, "And your father? Who should I contact about his disappearance slash murder? You... or your billionaire boyfriend rich enough to cover for you?"

I'm too stunned by her accusation to remain quiet. "I had nothing to do with my father's disappearance—"

"So you're saying it was him?" Detective Pascall nudges her head to an image announcing whose birthday is being celebrated today.

"No. Ark would never..." My words trail off when I recall Ark's reaction to finding out I had been raped.

I'm going to track down that fuck and make him regret the day he laid eyes on you.

I'm going to kill him.

Then there were his other multiple promises of protection as our wonderfully beautiful twenty-four hours of reprieve from the world went on.

He swore he'd never let anyone hurt me again. That he would do everything in his power to keep Tillie and me safe.

Would that have included murder?

I want to say no, but the evidence is worrying.

Scarcely breathing, I sling my eyes to Mrs. Bombae, as desperate to interrogate her as Detective Pascall is to interrogate me. Her timeline of my father's last known movements is damning. It could lead to a conviction if handed to the wrong person.

Before I can utter a syllable, the elevator doors I begged to miraculously open only minutes ago finally do, exposing both the man of the hour and the man I am almost certain maimed for me.

44

ARKADIY

*S*he knows.

One glance into Mara's pretty eyes exposes everything.

She knows what I did and how far I will go to protect her. She knows my deepest, darkest secret that has nothing to do with my childhood, and everything to do with ensuring her daughter wasn't forced to walk down the same dark corridor we were dragged down when we were children.

She knows, and I am as relieved as I am scared.

I take a moment to try to determine the cause of the groove between Mara's dark brows—*is it fear or relief?*—before I shut down the personal side of my head and rule with the power I once craved as much as I now do Mara's touch.

With a click of my fingers, I demand security to my side. "Please escort *Mrs.* Babkin from the premises. If she attempts re-entry, contact Myasnikov PD to advise them a *civilian* is impersonating an officer of the law."

Sanya's lips twist wryly but she remains quiet, aware she has no ruling here. She doesn't in the Trudny District anymore, either. She just fails to exert that she was let go from her position if it gets her foot in the door. I only found out when she pushed me so hard I had no choice but to shove back.

Charges are close to being filed.

It won't be my name on the arrest warrant. *Yet.*

Once Sanya is walked through the side entrance of the lobby, I shift my focus back to Mara. My heart is pounding, and my palms are drenched with sweat. I want to rush to her, to wipe away the tears on her cheeks, but I can't get my feet to move.

What if she pulls away?

What is she's so frightened of the monster I've become that she stammers while speaking to me?

God, please don't let her stutter.

It will kill me to know she fears me. That's why I pulled back. Just the thought of her being scared of me had me willing to serve life behind bars... or worse, a life without her in it.

I won't survive knowing she's frightened of me.

The shutter of cameras clicking draws me out of my stupor. Almost robotically, I push the call button on the elevator and gesture for Mara and Tillie to enter when the doors ding open.

I hold my breath when their feet remain rooted on the glossy marble floor, praying Mara still feels safe enough in my presence to enter the small confines of an elevator with me.

She stares at me, unmoving and unspeaking. Then, just as my lungs are about to scream for air, she unsteadily steps forward.

I snap my eyes shut and suck in the scent of her shampoo before following her inside the elevator. It kills me, but I stand at the far right of the car, giving her the space I'm confident she needs to feel safe in my presence.

I am the monster my mother warned I would become. But only because it was the only way I could keep them safe.

When we reach my apartment, we move through the motions similar to the ones we undertook last week when she was attacked. But this time, with Tillie's inclusion, we add additional steps I haven't undertaken since Karolina's suicide.

We make popcorn and start up the short-throw projector before selecting a channel I had installed when I had the deed of my apartment placed in Mara's name.

Tillie can feel the tension—it is too blistering to ignore—but after a brief hug with her mother and a quick smirk of encouragement flashed my way, she settles onto the sofa to watch one of her favorite Australian television programs and nervously nibble on her fingernails.

I dip my chin in thanks to Riley when she slips into the living room as Mara and I exit it.

Our steps to my third-floor office are done in silence. I won't lie. The quiet is killing me. It is so eerily similar to the lack of noise that projected from the bathroom Karolina had entered to wash off the tearstains our stepfather's sentencing had caused her cheeks.

The slash marks on her wrists when I found her made it obvious that she had been crying.

The truth hangs heavily between Mara and me when we enter my office. I leave the doors wide open, uncaring that my confession may be overheard.

I have every intention of handing myself in. I just can't do that until I'm confident Mara is safe—both physically and emotionally.

The wayward revenge plot concocted by Dr. Babkin's wife, who was left with next to nothing when her husband's victims sued his estate in a civil suit, is compromising her safety.

"Is she..." Mara tightens her arms over her chest, folding into herself. "Is she really Dr. Babkin's wife?"

I nod, incapable of speaking. Although she more stumbled over her sentence than stuttered her words, I'm still fearful some of the alarm in her eyes centers around me and what I did to protect her.

"Why is she here? What does she want with me?"

When she sways, I gesture for her to sit before she falls.

She refuses.

Not because she is stubborn.

Because she is strong.

"I can do this, Ark. You can trust me to know how much I can and can't handle."

Confident I am seconds from losing my battle not to touch her, too enamored by the sturdiness of her backbone not to react, I stuff my hands into my pockets before telling her everything I know.

"My team is still working through some facts, but from what we have gathered, your father was blackmailing Dr. Babkin for years before his death." She doesn't speak, move, or blink. She remains perfectly still. "He paid him two million dollars over a three-year period while you were under his care and for several years after it ceased." Her chest expands with a deep breath when I say, "Dr. Babkin was disinclined to pay once you... *became of age.*"

I wish I was better with my words, but it is a struggle to speak and not want to go on a rampage. Anger is burning through me, making it hard to do anything but flex and unflex my fists.

I am only achieving the impossible because I need Mara to know why I did what I did. I need her to know I didn't have a choice. Protecting her and Tillie was my only priority—it still is.

"Your father wasn't as willing to let things slide. He continued blackmailing Dr. Babkin until his death... and then he went after the money the courts set aside for his daughter."

Mara's hand shoots up to cover her mouth. "Dr. Babkin had a daughter?"

I nod. "Yes. She is around a year or two older than Tillie."

Her eyes search for answers to the question she doesn't want to ask. When she fails to get any, she proves how strong she is. "Did he...?"

She exhales a sigh, and in an instant, I know why I reacted the way I did while standing across from the man who was meant to protect her and failed.

Tears flood Mara's eyes when I confess, "Your father tried to blackmail me. He said he would release footage to the media that would hurt you if I didn't pay him three million dollars, thus not only outing your abuse for the world to see but the method of Tillie's conception as well."

She swallows past the lump in her throat to ensure her words are clear while asking, "Did you pay him?"

She gasps in a sharp breath when I nod.

It is released in a hurry when I murmur, "Then he noticed Tillie in the image that brought him to my door, and everything changed."

I move to my desk to gather the photograph that has given me more heartache than any of the scars I amassed in my childhood and hand it to Mara.

"I knew." I force my words through clenched teeth. "I knew the instant he looked at that picture what he had done to you. I could see it in his eyes, smell it on his skin. I saw the monster hiding deep inside him, and I knew he would hurt Tillie the same way if ever given the opportunity. He..."

I stop when I choke on my words, and then shake my head in anger while recalling the gleam his eyes got when he taunted me about getting Tillie's guardianship placed under his name.

"It wasn't love in his eyes when he looked at her. It was lust. It was predatory. He wanted to hurt her." I shift, needing to see her eyes when I confess to my greatest sin to date. "It happened so fast. I didn't realize what I was doing until it was too late. I killed him because I'd rather he be dead than contemplate what could have happened if he were ever near Tillie." I fall to my knees, my breaths coming out in a quiver. "And I would do it again in an instant if it were the only way I could protect her. I couldn't let him hurt her like he had hurt you. I just couldn't."

"Ark..." She stares at me like she is truly seeing me for the first time. I'd hang my head in shame if her look gave me any indication that she is ashamed or frightened of me.

Her watch isn't pronged with fear.

It's spiked with admiration.

After mirroring my pose, Mara lifts her shaky hands to my face. We share the same air when she brushes away a salty blob on my cheek I didn't realize was there before she bands her arms around my back. After tucking her head into my neck, she whispers her thanks into my ear on repeat until I stop believing that I am the villain in her story and start seeing myself as the hero.

45

MARA

*a*n uprising of emotions hits me at once when a shadow casts over the doorway of the room I'm settling Tillie in. The spare room closest to Ark's bedroom has a soft and inviting palette—*if* you exclude the inclusion of numerous Australian soap star posters tacked to the walls.

Ark's design team replicated Tillie's room to perfection. If it weren't triple the size and caked with that new furniture smell I've not experienced in years, I'd swear I was back in our apartment, slumming it with the less fortunate.

I don't mean people with no funds in their bank accounts.

I mean the people who don't have a love money can't buy.

I'd be worried Ark's request for us to spend the night was a mistake we couldn't come back from if I weren't aware how brilliantly smart he is. Barring a random photograph of two commuters sharing a cab fare, we have no known association before my father attempted to blackmail him.

As far as anyone is concerned, my father's contact, the request for a bribe, and the meetup it instigated occurred before a rogue detective put me back on Ark's radar.

My employment at the Chrysler building was always off the books, and my arrivals and departures over the past six months are wiped from the servers of this building and the many around it by Maksim's security team as per my request before I started working here.

As far as the world is concerned, Ark and I are strangers who have a hunger so strong for each other that we can see murder as a non-villainous act.

I wasn't lying when I said a mother knows who her children are safe with.

Tillie was not safe with my father. That is the sole reason I ran before she was born. I knew he would hurt her as Ark had imagined while standing across from him.

Although violence is rarely the solution, Ark reacted in the same manner I did when I saw the horrifying glint in Dr. Babkin's eyes when he tracked me down under my first alias.

I didn't have the means to hide my identity, so it didn't take much for him to find me.

He wasn't scared about possible prosecution for his crimes. He was more worried about his wife finding out about the money he had paid my father, and how he'd explain the mishap in accounting at her father's multimillion-dollar business.

He wanted me to write an affidavit that I was a willing participant during our "exchanges" and that I had both consented and was of age before our "affair" began.

His demands only stopped when the giggle of a child who was terrible at hide-and-seek alerted him to the fact that we were not alone.

It was then that I realized my mother hadn't told anyone about the positive pregnancy test that encouraged me to run. She somewhat protected me, though many years too late.

When I recognized the voice of the person banging on our motel room door, I made out to Tillie that we were playing a game. I shoved her under the mattress like it's normal for the seeker to know the hider's hiding spot before pleading for her to stay hidden.

Dr. Babkin burst into my room two seconds after I lowered the frilly bedspread until its hem tickled the carpet.

The look he gave Tillie when he told her to come out from beneath the mattress scarred me for life. I knew then and there that she wasn't safe, and I took immediate action to remove her from what I deemed a dangerous situation.

Like Ark, I don't recall much of what happened. I remember snatching up a lamp, swinging it hard enough for Dr. Babkin to fall onto the mattress Tillie had recently climbed out from under, and then collecting my minimal belongings and fleeing.

We haven't been back to the Trudny District ever since.

I never considered checking Dr. Babkin for a pulse or calling an ambulance. I ran as I am sure Ark wishes he could have after his fear got the better of him.

I smile at Ark to assure him the panic in his eyes isn't required before nodding at his mouthed question of if Tillie is asleep.

"You don't need to whisper," I say, my voice normal volume as I invite him into her room. "Tillie can sleep through a tornado."

The ache in my chest I haven't been able to shift since Ark begged us to stay the night clears away when he gently brushes back a curl flopped down the front of Tillie's forehead.

He loves her as much as I do. He's just confused as to what that means since his abuser is still a living, breathing part of his life.

With her wayward lock wrangled into submission, Ark gathers a box from a chest of drawers and hands it to me. I smile when I notice what it is. He bought Tillie a baby monitor.

I giggle. It is unexpected but very much needed. "She may never forgive us if we set this up. She appreciates her privacy. *Greatly*." I use couple terms to certify that that is what we now are. We're a team. "But I did show her the intercom and gave her a quick rundown on how it works, so she knows how to contact us if the need arises. But she has slept through the night since she was three months old, so I am confident she is out until the morning." There's no hiding my pride in my last two sentences. Tillie doesn't have nightmares because I did everything in my power to keep her sleep restful.

Now Ark has done the same.

I don't hate him for what he did. How could I? He protected my daughter when a threat presented. I could never hate someone for doing that.

Love is the only adequate word to describe my feelings about what he did.

Ark's exhale makes heating unnecessary when I slip my hand into his before guiding him out of Tillie's room. We're risking a lot spending the night together, but we both need this. We need to close out the world for twenty-four hours again and put the focus and energy we used to fight away our demons on each other.

"Mara... don't. Fuck," Ark pushes out breathlessly when a second after we enter his room, I commence removing my clothes. "This isn't why I asked you to stay. I just..."

I stare into his impossibly beautiful eyes when he struggles to express himself while I unzip my skirt and step out of it.

His chest expands with a big breath when my shirt is the next thing to go. Attraction fires through the air as the heady scent of lust wafts into my nostrils.

My body is drained both emotionally and physically, but as I said earlier, we need this.

I need to express how grateful I am for what he did to protect Tillie, and he needs to know that protecting someone you love no matter the cost doesn't make you a monster.

"Let us have this. They"—I point to the door I know he checked twice before coming to find me—"can have us tomorrow. But tonight... tonight is about us. Y-you..." I choke on a sob, and Ark is at my side in an instant.

"Don't. God." He breathes out slowly, his chest rising and falling faster than his mind works through the words he's struggling to express. "The thought of you being scared of me. It's killing me, Mara. I'll... I'll never forgive myself if I've scared you."

"Why in the world would I be scared of you? I love you, Ark."

"Don't. Fuck," he repeats. "I don't deserve it. I don't deserve you—"

I end his lies by propelling onto my tippy-toes and kissing him.

He hesitates for barely a second before he returns my embrace with just as much devotion, love, and respect. Our kiss is soul-stealing, above and beyond anything we shared.

His sacrifice gave us this.

After kissing me so tenderly I feel dizzy, Ark drags his lips down my chin and along my neck before he buries his nose into my loose locks and inhales deeply.

I washed my hair every day for a week, waiting for this moment.

"You smell"—I wait for the praise that always boosts my confidence. I get that and so much more when he finishes his sentence—"like home."

As we reacquaint our lips, we stumble back until the mattress folds my knees out from beneath me and I fall backward.

Ark catches me with one arm while the other gathers my wrists and pins them above my head. I squirm when the most intimate parts of our bodies collide before I rock my hips, grinding against the girth his pants are struggling to contain.

I barely get in two grinds when Ark's focus shifts lower. After pulling down on the cups of my bra, he licks my nipples and grazes them with his teeth before his five o'clock shadow tickles the squishy part of my stomach I've not been able to shed since giving birth.

My legs scissor when he kisses each little mark Tillie's growth caused my skin. His admiration is unmissable, and it has me teetering toward the brink of ecstasy.

Ark's thrilling kisses stop at the edge of my panties. He lifts his eyes to my face, searing me in place with a hungry stare, before he does something unexpected.

He frees my hands.

I keep them locked together and above my head when his focus shifts back to adoring my body. He kisses the bow at the top of my panties before he slowly peels them down my legs.

A tinge of self-consciousness should plague me when he stares at my pussy, but it doesn't. His stare is too hungry, too admiring, to instigate something as worthless as shame.

The praise I was seeking earlier bears down on me when he says,

"You smell so fucking good." He closes his eyes, enhancing his senses, before he flares his nostrils, sucking in the scent of my near arousal.

When his eyes open, the panic behind them earlier is gone, replaced with lust.

"I want to taste you again. Can I?"

The needy rumble of his deep timbre darts through my body, making me shake when I nod.

"Tell me, baby. Give me your words."

My nerves are too low to be heard in my voice. They're clustering in my pussy. "I want you to eat me, Ark. I need you to."

With a smirk that will highlight my dreams for years to come, he runs his index finger down the seam of my pussy before he teases my clit with his thumb.

"You have such a beautiful pussy, Mara. So pretty and pink."

My pussy sucks around him when he lowers his thumb and dips it ever so slightly into my pussy. He watches me under hooded lids, his body thrumming with as much excitement as mine is being bombarded with.

"I'll get you off like this first before bringing you to climax on my face. I need you wet enough so that my prickles don't chafe you when I eat you for dessert."

The eagerness in his voice almost sets me off. I dig my nails into my palms as the scent of my impending orgasm lingers in the air.

I moan when his thumb returns to my oversensitive clit, and he rolls it with precisely timed grinds.

One expert twang has my shoulders endeavoring to meet and my eyes rolling. I'm so close to the edge, so hot and raw, that I lose all sense of control after a handful more rotations.

His name tears from my throat as an uproar of devastation and elation rips through my body. My toes curl as a shake I'll never fear hands over the control of my body, its relinquish of the reins swift and without hesitation.

Just as the shudders making me a quivering, blubbering mess slowly surrender, Ark's mouth is on me. He devours my pussy with greedy licks and powerful sucks until I'm unsure if my climax is ever-lasting or if I am on the verge of orgasming again.

I'm almost certain it is a new one, but it is hard to tell.

It is intense. Blinding.

It makes me moan as if I am possessed.

But Ark never relents. He eats me until stars explode before my eyes and my nails claw at the bedding, desperate for something to cling to.

I lose all sense of control when he answers their private pleas. In a movement too quick for my heart to register, he pulls down my hand, rakes it through his sweat-damp hair, then sucks my clit into his mouth with so much power that my hips vault off the mattress.

I come with a cry, my climax toe-curling and immediate.

"*Oh...*" I moan, stunned by the power of the shivers racking through my body. I'm tugging on Ark's hair too firmly, screaming like I'm fighting for my life, but Ark can't get enough.

His growls as he licks, bites, and sucks me prolong the length of my orgasm.

My core spasms as sparks erupt around us.

It is such a beautiful moment I can't help the handful of tears that trickle down my cheeks and puddle around my ears.

Mercifully, this time, Ark doesn't see them as a bad thing.

He's just as moved by our exchange as I am, just as besieged.

His smile announces this, not to mention how he uses my hand to mop up any of my arousal left on his kiss-swollen lips before he lowers it to his bulky leather belt.

He wants my hands on him, and I'm more than a willing participant with his plan.

My legs feel like Jell-O when I crawl across the bed to assist Ark in undressing. I work on his belt as he undoes the buttons of his crisp midnight-black business shirt.

The stark material falls off his shoulders with a whoosh as the grind of his zipper lowering doubles the output of my heart.

He is such a beautiful man. Washboard abs, defined pecs, and the desirable V muscle all women imagine while idolizing their ideal man.

I could climax just looking at him, and the press of my thighs can't hide this.

"Go slow," Ark pleads after toeing off his shoes and kicking them and his trousers to the side.

I nod before wetting my lips, my mouth suddenly parched.

This is scary for him, but you wouldn't know it for how thick and long his cock is. It stands between us tall and proud, as jutted as the honor that fills my chest when he doesn't balk from me gently wrapping my hand around his shaft.

I could have started elsewhere, but if I want to switch his fears to desires, I need the sparks to turn into dynamite and his shakes to shift to shudders of lust.

He feels heavy in my hand when I drag it to the base of his cock and gently increase my pressure. I jack my hand up and down a handful of times in small, defined pumps before returning it to the crown.

Air hisses between his teeth when my thumb instinctively rolls over the slit to gather a droplet of pre-cum pooled there. It switches to a moan when I use it as lubricant to quicken my strokes.

I'm desperate to taste him again when a handful of pumps have a second salty drop beading at the end of his big cock, but I need to see his eyes, so I can't.

I have to guide him through this as well as he guided me through the realization that sex isn't dirty.

I stroke his cock hard and fast but also slow and easy, gauging the speed of my pumps by the desperateness of his moans.

If they get too hoarse, I go a little slower.

If they soften, I increase my speed.

I work out what he likes by watching his numerous expressions and feed off the euphoria that I'm responsible for the snippet of peace slowly slipping over his face.

The throbs of the vein feeding his magnificent manhood announce he is on the cusp of release. I'm right there with him. I hated Dr. Babkin's demand for touch. The emotions pummeling into me now are nowhere near disgust. I love the moans rumbling in Ark's chest, and the sheer bewilderment in his eyes as he watches me jerk him off. They have me so desperate to taste him again that my tongue darts out to lick up the pre-cum on his swollen crown without a single thought crossing my mind.

"Fuck..." Ark grunts as the rock of his hips greaten.

As I lick, stroke, and suck his cock, he keeps his eyes locked on mine.

His gaze is searingly intense, and it catapults my excitement to a never-before-reached level.

I moan against his knob, confident pleasing him orally is as good as when his head is buried between my legs.

I love that I can give this to him, that I can satisfy him like no one else has, and the knowledge has me losing all sense of control. I draw him to the back of my throat again and again, gagging when his thick crown plunges an inch too far.

"Fuck, Mara," Ark grunts again as his fingers get lost in my hair.

He holds me still as the veins in his cock pump furiously, his eyes never leaving mine.

Then, two seconds later, hot spurts of cum flood my tongue and slide down my throat.

I swallow eagerly, equally loving the taste of him in my mouth again and the utter relief on his face.

He looks at peace, at home.

He's finally content.

I'm so exhausted by the emotions pumping out of us that my body is limp when Ark crawls up it to re-lock our lips. I taste myself on his tongue when he licks a droplet of sweat off my top lip before he delves it inside my mouth, and I am sure he is experiencing the same, but his kiss is one for the memory books.

It conveys everything words never will.

His love, his devotion.

His protectiveness.

"Thank you," I whisper again, aware my words will never be enough to express my gratitude on how ruefully he protected my daughter, but optimistic that I have plenty of time to convey to him how much his sacrifice freed me from the shackles of my childhood.

Ark smiles as if we have the world at our feet before he lines up the crown of his still-throbbing cock with my pussy, digs his toes into the mattress, and then enters me with one ardent thrust.

The pain of taking a man of his girth and length exposes that the reward for those who persevere far exceeds the pain of those who give up.

It shows that quitting is never an option.

Fighting is the only choice, and I will fight for this man until I take my last breath.

46

ARKADIY

"*E*aston said it would take two hours at the most, so what's taking him so long?"

Rafael sinks in the chair opposite mine before he rests his left ankle on his right knee. "I don't know." My eyes lift from a stack of paperwork when he mutters under his breath, "Maybe he's buying you time he knows you desperately need."

He already has my focus, but he wholeheartedly demands it by bringing the only woman capable of making me believe I am not a monster into our conversation. "Mara wouldn't want you to do this, Ark. She wouldn't want you sacrificing everything you've worked for to take out the trash the authorities should have handled years ago."

When I remain quiet, incapable of fighting the truth, he drops his leg and leans forward to balance his elbows on my desk. "Tell her your plan before initiating it. Give her a chance to talk you out of it."

"I can't," I murmur, my words as weak and pathetic as the ones I used on Mara three nights ago when I pleaded for her to go slow.

I crave her touch as much as my lungs crave air, but I shook like my abuser hadn't died two years before Karolina committed suicide.

I guess Mara is right. My step-grandmother wasn't my sole abuser. My mother was, and still is, just as evil.

She has yet to admit to the depths of her crimes, but I wholeheartedly believe my mother was the reason Paarth was in the servants' corridor the night Mara was attacked. She ramped up his anger to the point of no return by saying his dismissal was unjust since Mara was a paid escort, so she should anticipate the unwanted gawks and leers of strangers.

I was so furious at the thought alone that I immediately removed her from the board of my companies and signed an affidavit on her decades of abuse that I will release to the media if she doesn't maintain her distance.

I'll even go as far as having her officially charged. That is how serious I am at ensuring she knows that I am no longer her sock puppet.

I tune back in just as Rafael hits the nail on the head. "Because you know if she asked you to stay, you would."

I *pfft* as if he is lying.

He isn't.

I'd stay without a second thought before burying what I did so deep inside me not even the woman with eyes that can see through to my soul would find it. But I can't do that to Mara. I can't ask her to look at me and not see me for what I am.

I am a murderer.

A monster.

I became what my mother said I would become.

But I am also a man in love, and at this moment, I want that to rate higher than everything else.

That is what the paperwork on my desk is about. Transferring every asset I own, every bank account, every vehicle, isn't about buying a way past my guilt. It is love. Support. It is giving Mara and Tillie the life they deserve.

I've tried my hardest over the past three days to do precisely that. Just like our first magical twenty-four hours, we crammed a lifetime of memories into three solid days. It was fast, but they've honestly been the best days of my life. Mara is amazing. Her daughter is the epitome of perfection. I couldn't be happier, but I can't hide from my responsibilities for a second longer.

It is time for me to be honest, which should also yank the scrutiny away from a woman who doesn't deserve it.

Upon following the direction of my gaze, Rafael reads me like a book. "They don't want possessions, Ark." He stares me dead set in the eyes. "They want you."

"I want them too," I say before I can stop myself.

Rafael sits up straighter, his suit straining against his back. "Then tell them that."

"I can't—"

"Why?" He doesn't give me a chance to speak. "Because you're afraid of the repercussions?" He sees my nod but acts as if he didn't. "Bull-fucking-shit. You allowed that woman"—he points to my office door as if my mother is on the other side—"to dictate your life for decades. *Decades*, Ark! But you ran her out of your life in a manner she can *never* come back from. You fucking told, Ark. You confessed to every horrible thing that woman let them do to you and your sisters..." He stops, swallows, then corrects. "To you, your sister, and your niece, but you're going to sit here and tell me you don't have the balls to tell *your* woman that you love her enough that you don't want to hand yourself in because not seeing her every day will be worse than death. That you love her enough that you don't just see her daughter as hers anymore. She's yours as well." He *pffts* me again, and it burns like an oil-ladened bath. "Fuck that. Fuck them. Fuck this entire existence, because what's the use? Why fight only to lie down just as you're about to win?"

My eyes jackknife to the servants' entry of my office when a voice I'll never stop missing sounds through the partially cracked-open door. "Because he's failed to remember not every fight is a solo endeavor. There are some comps that are a group event."

My cock throbs as fast as my heart when Mara enters my office without the slightest shudder to her thighs. There are as many people inside as there are exits, but she feels safe here. Protected. She knows this is her home as much as it is mine.

"I'm sorry to intrude, but I have an important meeting, and all the office spaces downstairs are full of the crockery and dishware from a party the man of the hour failed to attend."

When I look at her, lost as to whom she could possibly be meeting with, she nudges her head to the perch-like balcony hovering over the den.

Fury blasts through me when I notice who is being shown through my apartment. It isn't my mother as she attempted to do a minimum of four times a day after surveillance footage proved she sprayed my abuser's perfume into the vents of my room and office.

It is Detective Pascall—a.k.a. the widower of Mara's abuser. She is accompanied by the woman I had planned to confess my crimes to this afternoon: Detective Lara Sonova.

"Mara—"

She silences me how only she can, by flattening her hand on my chest, right above my heart, and whispering five words that will forever stop my crusade. "You can trust me, Ark."

I can, and I do.

After curling my hand over hers, initiating firmer contact, I grant her permission to flourish the strength brewing rapidly in her beautiful eyes.

She thanks me for my support with a quick peck on the side of my mouth, both fueling my campaign to protect her as much as it adds gas to the fire Detective Pascall is attempting to light under her ass.

"I thought you were unaware of Miskaela Palkova's whereabouts?"

Mara hits me with a wordless plea to play nice when my fists ball. I do. Somewhat.

"I guess I have you to thank for our coupling?" When Detective Pascall peers at me, confused, a smirk tugs at one side of my mouth. "I had forgotten about our run-in until you reminded me. Then, when it was only right that I warn Miskaela of your campaign to discredit her undoubtably clean character, I was reminded again in person how exceedingly beautiful my cab-sharer was."

She doesn't believe my lie for even a second, and her annoyance that I tried spoils my plans to Mara. "So I'm meant to believe you handed over every asset you have to someone you only met a week ago? No one is that stupid, Mr. Orlov."

I pretend not to hear Mara's exasperated gasp.

"I guess you've never been to Vegas, *Mrs.* Babkin." I sneer her title in the same way she sneered the last name I am no longer associated with, shocking both Rafael and Detective Sonova. "People there don't even wait a day."

I could be honest. There's no need for me to hide anymore. The only reason I'm remaining cautious is because I don't trust Sanya's motives. How could I when she's going after one of her husband's victims as if she seduced him instead of being terrorized by him?

There's something we're missing from this puzzle, but I'm almost out of time to admit what that is. A member of Myasnikov PD is in attendance of our meeting, and she knows it has something to do with Mara's father's disappearance.

I lower the severity of my scorn when Mara reminds me that she invited Detective Pascall back into our lives. "I couldn't work out where I had seen you before. It took hours, combing through footage in my head I wish to never see again, before I finally worked it out."

She assures me she feels my silent comfort with a ghostlike grin before she moves to my desk and spins my laptop around. The footage Easton was supposed to remove from Veronika's phone and destroy is on my laptop screen. Except it isn't stopped at the segment where Mara flees the motel with Tillie hidden under a bulky coat. It is the last known footage of Dr. Babkin still breathing.

"Don't," I plead, warning Mara against airing incriminating footage in front of witnesses bound by a code of conduct. It will defeat the purpose of my endeavor to hide it and give no reason to further delay handing myself in.

There are no witnesses to Dr. Babkin's exit of Mara's motel room. No evidence he was still breathing when she left. This footage could put her away for years. It could steal Tillie from her as her father threatened to do when he thought he could convince a God-fearing judge that he, an upstanding Christian man, was a better guardian for his granddaughter than a woman who birthed a child out of wedlock.

Against my advice, Mara hits play.

I've seen this footage a hundred times since Mara's father uploaded it to Veronika's phone for safekeeping in case I reneged on the agreement to pay him three million dollars, but I look at it from a different angle when Mara highlights someone in the far back corner of the frame.

"That's you."

"No," Detective Pascall denies, shaking her head. "I..."

She stops talking when Mara plays another clip. This one leaves no denial as to who is stalking Dr. Babkin's arrival at Mara's motel room. It shows every horrified thought that filters through her head when Mara freezes upon Dr. Babkin's illegal entry of her room.

She isn't excited to see him. She's petrified. But Detective Pascall's rant exposes only those who know Mara well can read her expressions. "I gave him over a decade of my life, I birthed his child and helped him set up his practice, and he repaid me by sleeping with a woman who was barely legal."

My fists clench so fast my knuckles pop when she has the gall to sneer at Mara at the end of her sentence, but before I can add words to my nonverbal response, Mara says, "I wasn't legal the first time he raped me. I was just a child."

Rafael's cuss is faint.

Mine is nowhere near as quiet.

I want to hold her again and promise I will never let anyone hurt her, but when a bull wants to charge, you must let it charge.

Mara needs this. She needs to dispel the fear, which hasn't stopped weighing down her shoulders since she learned how close her father was to Tillie's school, so she can start living again.

Her father was in the same town as Tillie, but he wouldn't have gotten close to her. Darius would have never allowed that to occur, and neither the hell would have I.

"I wasn't even the age your daughter is now." Tears gloss Mara's eyes as they flicker through horrid memories. "The first time *they* hurt me, I rode my bike to the emergency department." I have no regrets for what I did when she whispers, "My father used the hardness of my bike seat and the length of my trip to excuse the blood in my underwear when the hospital called him to advise him that I had sought medical assistance. The second time..." I'm at her side in an instant when she chokes on her words. "He blamed the saddle on the ponies he hired for my birthday party. The th-third—"

"That's enough. She's been through enough." I dance my begging eyes between Detective Pascall and Sonova. "Don't make her go through more. *Please.*"

After wiping away the tears streaming down her face, Mara says, "My father had an excuse for every horrible thing that had happened to me so he could hide his own malicious crimes." I see the train coming. I hear it clattering along the tracks. But the words leave her mouth before I can push her far enough away from the collision to stop her from getting hurt. "So when I thought he was going to do the same to my daughter, I made sure he couldn't."

"No!" I shout, my voice a roar. "She doesn't understand what she's saying. She is traumatized from me admitting to what I did." I cup Mara's cheeks and align our eyes. "Tell them the truth. Tell them what really happened."

Nothing but love beams from her eyes when she whispers, "I just did."

"No," I shout again as Detective Sonova stands to her feet, removing her cuffs on the way. "She's lying. She isn't telling the truth. She is trying to protect me." I return my eyes to Mara, wet and begging. "Please tell them the truth." I switch tactics when I realize there's only one person who can save her from herself. "Don't do this to Tillie, Mara. Save her from this."

She smiles like she didn't just confess to murder before saying, "I don't need to save her from this because you already did."

As she's cuffed and read her rights, Mara keeps her drenched eyes on me. They repeat the same three words again and again and again.

I trust you.

It is in that instance I know what I must do.

I fight, and I fight hard.

When Mara is walked out of my apartment, I bark orders like

everyone in my realm is beneath me. I order Detective Sonova to keep Mara in a private cell, I tell Mara not to talk to anyone without a lawyer present, and I instruct Rafael to get me the best defense attorney in the country like he isn't already on the phone doing precisely that.

I take control as I should have decades ago, my tirade only ending when the faintest snivel sounds through my one good ear.

Tillie's ashen cheeks as she hides behind Mrs. Lichard's somewhat curvy frame announces she is aware of her mother's plan, as does the quiver of the breath she releases when she spots her father on the open screen of my laptop. She is as devastated as me but vainly trying to keep it together because she trusts that her mother would never lead her astray.

Her faith is admirable, and it has me doing something I haven't done in years. I close my laptop screen before bobbing down and holding out my arms in offering.

She runs into my arms in an instant, almost knocking me over with the strength of her hug.

Once I have her tucked under my arm, I promise to make everything right.

"I won't let them take her from us, Tillie." I hug her in closer, lessening her shakes. "I won't let them win."

47

MARA

*M*y breath catches when the courtroom door opens, and Tillie enters two steps in front of Ark. The past week has been the longest we've been away from each other. I've missed her so much, but the pain has been manageable since I know deep in my heart that she is being well cared for.

Ark loves her as if she is his own. I have no doubt about that. What he did for her already proved it, but the way he included her in all aspects of his life in the three days following his confession outright verified it.

"Mommy!"

I hug Tillie the best I can in the prison shackles the guard has yet to remove, squeezing her tight and breathing in her scent. I almost cry. Now Ark's obsession with my shampoo makes sense. You don't realize how for-granted you take things until they are removed from your grasp.

Tillie inches back before I've had close to my fill and does a twirl. "Do you like my new dress? Riley made it for me."

She speaks at a million miles an hour, but I refuse to slow her down. She's flourishing under Ark's care, and it assures me that I made the right decision accepting a victim advocacy lawyer's advice.

The courts will be less harsh on me since I am a woman who has faced inexcusable abuse that is well-documented in numerous medical files.

They'd throw the book at Ark since none of his abuse made it into a file.

Well, they hadn't.

He has spoken out in the past week, and the stance he's taken against predators has made me incredibly proud. He is removing the stigma victims of abuse forever endure and touching the lives of many —Tillie and Riley included.

By speaking up, Ark's approval rating has surged to record highs.

The same can't be said for Veronika. When her plans to out an underage victim of abuse for personal gain were unearthed, she lost hundreds of thousands of followers in a day and was stripped of multiple endorsement deals.

She will be licking her wounds for years, if not decades.

I shift my focus back to the present when Tillie discloses, "Riley made a new dress for you, too. It's in your closet at home, next to Ark's clothes." Her giggle warms my heart. "Do you know he wears stuffy suits and ugly ties every day? Mrs. Lichard said it is because he's a business mogul." She peers up at me with her nose screwed up. "What is a mogul?"

She is given an answer from a man I will walk through hell to shelter as well as he protected her. "It is a man who won't stop fighting until he gets everything he wants *and* deserves." As I admire the crispness of Ark's designer suit and his gorgeous face, he drinks me in like I don't look wretched before he shifts his rapidly narrowed eyes to the bailiff. "Get the shackles off her, now."

"Sir—"

"Now!" Ark repeats, yelling.

"It's okay," I whisper, unbothered by the restraints.

I pled guilty to murder. I deserve to be in shackles.

I just hope they won't be on for much longer.

Since I pled guilty, I automatically waived my right for a trial. My lawyer said the ADA would rather plead out my case than see it go to court, but the DA took a stance no one anticipated. He left my fate in the hands of a judge I've never met.

I could have recanted my confession and faced a jury of my peers, but I couldn't risk them finding me not guilty or calling a mistrial. That would keep the case open, and the investigation into my relationship with Ark would be ongoing.

I don't want Ark to spend the rest of his life looking over his shoulder, waiting for the authorities to catch up with him. I want him to live his life as freely as a snap decision he made will allow Tillie to live hers.

He gave her the freedom I've been desperately seeking to unearth for the past ten years, and he has the means to make sure she lives her life to the fullest.

I could barely afford to buy a pair of gym shoes, so I'd serve thirty consecutive life sentences if it was the only way I could give my daughter the life she deserves.

When the bailiff instructs the court-goers to rise, I hug Tillie for a second time before I watch Ark guide her to an empty section of a pew near the front.

The courtroom is full. Journalists fill the back of the pews, victims of abuse take up the middle, and a small handful of people I class as family stretch across the front two pews.

The bailiff demands quiet when the tension in the room reaches fever pitch, and a handful of SA protestors can't help but shout their anger at the system that did them wrong.

"She wouldn't have needed to kill him if the courts had done their job."

"We should be paying her for taking out the trash."

"This is what is wrong with the system. They always make out the victims are the perpetrators."

The judge doesn't appear bothered by the catcalling and booing. He walks to his bench with a mountain load of files stuffed under his arm and his glasses balancing precariously on the end of his nose.

The room falls into silence when we're instructed to sit.

My backside has barely touched my seat when I am told to remain standing.

Here it comes. The outcome of my decision is about to be unearthed.

"I am of the belief you've pled guilty, Ms. Palkova?" When I nod, the judge looks down at me over his glasses. "Have you been threatened or coerced into pleading guilty?" Shock rains down on him when I switch my nod to a head-shake. "Would you like to say anything on your own behalf before I make my ruling?"

My attorney announced the verdict would be quick, but I didn't anticipate proceedings to move so fast.

After a big breath, endeavoring to remove the nerves from my voice, I nod. "Only that I trust your v-verdict and the process on which you took to reach it."

He dips his chin. Appreciation that I'm not going to hold up proceedings longer than necessary is seen all over his face. "Have you reviewed the pre-sentence report with your attorney?"

Again, I nod.

"So you are aware the ruling handed down today will be ratified immediately and without further endorsement from either the ADA or your attorney?"

I dip my chin, too choked with emotions to speak.

"Very well." He breathes out noisily, silencing everyone. "Under Section 272, if a person has assaulted another or provoked an assault from another, and the victim believes they need to use force to defend themselves or they will be killed or seriously harmed, the victim is not criminally responsible for the consequences." I lose the ability to breathe when he says, "However, in the case presented before me, there is no evidence that the victim caused grievous bodily harm to Ms. Palkova—"

"This time, your honor, but what about the multiple other times!"

The judge acts as if my attorney didn't speak. "And as such, I am under no obligation to accept the claimant's claims that the act was under the pursuant of self-defense." He pushes his glasses up his nose before peering down at me. "Your pledge of guilt is accepted by the court, and as so, I order a three-year non-probationary period to be served at a medium-security prison."

He whacks down his gavel, sending the court-goers into a frenzy.

I'm shocked but also relieved.

Three years is nothing compared to how many wonderful years Tillie has left to live, and I suffered almost daily abuse for far longer than that, but how could the judge have read my files and not understood why I would fear for my life while standing across from my father? Ark understood from nothing but a glance. That's why he killed my father. He knew if I were in the same predicament, I would have done the exact same thing.

He saved me that night as much as he did Tillie.

That's another reason I'm taking the blame for his crime.

"Mommy," Tillie whispers in confusion when the bailiff commences moving me back toward the dock before I get to say goodbye.

"It's okay, baby. Everything will be okay."

She's upset and crying but mercifully being comforted by the man I know is never capable of hurting her.

Ark bobs down to Tillie's level to wipe away her tears and whisper promises in her ear. He's shockingly calm. I shouldn't be surprised. The lengths a parent will go to safeguard their child is remarkable, second only to how honorably they love them.

I'm pulled partway through the dock's door by a correction services officer when his steps are thwarted by a raised voice. "Can I please approach the bench?"

I can't breathe when Detective Pascall bursts through the swinging doors that separate the court from the pews like permission was given. I haven't seen her since I invited her to Ark's apartment to hear my confession. Her presence wasn't necessary, but I needed her to hear my confession in person. Its impact wouldn't have been anywhere near as effective if she had read it on a piece of paper.

I needed her to identify the signs of abuse so she could make sure her daughter holds none of them.

"Ms. Pascall, the hearing is over," the judge says. "Any chance for rebuttal shall be saved for if the defendant chooses to appeal my verdict."

She nods as if familiar with court proceedings before wetting her lips. "It is important, your honor."

"It very well could be, but you have no jurisdiction here. The verdict has been handed down and already implemented."

When the judge gestures for the court officer to remove Detective Pascall from the courtroom, words shoot out of her mouth like bullets. "She didn't kill the man you found her guilty of murdering, your honor." The courtroom gasps in sync when she says, "I did." She shoots her eyes to Ark standing motionless with Tillie before she slowly trails them back to me. "I followed you to his hotel. He was bleeding and a little woozy"—she makes a gesture with her hand that shouldn't say as much as it does—"but he was still breathing."

The hurt in her eyes exposes that she isn't thinking about my father right now while recalling the scene she witnessed. Someone far more important is occupying her thoughts.

My heart sinks when recognition dawns as to the true cause of the pain in her eyes.

Oh god.

She found out too late.

She found out about her child's abuse *after* her daughter took steps to make it stop.

When I step closer to her, one mother desperate to comfort another, she holds her hand out, pleading for me to stop, like she doesn't deserve my sympathies.

"I met your father shortly after Luba's death." She sucks in a pained breath that she releases with a sigh. "He never disclosed your connection. He just said he had footage that proved I was there the day Luba died and that it could expose the true cause of his death." She spins to face the congregation as if they deserve more answers than me. "Luba's life insurance policy wouldn't have paid out for suicide, so when my unit was called to the motel, I made it seem as if he had been murdered. He owed a lot of people a lot of money, so it wasn't a hard stretch." Her eyes return to me. They're wet and somewhat honest. "But they took it all, anyway. Every cent. I would have gone under—"

"If it weren't for my father?" I murmur, recalling how he kept people's suspicions low by killing them with kindness. He had everyone fooled. Doctors, nurses, my teachers. Everyone believed that he was an admirable man.

Sanya nods, snot dribbling from her nose. "He made out you had been syphoning Luba's bank account for years by threatening to tell me about your relationship if he didn't pay up. He never disclosed the rest, and I never questioned him about it because..." She's too ashamed to admit her reason. No one wants to admit they fell in love with a monster.

"I heard what he said to you when he learned he had a grand-daughter." I picture the agony Ark went through when she whispers, "In an instant, he went from wanting money to wanting her." The disgust in her tone announces she heard the need in my father's tone as readily as Ark did. "When I confronted him about it, he became abusive. He hit me and told me my daughter's death was my fault. I snapped." Her eyes flicker as if this part of her story is a true confession. "I pushed him. He hit his head on the corner of the bar in his room on the way down."

"Did you call anyone?" the judge asks, as invested in her story as I am.

Detective Pascall shakes her head. "I watched him take his last breath, relieved that he couldn't hurt anyone anymore, before I had him cremated and buried as a John Doe."

There are holes in her story, many of them, but everyone but me seems oblivious to them.

The judge warns her as to the consequences of her confession in a court of law, and that acquitting me after a verdict has been decreed will shelter me from further prosecution, but she maintains her stance.

She takes blame for a murder she didn't commit, and I'm helpless to stop her.

48

ARKADIY

"*M*s. Palkova," the judge begins, silencing the court, "after hearing the confession of the true perpetrator, it is clear that a grave mistake has occurred today." The people shouting in anger only minutes ago cheer in glee when he bangs down his gavel while saying, "You are hereby exonerated of all charges."

Mara's eyes widen in disbelief as tears threaten to stream down her face. Her supporters mistake them as droplets of relief. I know that isn't true. She's upset for what Sanya went through and wondering if she had fought harder to have her father convicted of his crimes if she could have saved Sanya's daughter from being hurt.

It will take a lot to convince her she isn't at fault. Since I am confident I am the only man capable of achieving the seemingly impossible, I refuse to take steps that will deny me the opportunity anytime soon—if ever.

I've previously said Mara's safety is my utmost priority—both mentally and physically.

That hasn't changed.

Mara's wet eyes flick from me to the bailiff when he's instructed by the judge to remove her shackles. A wave of relief washes over me when their removal is swift and without incident.

The courtroom erupts into hushed whispers and murmurs as Mara rushes to embrace Tillie and me.

After a quick whiff of a scent no amount of desecration could alter, I step back, allowing Mara and Tillie to have this moment.

When I stray my eyes to Detective Pascall, who is in the process of being cuffed, a sense of triumph mixed with the sobering reality of how close we came to an irreversible injustice swamps me.

I had hoped it wouldn't come to this, that the justice system would, for once, protect the victim.

I should have known better.

The numerous injustices underaged victims of assault endure are one of the reasons I was running for president. I wanted to implement laws that would protect children like Karolina and Detective Pascall's twelve-year-old daughter who committed suicide last month.

They couldn't face the burden of an unjust world for a second longer, so they took matters into their own hands.

Technically, Mara did the same when she confessed to the crime I had committed. She has struggled for years to give Tillie the life she deserved, so when she thought an opportunity had presented to better her daughter's life, she took it.

I'd be angry if I didn't understand the incessant need to protect the people you love. It drove me to the playground of hell and added murderer to my list of achievements.

Detective Pascall's claim that Mara's father was alive when she returned to their hotel room is untruthful. Darius's security team worked as fast as Detective Pascall's partner did when he arrived at Mara's motel room six years ago and found Sanya standing over her husband's body with the knife Mara had used to cut up an apple for Tillie stabbed in his spleen.

Dr. Babkin's panic that Mara had living, breathing proof of his abhorrent crimes had him forgetting who he was purging to. He ranted and raved to his wife like she wasn't the mother of his child or a police officer.

Like me, Sanya blacked out in a fit of rage.

One minute, she was standing in front of Luba.

The next, she was standing over his corpse.

I let Sanya moderate how much she wanted to share about her involvement with Mara's father because, for now, while Mara's confidence is fractured so poorly that she believed handing her daughter's care to me was the safest option, I'd rather Mara believe Sanya had fallen in love with a monster than have her learn her father was never Sanya's intended target.

She wanted Tillie.

Sanya was so profoundly overwhelmed with grief that she thought she could replace her daughter.

A child with half her bloodline seemed like an easy target.

Sanya was getting desperate. If she had found Tillie before framing Mara for the murder of her husband, so Tillie's custody would be awarded to her grandfather, who had agreed to hand her over to Sanya for an undisclosed sum, I have no doubt she would have kidnapped her.

The time Sanya will serve for the crime she pled guilty to today won't be close to what she would face for what the courts would deem as the unprovoked murder of her husband and attempted kidnapping of a minor, but locking her up and throwing away the key isn't the right solution.

She needs help—medical and psychological. She will get that behind bars, and the charity I promised to establish in her daughter's name for her confession today will assist her once she is released.

For now, my priorities are needed closer to home, with my wife-to-be and my daughter, who prove time and time again there are no limits when it comes to protecting the people you love, and that trust isn't a word. It is a lifestyle.

If you enjoyed this book, please consider leaving a review.

Facebook: facebook.com/authorshandi

Instagram: instagram.com/authorshandi

Email: authorshandi@gmail.com

Reader's Group: bit.ly/ShandiBookBabes

Website: authorshandi.com

Newsletter: https://www.subscribepage.com/AuthorShandi

Made in the USA
Las Vegas, NV
28 August 2025

27090431R00174